Windows of the Heavens

Windows of the Heavens

A Novel

HENRY G. BRINTON

RESOURCE *Publications* • Eugene, Oregon

WINDOWS OF THE HEAVENS
A Novel

Copyright © 2021 Henry G. Brinton. All rights reserved. Except for brief quotations in critical publications or reviews, no part of this book may be reproduced in any manner without prior written permission from the publisher. Write: Permissions, Wipf and Stock Publishers, 199 W. 8th Ave., Suite 3, Eugene, OR 97401.

Resource Publications
An Imprint of Wipf and Stock Publishers
199 W. 8th Ave., Suite 3
Eugene, OR 97401

www.wipfandstock.com

PAPERBACK ISBN: 978-1-6667-3341-9
HARDCOVER ISBN: 978-1-6667-2900-9
EBOOK ISBN: 978-1-6667-2901-6

VERSION NUMBER 092022

Unless otherwise noted, Scripture quotations are from the New Revised Standard Version Bible, copyright © 1989 National Council of the Churches of Christ in the United States of America. Used by permission. All rights reserved worldwide.

To Bill Parent and Jay Tharp
Marathon Men

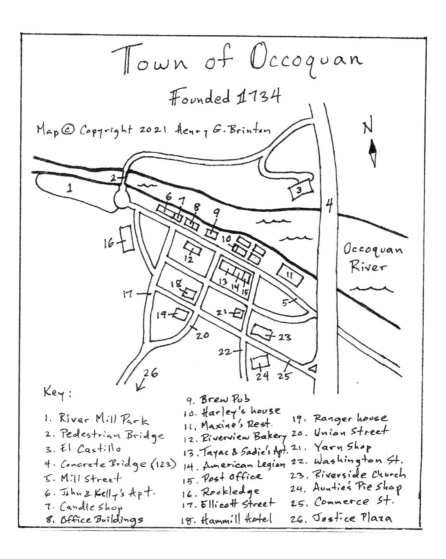

1

The steps of the Mayan temple were made for giants, not humans, but still Harley Camden climbed them, one by one, making slow upward progress on a windless summer day. Never had the sky been so clear and blue, nor the sun so powerfully bright, causing the tropical vegetation around the temple to wilt in its relentless radiation. Harley was soaked with sweat, and his clothing provided little relief since he was wearing his standard clergy uniform of blue blazer and red silk tie. *Why not my archaeological dig clothes? Or mission trip t-shirt and jeans?* It made no sense to him.

Harley's legs ached from climbing, and his arms were sore from his repeated pull-ups, stone after stone after stone. He wondered if it was the will of the Lord to destroy him. But why would God want him to suffer? He had done no violence, and there was no deceit in him. Stopping to catch his breath halfway up the staircase, he looked up and saw—what was it, feathers?—moving at the very top of the temple. *Are there chickens up there? Peacocks? Guacamayas?* Wiping perspiration from his eyes, he gazed out and saw a great crowd of raven-haired Mayans on the plaza, standing on lush green grass and looking up at him, watching his slow progress. He was an innocent man, and yet, here he was: climbing the temple with a burden of iniquity on his back.

Who could have imagined his fate? Cut off from the land of the living, he was sentenced for sins he did not commit. At the edge of the plaza was a strange ballgame being played by glistening athletes running up and down a rectangular court—the Mayan version of basketball. He knew that the winners of the game would be sacrificed, and that it would be an honor to die as victors. Spectators would elevate them as the greatest of athletes because they poured themselves out in death. *Is my fate the same?* As unjust as it seemed, he had been chosen. Scanning the edges of the plaza, he saw a number of majestic ceiba trees, two-hundred-footers with umbrella-shaped crowns. Called the "tree of life," they were sacred to the Mayan people—trees that made a connection between heaven, the earth, and the underworld. He would have so much preferred to be climbing a ceiba tree over a temple staircase. The leaves of that tree—*árbol de la vida*, tree of life—were for the healing of the nations.

Loosening his tie, he began to climb again, stone after stone. He remembered a line from the prophet Isaiah, "the Lord has laid on him the iniquity of us all." The prophet was speaking of a suffering servant, one who gave his life for others. He had always understood that line to be pointing to Jesus, but at that moment, on the monstrous steps of the Mayan temple, the words were coming true for Harley—it was he who was the lamb being led to slaughter.

∽

His journey to the temple had begun three weeks earlier, on an evening walk through River Mill Park in the town of Occoquan, Virginia. The streetlights that dotted the perimeter of the small park were not working on that September night, so the place was strangely dark, and its blacktopped walking path vanished quickly in front of him, disappearing into the void. At the entrance of the park, he hesitated, feeling as though he were about to jump into a dark and mysterious lake, not knowing the depth of the water or what hazards lay below the surface.

But Harley was well acquainted with the park, having lived in Occoquan for a little more than a year. He had been sent there by his bishop to serve as the pastor of tiny Riverside Methodist Church, after the deaths of his wife and daughter—a reassignment that had felt like a demotion. The town of one thousand was a peculiar little community in the suburban sprawl of the Nation's Capital, located on the river that separates the million residents of Fairfax County from the half-million citizens of Prince William County. Founded in 1734, the village was a mix of historic buildings and brand new structures, with run-down craft shops sitting right next to the trendiest of wine bars. Occoquan was a town in transition, and it was still too early to tell if it was moving up or sliding down. *Depends on the day,* Harley thought, *maybe even the hour.*

The park marked the western end of a stroll that Harley took almost every night, one which began with him leaving his Victorian townhouse and walking away from the park, eastward along a riverside boardwalk to a massive concrete bridge which carried six lanes of traffic across the Occoquan

River. Guitar music drifted out of an open-air bar on most nights, mixed with eruptions of laughter and the sound of sports commentary on television: noises that didn't make much sense in themselves but sent pulses of desire and delight out over the water. At the bridge, Harley made an about-face and walked along the quiet shops and restaurants of Mill Street to the park, watching the nightly transition of shopkeepers heading home and diners parking their cars in front of restaurants. A meeting at church had delayed the start of his walk on that particular night, and the sun was down by the time he set out. But he wasn't worried. Although he had seen drunks vomiting outside a brew pub along his route, and an occasional fight near the bar of a seafood restaurant called Maxine's, he had never feared street crime in his adopted hometown. Yes, there had been a murder the year before, but that was not a random act of violence.

Fortunately, the moon was full on that Monday night, and the park was bathed in an unearthly glow. Once the streetlights of the town were behind him and his eyes had time to adjust, the moonlight gave him sufficient illumination to find his way. Stepping into the park and beginning his walk along the path, he saw that the moon made everything look like it had been painted in various shades of teal, which was an odd color for the placid Occoquan River to his right and the hulking oak trees to his left. But Harley began to enjoy this unusual filter on the familiar scenery, and he soon noticed that there were eerie moon-shadows under the park's benches along the way.

Then, as he was nearing the western end of the park, he saw another light—yellow flames dancing out of the top of a large steel drum. Dark silhouettes were moving in front of the flames—figures walking slowly in a circle. His heart beat faster, and Harley wondered if he should turn around and head home. Caution pulled him one direction and curiosity the other, and as he stopped and stood in place, he began to hear people chanting in a strange, guttural language. The group was made up of about a dozen people dressed in loose, flowing clothing, and they seemed to be riveted on each other and on the flames at the center of their circle. Then his heart jumped as he realized what he was seeing—the witches of Occoquan.

Harley made a hard turn to the left and walked quickly out of the park, looking back only once to make sure that he wasn't being followed. His heart didn't return to its normal rhythm until he stepped through the front door of his townhouse.

"Yes, we've got a coven here in Occoquan." Tim Underwood had reported this fact to Harley while sitting in his golf cart one sunny afternoon that summer. Middle-aged with wire-rimmed glasses and a gray beard, the town maintenance man was wearing his standard outfit of a broad-brimmed hat and a tie-dye t-shirt, which led most people to call him "Tie-dye Tim." He was from an old Occoquan family and had been the first person that Harley had encountered on his initial visit to Riverside Methodist in June of the previous year. "You'll see them doing their services outside from time to time," Tim predicted. "Chanting, dancing, holding hands."

"Devil worshipers?" Harley asked.

"Dunno," Tim said, shrugging his shoulders. "They certainly aren't Methodists."

"Sounds evil," said the pastor, wondering why Tim wasn't more concerned. Harley didn't like what he was hearing.

"They *are* a bit odd," admitted Tim, "but they don't hurt anybody."

That you know of, thought Harley. But then, not wanting to sound overly concerned, he tried to lighten the mood. "Odd and harmless," he teased. "The same could be said of you, Tim."

Drinking coffee in his kitchen on the morning after his witch-sighting, Harley looked at the calendar on his wall and saw that it was Tuesday, September 25, 2018. He had experienced a full church year at Riverside, with a cycle of church holidays under his belt, and he was forging ever-stronger connections with the members of his small congregation. Flipping through the months of the calendar, he thought of the couple that was having marital problems, the senior citizen who had lost his spouse, the middle-aged woman who had received a cancer diagnosis. *I've learned the truth about these people, from the fragile to the resilient—the self-aware to the completely clueless.* He now knew who was struggling with alcohol, who had lost a series of jobs, who was abusive to her spouse, and who had a hard time coming to terms with his sexuality.

After rinsing his mug in the sink, Harley put on a navy-blue blazer and headed out the door. The coat was fitting him well after losing a few pounds over the summer. At age fifty-eight, he had to work at keeping his weight under control, especially with the sedentary life of a parish pastor, so he had increased his running and cut down on his eating. In his forties, Harley had been a marathon man, running at least one a year for ten years, and during that period he burned so many calories in training and competing that he had no trouble with his weight. But now his runs were much shorter, just a few miles in length, so he could no longer count on his exercise program to keep him healthy and fit.

One of his favorite runs was a figure-eight which took him along the southern bank of the Occoquan River to the Lake Ridge Marina, then a sweeping right turn that sent him back along Route 123 and over the concrete bridge into Fairfax County, where he always kept his eyes open for a bald eagle who liked to perch high in a tree on the riverbank. That completed the top loop. Then he turned left and ran through the woods on the north side of the river, past ancient rocks that stood as tall and strong as Easter Island heads, until he turned left again and crossed over the pedestrian bridge. He finished the bottom loop by returning through the streets of Occoquan along the south side of the river until he reached his home, out of breath but not completely exhausted. Two and one-half miles. *Not a marathon, but not bad for an old man.*

Harley looked at himself in the plate-glass window of a jewelry shop as he walked westward on Mill Street, and he was pleased with what he saw. His face was a little thinner than it had been a year earlier, and he had shaved the goatee that he had sported for years. *Good choice; makes me look younger.* His hair was gray and getting thinner all the time, but there was not much he could do about that—at least he *had* hair. On the whole, he looked decent for a middle-aged minister, and that made him happy since he was heading to the Riverview Bakery for coffee with Tawnya Jones, a beautiful woman on whom he'd had a crush since he arrived in town.

"Reverend Camden!" she called out from the door of the bakery. "Don't you look nice today?"

Harley blushed, but was delighted by the compliment. Tawnya was not a member of Riverside Methodist, but had been active in the African-American congregation that had occupied the church building when it was called Emanuel Baptist Church. Outgoing and flirtatious, she was someone that Harley could enjoy without running the risk of violating his professional ethics. Although he knew that she saw him only as a pastor and a neighbor, her attention made him feel young and virile and alive.

"I should say the same about you," Harley replied. Her black hair was tightly braided and she was dressed in a beautifully-tailored linen suit. "You sure dress well for your work in the Department of Justice."

"I'm going places at work," she said with a toothy smile. "You know what they say: Dress for the job you want."

"In that case, you should be Attorney General."

"Aren't you nice?" she said with a wink, and then held the door open for him. "Better stop talking like that, or my husband will get jealous."

"I have that effect," Harley said, smiling.

Joining the line of customers, he asked Tawnya what he could get her. She asked for a cinnamon scone and a black coffee, and he ordered the same for himself. Serving them was Sarah Bayati, a woman with a round face and brown eyes, a younger version of her Iraqi immigrant mother. Harley knew the family well, and normally would have engaged her in conversation, but she was moving quickly to serve the rush of morning customers. Harley simply asked how she and her family were doing, and when she grinned and said "busy," he gave her a thumbs-up and took his order out the door.

"Sweet young woman," said Tawnya as they sat on a bench along Mill Street to have their breakfast. The sky was a brilliant blue, what Harley always called "Carolina Blue," with just a few clouds on the western horizon. *If God is not a Tarheel, why is the sky Carolina blue?* Harley remembered that saying from his days at Duke Divinity School, just a few miles from the University of North Carolina. As a fierce rival of UNC, he hated to admit that the saying was actually quite true.

"Indeed, she is," nodded Harley as he handed Tawnya her coffee and scone. He noticed that her nails were brightly colored and polished to perfection, as usual.

Harley bit into his scone and looked across the street at the gravel parking lot. Beyond the lot was the river, sparkling as though someone had scattered a handful of diamonds across the water. Even after a year in Occoquan, Harley was amazed that there was nothing more than a parking lot on this valuable stretch of the main street of the town, since in most comparable Virginia communities the edge of the water would be filled with an unbroken string of restaurants, shops, and bars. For most of its history, Occoquan's riverfront had been covered with wharves and warehouses, with no trendy spots to eat, shop, or drink. But in the late twentieth century, developers moved in, sensing that a riverfront town in the DC-area could be a magnet for suburbanites and their money. Slowly, the town was changing into a boutique-filled tourist destination, with only two gravel lots and the ruins of the old mill remaining as evidence of its industrial past.

"She is still grieving her sister's death," Harley said after swallowing his bite, "but trying to stay positive."

"That whole situation still seems like a bad dream," said Tawnya, taking a second to blow on her hot coffee. "Growing up here in Occoquan, I never heard of anyone being murdered. All of a sudden, a woman is smothered in her bed."

"It is still hard to believe."

Loud honking came from the sky, and the two of them looked up as a V formation of geese soared over their heads. Tawnya took a drink of coffee, looked toward the river, and asked, "How is your boat, pastor?"

"Broken," Harley sighed. He loved his twenty-three-foot powerboat, a consolation prize that he awarded himself after being demoted to Riverside

Methodist. "It started running rough in July, and by mid-August I couldn't get it started. At the marina, they said that water was getting in the cylinders, which is pretty serious. They are still working on it."

"Sorry to hear it. I guess what they say about boats is true: A hole in the water . . ."

". . . into which you pour money," said Harley, smiling. "And you know what BOAT stands for, don't you? Bring Out Another Thousand."

Tawnya laughed. "At least the timing is not bad. I hear we are supposed to get some nasty weather. Something about a hurricane."

"Well, this is the time of year. I hope we don't get hit when I am trying to fly to Honduras."

"What's that about?" Tawnya asked.

"A mission trip," said Harley, sipping his coffee. "End of next week. One of my church members is a dentist who goes down there once a year to do a dental brigade. When he heard I had been on an archaeological dig in Honduras, he asked if I wanted to go back."

"Are you going to pull teeth?" asked Tawnya with a grin.

"Not if I can help it," said Harley. "The brigade always includes non-dental helpers. Maybe I'll paint a wall or help in the waiting room. I know *un poco de español.*"

"When did you do your dig?"

"Over thirty years ago," said Harley. "Summer of 1986. I was part of a team that worked at the Mayan ruins in Copán."

"But someone told me that you were an archaeologist in Israel."

"That was the summer before, 1985. Digging was kind of my thing, back in my twenties."

"A regular Indiana Jones!" flirted Tawnya.

"Hardly," said Harley, smiling. "No whips for me." Pleased by the attention but also a little embarrassed, Harley looked down. As he did, his eyes fell on her slender legs, which he knew was not where his eyes should be. *Don't want to be in the news for harassment,* he thought, recalling the string of politicians and media giants recently called to account. So, he brought his gaze back to her face and said, "I know you didn't ask to meet so that we could talk archaeology. What can I do for you?"

"I have a request for you, pastor," she said. "I hope you can help me out."

"Happy to do what I can."

"You know that my family has been part of Emanuel Baptist for generations. We have a reunion every five years, and this year we would like to gather in Occoquan. I was wondering if we could rent the social hall of your church, since our congregation was in the building for so many years."

"I don't see why not," said Harley. "Your family practically built the church."

"Well, not exactly," Tawnya replied, brushing off the compliment. "But it is certainly very special to us, especially to my father."

"Yes, Jefferson mentioned how much he loved the place. When he visited me last summer, he said that the desk in my office had been used by his uncle."

"That's right," Tawnya nodded. "My great-uncle served there. Many years."

"So, when would you like it?" Deep down, Harley was thrilled to be helping her out. "I can check the church calendar and get back to you."

"Saturday, October 20. We'll have a picnic lunch and be out before dinnertime," she said. "I promise we'll have everything straightened up for Sunday."

"My guess: You'll leave it cleaner than you found it."

Tawnya smiled but seemed distracted. "This will really mean a lot to us, especially to my father." She paused, sipped the last of her coffee, and then said, "I'm not sure if I should mention this, but my father has cancer."

"Jefferson?" asked Harley. He was stunned.

"Yes," she said, tears welling up. "It's very serious. Pancreatic. This might be his last family reunion." She covered her eyes with her glistening nails.

"Tawnya, I am so very sorry." He put his arm around her shoulders and drew her close. But not too close. For a minute they sat in silence. A breeze had begun to blow, and Harley looked up to see that clouds from the west now covered half the sky.

"He doesn't want anyone to know," she said, sniffing. "He has some business deals in the works, including the sale of Justice Plaza. He wants to remain strong in his negotiations." Looking Harley in the eyes, she said, "But you are confidential, right?"

"Of course," he said. "I'll keep him in my prayers."

"He needs prayer," Tawnya continued, composing herself. "He is a proud man, so hard-headed. He wants to get rid of the plaza and then complete the redevelopment of the old buildings up the street here, near the park. Can you believe he would care about such a thing while fighting cancer?"

"That's how some people cope. Staying busy."

Tawnya nodded. "The redevelopment is a tough and tricky job, because he is displacing a number of tenants who have been here a long time—including those crazy witches."

The witches, thought Harley. "Yes, I've heard about them," he said, removing his arm from her shoulder. "And I think I've even seen them."

"Please do pray for him," Tawnya concluded. "And let's keep this between us." Harley nodded, and Tawnya gave him a hug before she said goodbye and headed for her office. Harley took his time walking to the church, thinking about the struggle that lay ahead for Jefferson and his beautiful daughter. Although he was not their pastor, he had come to care for them as though they were part of his flock.

The skies got darker as the day progressed, and Harley learned that a full-blown hurricane was making its way up the coast. By the time he left the church and headed home at dinnertime, the wind was howling, rain was coming down in sheets, and he became drenched when his umbrella blew upside down and inside out. Harley had never seen such a volume of water coming down from the sky, hour after hour after hour, and his anxiety rose as a deep darkness settled on Occoquan. As he turned off the lights to go to bed, he looked out a window onto Mill Street and saw that the storm sewers were beginning to overflow and flood the pavement. Water was coming from above and below, and as he lay in bed he remembered the line from Genesis, "all the fountains of the great deep burst forth, and the windows of the heavens were opened." Surely, he thought to himself as he drifted off to sleep, his riverside townhouse had been built to survive such a deluge.

2

Rain pounded on the roof of Harley's house, banged on the windows, and rattled down the gutters all through the night. The cascading water provided the soundtrack for a vivid dream, one in which three women were standing around a huge iron cauldron at the western end of River Mill Park. The night was as black as India ink, and a raging wind whipped the hair and clothes of the women as they chanted the words, "Double, double, toil and trouble; fire burn and cauldron bubble." The words were familiar. *Shakespeare, perhaps?*

As Harley neared the cauldron, he could see the faces of the women in the glow of the fire beneath it, and he was shocked by who they were: Mary Ranger, the Occoquan postmistress; Doris King, co-owner of the Yarn Shop; and Leah Silverman, a neighbor and old friend. "When shall we three meet again," Mary asked the other two. "In thunder, lightning, or in rain?" Moving closer, he saw black clouds, not in the sky but in the cauldron, swirled by a fierce and unearthly wind. As the witches chanted, the spinning mass of liquid began to exert a pull on him, drawing him closer and closer to the edge of the iron pot, and soon his face was within inches of the bubbling, swirling fluid. Then it sucked him in.

Spinning down the vortex, he saw two figures ahead of him: His dead wife and daughter, Karen and Jessica. He reached out and tried to grab them, wanting to catch them and hold them, pull them close and protect them. But he couldn't reach them. Over the roar of the whirling liquid, Harley heard strange names being chanted by the witches behind him, "Fire Dolphin, Earth Eagle, Fire Dolphin, Earth Eagle." His wife and daughter just kept moving ahead of him and disappearing into the whirlpool. Once again, Harley was losing them.

Then a wail cut through the sound of the spinning liquid and woke him. Startled and confused, Harley came to the surface not knowing where he was, or what was happening around him. The shrieking was accompanied by pulses of blue light on his bedroom wall, images that flowed like glowing liquid from ceiling to floor. Harley realized that the shimmering was being caused by sheets of rain on his windows, and that the pulses were coming from a lightbar. *Of what? A firetruck? A police cruiser?* Yes, he remembered slowly, must be a police cruiser—red means fire, blue means police. He rubbed his eyes and went to the window on the west side of his bedroom, and saw that the light was not actually outside his window, but was bouncing off the windows of the building next door. Putting on his bathrobe, he proceeded to the bedroom overlooking Mill Street, and there he looked southward and saw a cruiser up the hill from his house, parked at the corner of Commerce and Union Streets. For a second, he assumed that it was a traffic stop, but when his eyes adjusted to the darkness, he saw something more surreal than anything in his dream.

Union Street, which runs from Commerce down to Mill Street, had become a river. A torrent of black water, several feet deep, was running toward the Occoquan River, swelling, rolling, and ripping merchandise from the porches of shops along the street. Harley thought he heard a train, but then realized that the sound was being made by the water as it roared through town, even causing parked cars to rise up, spin around, and crash into buildings. Logs and large branches were being carried downhill, along with lawn chairs and pieces of fencing, and while some of the debris spilled left and right onto Mill Street, most of it flowed directly into the Occoquan River. In the glow of the streetlights, he could see that the gravel parking lot that stood between Mill Street and the river was now submerged—it had become a muddy delta linking the two rising, churning, bodies of water. Up the hill were two police officers on Commerce Street, trying to set up barricades in the pouring rain, but the sawhorses they tried to put in place were immediately swept away.

Harley was breathing quickly, frightened by what he was seeing but also awestruck, witnessing a force that could destroy anything in its path. A line from Genesis came to mind, "The waters swelled so mightily on the earth that all the high mountains under the whole heaven were covered." *Surely an exaggeration, but not too far from the truth.* Pulling his bathrobe tightly around him, he watched the black water rush down the hill like a gusher of crude oil, carrying objects past the glow of the streetlights and then into the darkness: A large barrel, three or four trash cans, a floating window box, and an empty kayak. All were being spirited away, effortlessly, by the dark and roaring floodwaters. Then, looking at the gift shop on the corner of Union and Mill, Harley saw a wooden porch begin to wobble as the rushing water undermined it. The posts which held up the roof began to sway, and then the supports gave way and the roof crashed down, splintering with a crack like breaking bones. Immediately the pieces were swept away, leaving the front door of the shop looking ridiculously naked and exposed.

The Town of Occoquan was being transformed by the flood. Another car floated down the street, and then a small pickup truck, spinning like leaves in a stream. *How could that be? They weigh . . . what? Thousands of pounds?* Water filled the streets for as far as Harley could see, including another set of rapids on Ellicott Street, which ran parallel to Union, one block to the west. Sticking his head over the porch railing and into the rain, he looked down and could see that the storm sewers on Mill Street were completely overwhelmed, causing water to rise around his building. His breathing quickened further as he thought about how high it might rise, remembering that the biblical flood covered everything with fifteen cubits of water—*whatever that was.* His mind began to race as he thought of the carport beneath him, which contained his new car, which he loved and really hated to lose. He had nothing else down there, but any neighbor with storage in the carport was going to find their possessions ruined, if not washed away.

Looking across Mill Street, Harley could see lights in the apartments above the first-floor businesses, and a few silhouettes looking down into the street. One was a tall man with long hair, a figure who had, in profile, the features of a Native American—not anyone that Harley had seen on the streets of Occoquan. He squinted to sharpen his focus, but couldn't make out any details of the unknown neighbors through the rain. Giving up, he glanced at the clock in the guest bedroom and saw that it was almost seven, his normal wakeup time. *Better get dressed, no sense standing around.* After walking barefoot to his bedroom, he found a pair of blue jeans and a wool work shirt, remembering the old adage about wool being warm when wet. Then he dusted off some work boots that he had stashed in the back of his closet, and put on a pair of wool hiking socks.

Opening the curtains of the turret in his bedroom, he looked north toward the river. The rain was still coming down hard, but the rising sun was beginning to backlight the dark clouds with an eerie glow. The clouds were rolling from west to east like enormous tumbleweeds, scraping the tops of the trees on the ridge across the river. The Occoquan River was higher than Harley had ever seen it, close to breaching the boardwalk in front of the first row of townhouses. Looking down, Harley could see that the parking lot that sat between the rows of houses was now a lake, at least a couple of feet deep, and he guessed that it wouldn't be long before the water in the river merged with the water in the parking lot, forming one large, churning body. His housing development had ten houses on the river and ten on the street, and as Harley looked at the riverside houses, he realized that they were about to become an island.

Trudging down the stairs to his kitchen, he started a pot of coffee and pulled a bagel out of the refrigerator. His stomach was growling, but he didn't want to drink coffee without food, so he gnawed the cold bagel while the coffee was dripping into the carafe. Looking out the kitchen window onto Mill Street, he felt a sudden wave of panic. *What will happen if the waters keep rising? Will my house be swept off of its piers? Collapse around me and crush me?* Harley threw the half-eaten bagel into the trash and began to pace the hardwood floors of the dining room and living room, looking outside each time he passed a window. The house was creaking and rattling as the wind whipped at its sides, and Harley got the feeling that the structure itself was beginning to sway. *This is not how I want my life to end, trapped like an animal in a cage.*

But on his third circuit from the kitchen to the living room and back, he realized that he had no control over how his life would end, that morning or any morning. His wife Karen and daughter Jessica had probably started their day with coffee and a croissant, one of many numerous daily decisions that lull us all into thinking that we are in control of our lives. They may have bickered in the cab to the Brussels airport, with one blaming the other for a poor restaurant choice the night before. But then they walked into the departure hall and were killed by the nail bombs of a terrorist cell. They had no say in their final moments, and nothing short of a flat tire on the cab could have saved them. Harley was coming to realize that whether you are pierced by nails or crushed by collapsing walls, death will have its way with you. *In the end, there is nothing you can do about it.*

Harley swallowed hard and looked out the kitchen window again, expecting to see the water swelling even higher. But instead, he saw the Native American stranger, standing tall in his second-floor window, looking stoically down onto the street. A woman with blond hair came up behind him and put her arms around him, nestling her head in his shoulder-length black hair. *Who are you,* he wondered, *and why have I never seen you before?* Their features were clearer because the sheeting rainfall had ended, replaced by rapid-fire raindrops making splashes in the street. Realizing that he was staring at the couple, he felt a rush of embarrassment and turned away quickly. *Don't want to be the creepy guy, the voyeuristic pastor, across the street.* But even as he averted his eyes, he hoped that they had noticed him. He longed for a connection, even a fleeting one, in that perilous moment.

Shifting his attention westward, he saw that the river on Union Street was no longer gaining ground. This gave him a sense of relief, so he turned back to give a wave to the couple across the street. But they were gone.

Shafts of light began to cut through the clouds and illuminate the town, revealing piles of debris on the sides of houses and shops along the waterfront. Rainbows arced across the sky and then quickly disappeared, as the wind propelled the clouds across the face of the sun. The water level dropped quickly as the rain tapered off, and within a few minutes the tops of the curbs were once again visible. Like Noah, Harley could see that the waters were subsiding from the earth, and that "the face of the ground" would again become dry. Soon, the flood dropped to a level that could be traversed by a truck, steam began to rise from the water all around, and residents up the hill began to leave their homes to survey the damage. Harley wanted to get out of his house to join them, but the storm sewers on Mill Street were still submerged, and it would take time for the Occoquan River to drop far enough to drain them.

Just then, a large SUV with a flashing blue light appeared on Mill Street, moving slowly from east to west. Harley had never seen the vehicle before and assumed it must have come from Prince William County to assist the two members of the Occoquan sheriff's department. The siren was being sounded in bursts, and an officer was using the loudspeaker to ask if anyone needed assistance. Harley stepped onto his front porch and gave a thumbs-up, signaling that he was okay. The officer in the passenger side of the vehicle returned the gesture, and the vehicle kept moving toward the Union Street rapids. When the driver revved the engine, Harley assumed that they were going to ford the river, but then they stopped—the water was still deep in the intersection, and moving fast. The officers had enough sense to wait for the water to drop even farther, and they used the time to check in with residents who were sticking their heads out of the second-story apartments. He heard the officer who was driving the SUV shout something about a building collapse . . . Ellicott Street . . . with debris going into the river.

When the water flowing down Union Street dropped to a fordable level, the police SUV continued its progress. Then Harley heard the wail of another siren and saw a firetruck and an ambulance appear on Mill Street, with red lights flashing. They followed the SUV on its slow westward journey, and the three vehicles stopped at the intersection of Ellicott and Mill. Harley went upstairs to the porch of the Mill Street bedroom to try to get a better view of the damage but couldn't see anything except the spinning blue and red lights of the police and fire vehicles. Up the hill, a stream of residents was flowing westward along a parallel street, and Harley itched to join them. He hated to miss the excitement. The fear he had felt for his own safety had been quickly replaced by an intense curiosity about the misfortune of others. *Schadenfreude. The pleasure you feel at another person's troubles. Such an unattractive emotion.*

But instead of berating himself, Harley seized an opportunity. The official Occoquan pickup truck appeared, slowly cutting through the water on the street below him, driven by the town maintenance man. "Tim!" shouted Harley, waving from the porch. "Stop!" Tim hunched over the steering wheel and looked up at him. "Meet me at my porch," said the pastor, pointing downward.

Tim came to a stop, and Harley ran down the stairs to the porch on the west side of his townhouse, off the kitchen. Looking down the wrought-iron stairs, he could see that the receding water was now only about half-way up the first step. He bounded down the stairs, a bit too fast for the conditions, and then splashed through the water in his work boots. Tim threw open the passenger door and Harley climbed in. The maintenance man looked more serious than Harley had ever seen him.

"What do you need, Harley?"

"Just a ride, Tim. I want to see what happened."

"This is serious," said Tim, shaking his head. "Worst I've seen since seventy-two. You really shouldn't be outside."

Harley felt a flush of shame. He knew he was being a voyeur, but at this point he wasn't going to turn around. "Terrible," he agreed. "What happened in seventy-two?"

"Hurricane Agnes. The rain from that storm caused the Occoquan River to overflow the dam. A steel bridge was completely swept away. And downtown Occoquan was completely flooded."

"That's awful," said Harley. "Did anyone die?"

"No, thank God. But if the dam had broken, people would have. This is the worst since Agnes." Tim put the truck in gear, and as he began to inch forward, he said, "Since you're in the truck, you may as well come along."

As they crossed Union Street, Harley looked to the right at the delta in the gravel parking lot. Water was flowing through a trench cut through the middle of it, and several inches of thick mud and scattered debris covered the rest of the lot. The Occoquan River was still running high, with its water spilling into the first floors of shops along the bank. *Hope they paid their flood insurance*, thought Harley.

"What happened to the porch of the gift shop?" asked Tim, looking to the left.

"Washed away," said Harley. "I watched it collapse and get swept way."

"Unbelievable," Tim said.

On the south side of Mill Street, the Riverview Bakery seemed to have escaped major damage, but the first floor of the brew pub on the north side, next to the river, was full of water. Overall, it appeared that the buildings on the river side had suffered the worst, but everyone had been hit. When Tim waved to the owner of a card shop and asked how he was doing, the man replied, "Flooded basement! Can't even get down the stairs!"

Then they pulled up beside the firetruck at the corner of Ellicott and Mill, and saw a sight that put the rest of the town's damage into perspective. At the end of Ellicott was a three-story brick apartment building that had been connected to a white clapboard candle shop. Above the candle shop was a single apartment in which the owner lived, and a narrow alley separated the shop from a row of old but well-maintained brick office buildings on the other side. Now the brick apartment building stood at an odd and unexpected distance from the office buildings, looking like a row of teeth with one knocked out. The candle shop had been washed away.

Tie-dye Tim and Harley were stunned. Only a few pieces of lumber remained on the side of the apartment building, remnants of the candle shop. The Ellicott Street rapids had been as powerful as the river on Union Street, and had unleashed their full force on the shop at the bottom of the hill.

Stepping into the drizzle, Tim walked over to the Prince William County police officers who were trying to assess the damage. "Where's Beau?" he asked, his voice croaking.

"Who are you?" replied the taller of the two. He was a burly guy who didn't seem interested in small talk.

"Tim Underwood, town maintenance. Where is Beau Harper, the owner of the candle shop?"

"In the ambulance," said the second officer. "Got out of the building but fell and hit his head."

Tim nodded and headed for the ambulance. Since Occoquan had only a thousand residents, the maintenance man knew everyone.

Harley felt out of place near the police SUV, the firetruck, and the ambulance. The red and blue lights continued to pulse, police tape had been strung around the area, and the officers and firefighters were conferring on how to secure the area. Sensing that the police were going to shoo him away, he walked toward the brick apartment building and surveyed the debris that filled the cavity where the shop had stood just hours before. Most of the wood of the building had washed away, but on the muddy foundation lay a bathtub, a toilet, and a tangle of pipes and wires. A steel filing cabinet poked out of the mud, but the rest of the contents of the building had been swept into the river. Not a single candle remained.

Harley stepped onto the concrete landing of the apartment building to get his feet out of the muddy water in the street. Just inside the front door of the building were a man and a woman who appeared to be in their late thirties or early forties. She had long auburn hair, pale skin, and multiple piercings. He had a bushy brown beard, dark eyes, and tattoos covering both arms. They were talking quite intensely, but when Harley stepped onto the landing they moved outside.

"Hello," said Harley, extending his hand. "I'm Harley Camden. I live down the street."

"Good to meet you," said the woman, shaking his hand. She had a strong grip, and Harley couldn't help noticing that her arms were very toned. In fact, her entire body was lean and muscular, covered only by a form-fitting athletic shirt and yoga pants. "I'm Kelly Westbrook. And this is John Jonas," she said, pointing to her partner. "We live in this building, on the top floor." Harley reached out and shook his hand as well. John was in good shape, but not as ripped as Kelly. He seemed to be more of an outdoorsy, hiker type.

"Quite a disaster," Harley said, sweeping his arm across the destruction.

"Yes," Kelly nodded. "Very unnatural."

Harley tilted his head, wondering what she meant. *Unnatural?* A torrential downpour seemed to him to be the definition of a natural disaster.

"Unsettling," added John.

"At least your neighbor is okay," Harley said. "That's a relief."

"Yes, we are glad," said Kelly. She glanced at John, and seemed to be struggling with what to say. After a moment, she said, "He had issues with us, but we did not wish him ill."

"Issues?" asked Harley, wondering if they too were feeling *schadenfreude*. "Neighborhood issues?"

"You might say that," John replied. "He did not care for our religion."

"That's a shame," said Harley. "I'm all about religious freedom. I'm pastor of Riverside Methodist."

"Oh, a pastor?" Kelly said, her green eyes lighting up. "We're religious leaders, too. Wiccans."

"Wiccans?" asked Harley. "As in witches?"

"Yes," she said. "I'm Fire Dolphin."

"And I," said John, "am Earth Eagle."

3

"You can't stand here," said the burly police officer to the pastor and the witches. Harley usually resented being bossed around, but not this time. "Need to clear the area," directed the officer with a sweep of his arm.

Giving a quick nod to Kelly and John, Harley stepped back into the muddy stream running down the street and began to look for Tim Underwood. The maintenance man was finishing his conversation with the owner of the candle shop, and he motioned for Harley to meet him at his truck. When they climbed into the cab, Tim said, "He'll be okay. Just a knock on the head."

"I met the witches," said Harley.

Tim looked at him as though he were missing the point, and Harley realized he was being insensitive.

"That's good about his injury," said Harley. But his focus was clearly elsewhere. "I met them," he said again.

"John and Kelly," nodded Tim.

"What are they like?"

"Pretty normal, I think."

"Normal? But they're witches."

"Not full-time. Kelly is a fitness instructor at a gym in Lorton . . ."

"A fitness instructor?"

"Yeah, does classes and personal training. And John works in IT, for the county. He's also a hell of a softball player; he swings a mean bat."

"But they said they are leaders—religious leaders."

"That's right," said Tim, smiling. "But not paid professionals. Not like you."

Harley locked eyes with Tim, sensing sarcasm. Then he said, "Yeah, the *big money* is in being a Methodist pastor."

"Speaking of which," said Tim, firing up the truck's ignition, "let's go see how your church is doing." He gunned the engine and headed up Ellicott Street, which had been a torrent just an hour before. Now the last vestiges of the flood were flowing gently down the street, glistening in the morning sun. "And the waters gradually receded from the earth," Harley remembered from Genesis. He was amazed at how quickly the crisis had passed, as well as how much destruction had been left behind.

Tim hung a left on Commerce Street and drove carefully eastward, dodging debris and stopping to check with residents along the way. Dozens of people were on the sidewalk and in the street, picking up branches and lawn chairs and other items displaced by the rain, and most of them looked discouraged and exhausted—even though the day was just beginning. One man stood on his front lawn, looking forlornly at a missing section of his roof. Others were pointing to their basements and using their hands to show each other how much water had accumulated. It appeared that everyone on Commerce Street had some flooding, although the damage seemed to be less catastrophic than what had been suffered down the hill.

Mary Ranger, the Occoquan postmistress, stepped out of her small brick house on the corner of Commerce and Union and gave a wave to Tim and Harley. Her bleach-blonde hair was tousled, and she looked bigger than usual in a loose-fitting sweat-suit. She normally flashed a toothy smile, but she looked absolutely miserable that morning. Harley felt a rush of sympathy for her, even though she had been a witch in his dream.

"I need your help, guys," she said as she approached the truck. "Paul is trying to rescue his rare book collection, and I'm afraid he's going to give himself a heart attack."

"Sure thing," said Tim, steering the truck to the curb and putting it in park. "What exactly is he trying to do?"

"His books are in the basement, and he's afraid the water will ruin them. He's throwing them in boxes and running them upstairs as fast as he can."

"That's not good," said Harley.

"He won't listen to me," Mary lamented. "He's a man on a mission."

As the three of them stepped through the front door, Harley realized that Mary wasn't a witch. She was a Methodist. A pretty typical member of his congregation, to be exact. He had never been in her home before, but it was exactly as he expected it would be: Framed photos of children and grandchildren on the living room wall, comfortable overstuffed furniture facing a fireplace, and a coffee table with a large, colorful, book about Jerusalem—Harley had heard about their trip to Israel with a group from the church. Why she popped up in his dream about the three witches was a mystery.

Pounding footsteps echoed through the house, and Mary said, "There he goes, running a box upstairs."

"Paul!" shouted Tim. "Let us give you a hand."

Tim led Harley to the back of the house, where they encountered a thin man in his early sixties, carrying a heavy box of books. His gaunt face looked panicked as he came up from the basement and pushed past them on his way to the upstairs bedrooms. "I got this," he said, without looking them in the eyes.

"You're going to give yourself a heart attack," said Harley as the man disappeared up the stairs. "Let us help."

Standing in the kitchen, near the door to the basement stairs, Harley and Tim waited for Paul to return from his trip upstairs. When he headed down with an empty box, they offered again to give him a hand. He was breathing hard and seemed exhausted. "Well, okay," he said. "Let me pack and you carry. Upstairs, Mary can unpack."

"Okay," said Tim. "Deal."

The two men followed Paul down the basement steps to a subterranean room that was illuminated by a single bare lightbulb. When they reached the concrete floor, they stepped into a half-inch of standing water. Looking to his right, Harley saw an old furnace and hot water heater; to his left, a row of cardboard boxes marked "Christmas" and "Winter clothes" and "Taxes"—boxes that were now soaking up water from the floor. Straight ahead was a wall of shelves containing rows and rows of old books, which could be reached only by dodging a stationary exercise bike and a rack of barbells. Paul led them across the room, placed an empty box on a weight-lifting bench, and began to fill it up. "This basement has always been dry as a bone," he lamented. "Now, look at it."

"Yeah," said Tim. "You got hit hard. But the people downhill got it even worse."

Harley was curious about the books that Paul was packing, but he didn't want to pry. The single bulb didn't shed much light on that section of the room, so all he could make out was that the books were old, and many had well-worn leather bindings. Paul finished packing the first box, closed the lid and handed it to Tim. Then, as Tim headed for the stairs, he began to fill a second box for Harley.

Moving closer, Harley caught sight of one title: *Aphrodite*. Then another: *Casanova*. Next, a book called *Marriage Ceremonies & Priapic Rites in India & the East*. For Harley, a light was beginning to dawn about the nature of the man's rare book collection. Then, just as Paul closed the lid on the box, Harley saw the title *Epistolai Erotikai*. "Need something?" Paul asked sharply, looking Harley in the eye as he lifted the box and passed it to him.

"No," said the pastor. "Nothing."

Trudging up the stairs, Harley thought back to his Greek classes in divinity school and tried to translate the title. "*Epistolai Erotikai*," he said to himself. "Must be *Letters of . . . Erotic Love*." Kinky. But what are *Priapic Rites*? He thought that the word priapic sounded Greek, but he had no idea what it meant. Pulling back the lid of the box, he saw another title, *Erotische Szenen*. Although terrible in German classes back in college, he didn't have to be a linguist to figure out that it too was an erotic book. *What dark desires were being fed by this collection?* Harley realized that he was now an accessory to an act of saving dirty books.

Stepping into the kitchen, he encountered the maintenance man as he was heading back to the basement with an empty box. "Tim," asked Harley, "what does 'priapic' mean?"

"Phallic," he said, without missing a beat. "Relating to male sexuality."

"How do you *know* that?" asked Harley, shaking his head.

"I read a lot," he said with a smirk.

Harley took his load upstairs to the bedroom, where Mary was stacking the books in a corner. *Does she crave this material, too?* She looked up at him and blushed. *No, she's embarrassed*. Harley put the box of books on the bed, and stepped back so that she could unpack them. "Paul is a good man," she said as she opened the box.

Harley stood silently in front of her, not sure what to say.

"Collecting these books is his hobby," she said as she pulled out *Erotische Szenen*. "They are an investment as well. Some of them are worth hundreds of dollars."

"I'm not judging," said the pastor—although he was.

"It is a little weird," Mary admitted, "but Paul's not a pervert. He's been faithful to me throughout our marriage. But he got interested in this early."

"Most guys do," quipped Harley.

"Yeah, I know," she said, nodding. "But Paul grew up in Indiana, and went to Indiana University. He had a part-time job at the Kinsey Institute."

"Ah. Sex research."

"Not that he was a participant," she said, tipping the box to remove the last book, *The Phallic Idea*. "He worked in the library. But it aroused his . . ."

At that moment, Tim entered the room and said, "Chop, chop, pastor. Get down there with your empty box. We have a lot of books to move." Harley gave a half-hearted nod, took the box from Mary and headed out of the room. Before disappearing, he turned and caught Mary's eye, trying to show his sympathy.

What else was being flushed out of the basements of Occoquan? "Adder's fork and blind-worm's sting," the witches had said in his dream, "lizard's leg and howlet's wing." As he descended into the dark, dank cellar, Harley wondered if there were other strange collections being brought to the surface after the flood. When weather is good and basements are dry, obsessions remain hidden, but when the heavens open . . . all is revealed. He imagined that people across town were responding to the flood by rescuing hidden porn videos and drug paraphernalia and books on the occult. He guessed that they feared the loss of these possessions, but also hoped that they would be destroyed by the waters. *Love and hate; how often they mix.*

Harley saw this conflict in Paul's eyes as he sloshed toward him across the basement floor. The man was all business, wanting to get his books to safety but at the same time being haunted by something. *Shame, perhaps. Humiliation.* "Here's another load," he said, quickly filling Harley's box. He then paused for a moment, as though he wanted to offer an explanation. But all he said was, "I do appreciate your help." The pastor replied, "No problem," and then turned to climb the stairs.

But are erotic books really such a dark secret? Harley pondered this as he made a number of runs between the basement and the bedroom. He remembered that in Dante's *Inferno,* the lustful were sent to the second ring of hell, where they were punished by being blown back and forth by strong winds—like the winds that blasted Occoquan all night. This was a terrible fate for the lustful, and it prevented them from finding any peace or rest. But at the same time, Harley knew that this was simply the second ring of hell. These souls were not being punished as severely as the people in rings three through nine, who had committed the sins of gluttony, greed, anger, heresy, violence, fraud, or worst of all, treachery. For Dante, lust was bad enough to deserve condemnation, but it was far less serious than all of the other sins.

Perhaps, thought Harley, a penchant for erotic books could be tolerated because the human body was a gift of God, part of the creation that God had declared to be good. The ancient Hebrews believed that the spirit and the body were united—"psychosomatic unity" is what Harley's divinity school professors called it—and they saw feasting and dancing and touching and lovemaking as part of a good and faithful life. Jesus himself had no problem with human bodies, and was well known for the ways in which he fed people and healed them, often with a physical touch. It was the Greeks who saw the spirit and the body as separate, and their high view of the spirit and low view of the body eventually influenced Christianity, leading many people to believe that their bodily appetites were dirty, disgusting, and evil. Harley knew that suspicion of the body and its natural impulses, grounded in Greek philosophy, had caused many members of his church to become overly obsessed with their weight or their sexuality, leading to self-loathing and even self-destructive behaviors. Paul Ranger may very well have been one of them, but his rare book collection, by itself, was not proof that he had a problem.

"Hey, check this out," said Tim, meeting Harley on the stairs on his final run from the basement. He had plucked a book out of the last box that he had carried to the bedroom. "*120 Days of Sodom,* by Marquis de Sade," he said. "Sadism, right?"

"Yeah, that's some sick stuff," admitted Harley. Maybe Paul *did* have a problem.

"Here, you can make the delivery," said Paul, sticking it in the top of Harley's box. "I'm done, and I'll meet you out front."

Harley carried his last box to Mary, and again stepped back to give her some space. "I'm grateful to you, Harley," she said. "And to Tim. I really thought that Paul was going to hurt himself with all these heavy books."

"Are you okay with this?" asked Harley, feeling concern. He would have felt guilty if he left the house without raising the question.

Mary stopped unpacking and sat down on the edge of the bed. "People are complicated," she admitted, not meeting Harley's eyes but looking out the window. "I see it every day at the post office. Wrappers and packaging can hide a lot, but you wouldn't believe what I see in the return addresses alone."

"Does Paul's collection bother you?"

"Well, it's not the hobby I would choose for him," she said, turning to face her pastor. "But you know what? We are all pleasure-seeking creatures. It's the way we are made. I get pleasure from cooking a decadent meal. He gets pleasure from these books. As long as it doesn't hurt anyone, I guess it's okay."

"Are you sure about that?" asked Harley. *Who knows what harm is being done every time Paul pores over one of these books?* Mary didn't answer, but sat there looking past him toward the door. Then Harley heard a floorboard squeak, and he turned around. Paul was standing in the doorway.

"Thank you, Harley," he said. "You and Tim were a huge help. I'm sorry to take so much of your time."

"You're welcome. We've got to pull together at a time like this."

"Maybe we can talk someday," Paul offered. "I know these books are . . . uh, unexpected. Concerning, perhaps. I'd like to explain."

"Look, Paul, I'm not here to snoop. But if you'd like to talk, that would be great." With that, Harley stuck out his hand, Paul gave him a two-handed shake, and Harley headed down the stairs.

"Well, that was weird," said Tim, as the pastor climbed into the truck.

"You *think*?" Harley replied, smiling. "I really like to see you surprised, Tim. I figured you knew everything about everybody, and that nothing could shock you."

"Learn something new every day." With that, Tim put the truck in gear, and continued down Commerce Street toward Riverside Methodist Church. The sky had turned a bright blue while they were working at the Ranger house, and the wind had all but disappeared. Looking to the left, they could see the Occoquan River rushing wildly from west to east, carrying a thick load of debris from upriver. The streets of the town were full of refuse as well, and coated with an inch of mud. "I've got my work cut out for me," said the Occoquan maintenance man. "Cleaning the streets alone is going to take weeks."

Riverside Methodist Church stood on the corner of Commerce and Washington Streets, as it had since its founding as Emanuel Baptist in 1885. As soon as the church came into view, Harley gave a gasp. The cross that had perched on the top of the stubby steeple was missing. As Tim turned left on Washington and then right into the church parking lot, Harley craned his neck to see where it was, and then spotted it on the ground near the front door of the church. It was surrounded by splinters of wood from the shattered steeple.

Jumping out of the truck, Harley picked up the heavy iron cross, which was fortunately undamaged by its fall. Tim kicked the toe of one of his boots in the pieces of wood on the ground and said, "Looks like you had a thoroughly rotten steeple, pastor. Lots of water damage over the years, I would guess."

The two men gazed up at the stub of the white steeple, which looked like a broken tooth. "That's going to be tough to fix," said Harley. "Who even does that kind of work?"

"It'll be a challenge," said Tim. "But a good carpenter should be able to do the job. I know a guy."

"Never would have guessed I had steeple rot," Harley mused. "Wonder how deep it goes?"

"Won't know till someone gets up there and starts poking around."

"Steeple rot," Harley said with a grin. "Sounds like a medical term."

"For sick pastors," teased Tim.

At that moment, a siren began wailing and one of Occoquan's two patrol cars roared down Washington Street with its blue lights pulsing. "Looks like Terry Stone," said Tim, watching the car as it took a screeching left onto Mill Street. Stone was Occoquan's sheriff, who along with deputy Sharon Madison comprised the entire department. The two did a good job of traffic enforcement and inebriation control, but for any major criminal activity they needed the help of the Prince William County Police.

"Where do you think he's heading?" Harley asked.

"Probably back to the candle shop," Tim guessed. "Throw the cross in the back of the truck, and let's go see."

In a matter of minutes, they were back at the corner of Mill and Ellicott. The burly Prince William cop was still there, along with several other officers, paramedics, and firefighters. The atmosphere was highly charged, even though the danger of the hurricane was now long gone. Sheriff Terry Stone was talking with them, and one officer was pointing down to the edge of the water, which had receded several feet in the last hour. More of the wreckage of the candle shop was now visible, and several firefighters and officers were gathered around something in the debris.

When Stone began to walk toward the water, Tim and Harley fell in behind him. The Prince William cop put his hand up to stop them, but Stone turned around, saw who it was, and said, "It's okay." Tim was a big help to the sheriffs in various town events, and Harley was, well, a pastor. He had accompanied Stone on several calls in the past year, most recently to comfort the wife of a man who had put a gun in his mouth and shot himself. That was a blood-spattered scene that Harley would never forget.

They walked carefully through the muddy debris, trying to maintain good footing in the muck, and when they reached the water's edge, they saw what the officers and firefighters had discovered: A body. It appeared to be that of a young man in his early 20s, a Latino with numerous tattoos and long dark hair. His face was battered and swollen, and his right arm was twisted in an impossible angle over his head. Numerous lacerations covered his naked torso, and several fingers were missing from his left hand. Harley had seen many corpses over the course of his ministry, but none this disfigured, and he suddenly felt himself overcome by nausea. Not wanting to embarrass himself by vomiting, he turned away from the body and faced Mill Street. But then he heard the burly cop say to Sheriff Stone, "Look, the claw."

Harley swallowed hard, and turned back toward the body. Carved into the man's back was a crude and bloody rendering of Satan's claws.

4

A team of retirees assembled outside Riverside Methodist on Thursday morning, armed with buckets, mops, and a couple of Shop-Vacs. The church members ranged in age from sixty to ninety-three, and although they were joking and trash-talking like young men, they had long ago lost the stamina and muscle needed for the heavy lifting of storm cleanup. What they lacked in strength they made up for in volume, joshing with each other loud enough to overcome the limitations of their hearing aids. Most had spindly arms and big bellies, and several had scars on their hairless legs from knee replacements. But Andy Stackhouse, a former Navy officer, approached the clean-up of the social hall like a military operation, addressing his fellow volunteers as though they were highly-trained troops about to storm a beach. "We found an inch of water on the lower level yesterday afternoon," he reported to the group. "It has drained to about a half an inch now, but we have got to get the rest out or we'll have mold and mildew. We'll begin with Shop-Vacs, then use mops and buckets, and finally we'll open windows and doors and set up large fans. Any questions?"

"Where's the coffee?" asked Arvin Natwick, the oldest man in the group and a veteran of the Second World War.

"And donuts?" added Sid Bennett, a former high school teacher.

"You think you deserve coffee and donuts?" asked Andy. "Really? Right now? Let's move some water first."

"Oh, my back!" said Sid, hunching over.

Gretchen Bennett, the only woman in the group, said to the leader, "Don't let Sid sit down. He'll never get up."

"Sounds like you speak from experience," said Andy. "Guys, you'll get your break, don't worry. I don't want to upset your union."

"*Vamanos, amigos,*" said Juan Erazo, a 70-year-old immigrant who had joined the church a year earlier. "Remember the Puerto Rico clean-up? We can do better."

Standing at the door, Harley gave them high-fives as they took their equipment into the social hall, thanking them and saying to the last one, Arvin, "Don't know what I'd do without you."

"You'd have a moldy church," said the old soldier. "Or, should I say, a *moldier* church." Arvin fancied himself a comedian.

Just as they were firing up their Shop-Vacs, a midnight-blue Mercedes Benz pulled into the parking lot. Harley saw rat-faced Jefferson Jones behind the wheel, next to his colleague Abdul, whose head looked like it had been carved out of a block of cappuccino granite. Jefferson was a member of Emanuel Baptist Church, which had moved from Occoquan to nearby Woodbridge when the congregation outgrew the Occoquan church building, and Abdul was an African American who had converted to Islam while in jail. Jefferson was dressed impeccably, as usual, in a beautifully-tailored brown suit, while Abdul was wearing workout clothes that were stretched to the limit by his enormous muscles. They were powerful men, each in his own way, and the two had a close bond despite the fact that Jefferson was thirty years older than Abdul.

As they got out of the car, Harley noticed that both men had shaved their heads. This was normal for Abdul but not for Jefferson, who had always kept his gray hair perfectly trimmed. Perhaps he had shaved his head in anticipation of chemo, to keep people from asking about why he was losing his hair. Harley remembered his promise of confidentiality, and didn't say a word about it.

"Jefferson, good to see you," said the pastor, extending his hand. "And you as well, Abdul."

"A pleasure," responded Jefferson, formal as always. "How is your church faring after the flood?"

"Water in the basement and a broken steeple. But not bad, given the circumstances."

"I remember Agnes," said Jefferson, turning his pointy face toward the river. He was a dignified man but terribly ugly, and it was a mystery to Harley how he could produce a daughter as gorgeous as Tawnya. "So much destruction from that storm, up and down Mill Street," said Jefferson. "I remember a fishing boat sitting in front of the post office. But since this church is uphill, nothing but a flooded basement."

"Well, it's happened again," Harley said. "Guess we were due, after almost fifty years."

"I don't know about 'due,'" Jefferson responded, skeptically. "Seems unnatural to me." Like the witches, Jefferson was seeing the flood as something other than a *natural* disaster.

"You know," said the pastor, "they talk about fifty-year floods. Maybe this was one of those."

"Or something else," Jefferson suggested, raising an eyebrow.

The door of the church basement opened, and Arvin and Sid struggled to push a Shop-Vac into the parking lot. Already full of water, the vacuum was heavier than the older men could handle. "May I help?" Abdul asked Harley.

"Be my guest."

The strapping Muslim made his way to the basement door and greeted the church volunteers. Then he leaned over, picked up the Shop-Vac, and easily dumped the water into the parking lot so that it could flow away from the building. "Water is heavy," he commented in a matter-of-fact sort of way, "8.34 pounds per gallon."

"Felt like at least 8.5 pounds per gallon to me," said Arvin the jokester.

"No, 8.34," said Abdul. "Unless you are talking about imperial gallons." With the hint of a smile, he said, "Imperial gallons are lighter, of course."

"Of course!" said Arvin, holding out his hands to take back the empty vacuum. Abdul held on to the vacuum and offered to help with the cleanup. The older men seem delighted.

"Is this taking Abdul away from you?" Harley asked Jefferson.

"No," said the older man. "We're here to help. But he is in better shape than I." Harley didn't know if he was alluding to his age or illness. Jefferson did not elaborate.

"Want to come inside?" Harley asked, pointing to his office, up a flight of outdoor stairs.

"Sounds good," said Jefferson. He seemed older and wearier than he had just a few months before.

Harley's office on the side of the church was small, not much bigger than a broom closet. Jefferson took a seat in a wooden arm chair in front of the pastor's desk, and Harley sat down in an identical chair just a few feet away. Jefferson ran his fingers across the top of the solid oak desk that had belonged to his uncle when he was the pastor of Emanuel Baptist, a piece of furniture that had been left behind when the congregation moved to larger and more modern quarters. "I don't think I've been in here since Abdul and I made our donation," said Jefferson.

"I think you're right," Harley agreed. "Your gift was very helpful to the Bayatis."

"I'm glad," said Jefferson. "They got justice. Not everyone does." Harley sat quietly, thinking that the older man would say more about the Iraqi family, but he changed the subject. "'Justice' was the name of my first shopping center," he said.

"Up at the top of Tanyard Hill?"

"Exactly," said the older man. "Bought the land and developed it while I was still a shopkeeper here in Occoquan."

"Must have been expensive," Harley surmised.

"Not too bad," said Jefferson. "The owner stopped paying his property taxes, so I got the land in a tax sale."

"Poor guy."

Jefferson shook his head. "No, I cannot feel sorry for him. He was a total racist, a member of the KKK. I was happy to take his land and develop Justice Plaza. Good name, don't you think?"

"Absolutely," Harley nodded. "I had no idea where the name came from."

"Most people don't," acknowledged Jefferson. "Justice seems innocuous. You know, like the line from . . . what was it . . . Superman? Yes, I think it was Superman: 'Truth, Justice and the American Way.' But for me it has a very special and specific meaning, unrelated to the comics. For me, justice is very concrete."

Harley had driven by Justice Plaza many times, not knowing its history and hardly noticing its name. A huge enclosed mall with an enormous parking lot, like so many of the retail monsters that were developed in the 1970s, it was probably nearing the end of its useful life. But the shopping center continued to operate, surrounded by acres and acres of blacktop at the top of the hill by the intersection of Tanyard Hill Road and Old Bridge Road.

He knew from his conversation with Tawnya that Jefferson wanted to sell Justice Plaza, but he didn't raise the topic since the information was given in confidence. Instead, he asked, "So what effect has the flood had on you?"

Jefferson sighed and said, "I was the owner of the candle shop."

"Really?" replied Harley.

"Yes, I'm afraid so. I bought it last year, as part of my planned redevelopment of the waterfront."

"Right," Harley remembered, thinking back to when he first met Jefferson and Abdul by the river, in July of the previous year. "I knew you were trying to do something in that area. I'm just glad that Beau Harper is okay."

"As am I," Jefferson agreed. "Although, tragically, I've lost him as a rent-paying tenant." His words seemed harsh, but then he smiled. "I'm kidding, of course. Beau is a good man. I'm glad he survived."

"So, what were your plans for the shop?" Harley asked.

"Well, I was going to remove all of the antique fixtures and fine woodwork before tearing it down. I don't know if you ever went inside it, but it was a treasure."

"No, I never did," said Harley. "I'm not much of a candle guy."

"Neither am I," said Jefferson, "but the interior of the building was beautiful. Now it's a total loss."

"Sorry to hear it. I really am."

"I just wish that Beau hadn't been feuding with the witches."

Okay, thought Harley. *Where is Jefferson going with this?* "Tell me more," he said.

"Beau is a member of an evangelical church, New Life Community Church."

"Pastor White's church?" asked Harley.

"Exactly," said Jefferson. "Pastor Tony White. Anyway, Beau became very upset that there were witches living next door to him and having their ceremonies in River Mill Park. He organized a group from his church to do a picket line when the witches had a ceremony."

"Interesting," said Harley. "How did the witches respond?"

"Ignored them, mostly," said Jefferson. "But one time there was a shouting match, along with some pushing and shoving."

"Who started it?"

"One of the Christians, I'm sorry to say."

"I guess they were taking a stand for their faith," offered Harley.

"I suppose," said Jefferson, taking a deep breath. "But I don't approve of violence, even in support of my faith. Picket lines are fine. Prayer vigils are fine. But pushing and shoving? No."

"That must have created some bad blood."

"Indeed," said Jefferson. "Beau told me that the witches were casting spells on him, trying to bind him and make him fail."

"Where did he get that idea?" asked Harley.

"I'm not sure," Jefferson shrugged. "But I do remember that about a year ago, around Halloween, there were reports of thousands of witches casting spells against President Trump."

Harley hated to talk politics, inside or outside his church. He knew that Jefferson was a Republican, a proud member of the Party of Lincoln, but he couldn't imagine him supporting Trump. So, he played it safe and said, "That's right. I do remember hearing that." An image from the news popped into his mind: Witches burning yellow yarn and crying out, "Lose all of your hair!" At the time, it seemed funny to him. But not now.

"Beau got the idea that the witches were against him, summoning evil powers to destroy him. And you know what? After the flood, I think he may be right."

"How so?"

"The flood," Jefferson said in a calm and measured way. "I think the witches may have caused the flood. If you wrong them, they're going to wrong you back."

At that moment, Harley's cellphone rang, and he looked at the number. "Excuse me, Jefferson," he said, "I need to get this." He talked for a moment with Bill Stanford, a member of Riverside who was the dentist in charge of the mission trip to Honduras. Although Harley was usually annoyed by such interruptions, this one came as a relief since his conversation with Jefferson was turning surreal. Bill helped him to clear his head for a moment. *Witches. Spells. Evil powers . . . causing the flood? For real?* After hanging up, Harley said, "So you think the witches might have put a spell on Beau?"

"Or used their power to bring down the waters," suggested Jefferson. "I don't know exactly what witches do, or what power they have. And frankly, as a Christian, I don't want to know. I don't want to get close to the occult."

Harley sat quietly for a moment, and then said, "I've never heard of such a thing, not in all my years of ministry. But who knows? 'There are more things in heaven and earth . . .'"

"'Than are dreamt of in your philosophy,'" said the older man, completing the quotation. "Hamlet, right?"

"Exactly."

"There *is* something wicked going on," said Jefferson. "How about that dead man, found in the rubble of Beau's shop? Was he killed by the flood? Or by witches? I hear that he had satanic markings on him."

"Yes, that's true," Harley agreed. "I saw them. Gruesome. But two of the witches were questioned about him—the two who live next door—and they said they didn't know the dead man."

"I heard the same," said Jefferson. "But you know what they say about Satan: He is the father of lies."

"You know your Bible, Jefferson."

"That's how I was raised."

"I can't say if the witches were telling the truth or not," admitted Harley.

Just then, a knock came at the door. "Excuse me," said Abdul, sticking his large shaved head into the pastor's office. Harley waved him in. "This clean-up will go a lot faster with additional Shop-Vacs. Jefferson, if you can drive me to the rental center, I'll get a couple more and we'll knock this out."

"Thank you, Abdul," said Harley. "Let me cover the cost."

"No, we've got it," the big man said, holding up his right hand. "Jefferson wants this place looking good for his family reunion."

"He's right," said the older man, smiling. "The women of my family have made their expectations clear. If it's not clean and dry, *you* will not be held responsible. *I* will."

Harley walked the two men to the door, and stood on the landing as they headed down the wooden stairs to the parking lot. He gazed north toward the swirling coffee-colored river, and saw that it was still running high, with logs and large branches being carried by the strong current toward the bay. Although the foam on the surface made the water look as harmless as a frothy latte, he knew that anyone who dared to take a boat on the water would quickly lose control and be sucked into the vortex. Down, down, down, just like the waters of the cauldron in his dream. A feeling of dread began to well up inside him, a sense that something horrible was lurking beneath the surface, something that could spin him around and suck him in.

He turned to go inside, wanting just a minute to settle himself—but then a car horn sounded. Harley looked over his shoulder, squinted his eyes and saw that Bill Stanford was pulling into the parking lot. *Come on, man,* he thought to himself, *wasn't our phone call enough for you?* Although he really didn't want to take the time to talk, he had learned decades earlier that ministry was all about interruptions. A short conversation would be the right thing to do. "Dr. Stanford, *cómo está?*" Harley asked with forced enthusiasm, as the man walked up the stairs.

"*Muy bien, amigo,*" responded the dentist.

"Come on in."

Bill Stanford plopped into the chair that was still warm from Jefferson Jones and spread his long legs. He was a tall guy with red hair, about Harley's age, who had played basketball at Virginia in the early eighties, alongside superstar Ralph Sampson. "I know we just talked, but I was driving by and realized I had some Cipro you might want to take to Honduras."

"Cipro?" asked Harley. "Don't know what that is."

"It's a powerful antibiotic," said the dentist. "Ciprofloxacin, to be exact. Might be very helpful if you get infectious diarrhea on our trip."

"Sounds like fun," Harley said.

"This stuff will knock out whatever bugs you pick up," Bill promised, tossing the plastic medicine bottle to Harley.

"So, what other meds should I be taking?" Harley figured that if they were going to chat, he might as well learn something. "It's been over thirty years since I was in Honduras."

"Let's see," said the dentist. "You've got your hepatitis shots, right? And typhoid. I assume your tetanus is up to date."

"Yes, I checked. It is."

"Then you really just need to start your anti-malarial meds. What are you taking?"

"Let me look," said Harley, opening his desk drawer. Pulling out a bottle, he read the name, "Melial."

"Okay," Bill said, nodding. "That one is new to me. When do you take it?"

"Started last Wednesday, one tablet a week for three weeks before departure." Looking at a calendar on his wall, he realized he had missed a dose. "Should have taken one yesterday," he admitted.

"Then you better take it today."

"Okay, I will. The third dose comes three days before we leave. And then once a day in Honduras."

"We're at a decent elevation, so the mosquitos aren't too bad," Bill said, "but better safe than sorry."

"Agreed. Don't want to come back sick."

"The real dangers are elsewhere," said the dentist. "For starters: The roads. They're terrible. I've seen some horrible accidents."

"Yes, I remember. Potholes everywhere."

"And the gangs, *Mara Salvatrucha* and the *Barrio 18*. We won't have any trouble where we'll be staying, but there are neighborhoods in the big cities that are war zones."

"Murder capital of the world," said Harley, shaking his head.

"All driven by drugs. And I hate to say it, but North America is creating the demand that Central America is trying to fill. We've got blood on our hands, for sure."

Harley had thought of Bill as a Christian do-gooder, not particularly tuned into global politics. But then he realized that the dentist had been going to Honduras for at least a decade. You cannot spend time with the locals without getting a sense of what is going on in the *barrio*.

"And don't even get me started on the corruption in Honduran politics," Bill continued. "The president was losing the election last fall, and then suddenly the vote count was suspended. When it resumed, the president won!"

"And we think we've got problems," Harley said.

"No comparison," Bill concluded. "But the people of La Entrada need dental care, so I'll continue to go down there." Rising out of his chair, he said, "I'm going to head out. Glad you'll be part of the trip, Harley."

"Me too," he responded. Then, remembering something he had found while moving to Occoquan, he pushed aside a stack of papers on his desk and picked up an old notebook. "Check this out: My Honduras journal." Opening it to the first page, he gave it to Bill to read.

> *May 20, 1986. Flew into San Pedro Sula with the dig team, and took a charter bus to La Entrada. Spent my first night in Honduras and was introduced to Salva Vida beer at the hotel bar. Tasted so good after a long, hot day. Didn't think I'd be doing archaeology again this summer, but professor Larry Baker heard about my work at Sepphoris and asked me to come along and supervise a square. Next day, the bus continued to Copán Ruinas, dodging potholes all the way. Larry gave a lecture on the bus about Copán, one of the centers of the Mayan world in the classical period, 250 to 900 CE. The area around Copán had a population of about 28,000 people, and was a center of extraordinary stone carving and other forms of visual art. Archaeologists disagree about what caused the kingdom to collapse.*

"Ah, *Salva Vida*," said Bill. "A good beer. You'll have some again."

"Could use one right now," said Harley, opening his bottle of Melial tablets. "Although it still is a little early." Picking up a glass that had an inch of water in the bottom, he popped a tablet in his mouth and washed it down. Although he had been telling himself that he was an experienced Honduras traveler, he had no idea what he was getting himself into.

5

"We've seen some mighty waters this week." The shell-shocked congregation nodded as Harley began his sermon at Riverside Methodist Church on the first Sunday after the flood. The standing water had been removed from the social hall, but large fans were still running in the lower level and a moldy smell was wafting up from below. Fortunately, the air had turned cooler—the first taste of fall—so all the windows in the Sanctuary were wide open, and a refreshing breeze was blowing through the congregation.

"The Bible understands this, speaking clearly about the mighty waters that can drench, drown, and destroy us. Scripture talks of floods sweeping over us, waters roaring and foaming, deep mire pulling us down." Pointing toward the river, Harley said, "I guarantee that if you go to the edge of the Occoquan River today, you'll sink . . . sink in deep mire."

Although the people in the pews were exhausted from the cleanup of the past few days, they came to church because they needed to make sense of the disaster they had just suffered, and they wondered what their pastor would say about it. As he looked out over the congregation, Harley remembered how churches across the country had been absolutely packed on the Sunday after the terrorist attacks of 9/11. Times of communal trauma are, oddly enough, a good time to be the church.

Erotica-buff Paul Ranger was in the congregation, which was unusual since he typically came only on high holy days. So was Tie-dye Tim Underwood, who had become a regular visitor over the past year, although he had not joined the church. Tie-dye looked like an old mop that had been put through a wringer, having toiled overtime to coordinate the town's cleanup efforts. "A hurricane hit us hard this past week," Harley continued. "Basements have been flooded, structures have been damaged, possessions have been ruined, and a young man has lost his life. We have a hard time making sense of this, and it will take us many months to recover." He thought of Beau Harper, homeless after the destruction of the candle shop, and the merchants along Mill Street who wouldn't be able to reopen until they were able to replace their ruined flooring, furniture, and merchandise. Years of business development had been wiped out in a single night.

"But Jesus is with us when the waters roar and foam, and he always has been. Never forget that Jesus is with you in the storm." With these words, Harley swept his arm toward the black Jesus in the stained-glass window over his head. The figure had been installed in 1885, when the church was founded as Emanuel Baptist by a formerly enslaved person named Bailey. This particular Jesus had been ahead of his time, installed in an era in which most stained-glass figures were as white as Scandinavians. But this image was a perfect fit for 21st-century Occoquan, as the town became more multicultural every day. For generations, African-American worshipers had found strength to live with dignity and hope by gathering under this dark-skinned Jesus, a savior who was eternally calming the waves of a stormy Sea of Galilee, and Harley knew how important such a figure could be. In the archaeological work he did as a young man, Harley had discovered that visual images were soothing and stabilizing to a community experiencing stress, whether the artwork was a mosaic in Galilee or a stone carving in Honduras.

"But storms involve more than water," Harley continued. "Sometimes life overwhelms us with personal and professional problems. These, too, can feel like a flood of mighty waters. We feel overpowered by difficulties rushing towards us, whether they be financial, relational, vocational, or emotional. They knock us over, spin us around, and cause us to lose control." Out of nowhere, Harley felt himself hit by a rogue wave of grief, as powerful as the one that had overwhelmed him when he first learned of the deaths of his wife and daughter. He paused and looked down at his notes, but they were a blur. How could this wave be swamping him again? It had been more than two years. Grief was supposed to lose its power over time, not get stronger. He found himself beginning to panic, and his mind began to race. A strange set of words began to repeat rapid-fire in his head—*ancient foe, ancient foe, ancient foe*—a phrase from "A Mighty Fortress Is Our God," a familiar old hymn that the congregation had just sung: "For still our ancient foe / doth seek to work us woe." Harley closed his eyes and tried to clear his head.

After a few awkward moments of silence, he looked down again and the notes on the pulpit were clear. "We find ourselves gasping for breath," he continued, "with the waters coming up to our necks and our feet in deep mire. At times like these, we need an ark. A shelter from the flood. A refuge from the mighty waters. A vessel to carry us across the waves to a place of safety and salvation. An ark for our spirits." This was a good image, and Harley knew it. The idea of the church as a spiritual ark was strong and memorable, and it would comfort his people. But instead of being able to rest in the security of this image, Harley found himself being assaulted by more words from the morning hymn—*devils filled, devils filled, devils filled*—and though this world, with devils filled / should threaten to undo us. Once again, his sermon notes began to swim on the page. He had no idea what was going on.

Harley locked eyes with gaunt-faced Paul Ranger, who looked even more haunted than he had on Tuesday morning. *Ancient foe.* Mary wasn't with him, which made Harley wonder if they had been arguing over the erotica in their bedroom. *Devils filled.* Harley feared that his message was spiraling out of control, and that he wouldn't be able to finish. *Ancient foe.* He had always been a clear and focused preacher, priding himself on delivering a quality message. *Devils filled.* He said a quick prayer under his breath, asking God to help him get through this, and when he opened his eyes the words on the pulpit were clear again. "Of course," he continued, "I'm not talking about a physical ark. There is no boat that can give us the help we need, even though some people today think otherwise."

What a relief. Under his breath, Harley thanked God for saving him, and then lifted his head to tell a story. "Up in Frostburg, Maryland, you can see 'God's Ark of Safety,' an actual Noah's ark under construction next to Interstate 64. No kidding: A life-sized ark. It was started by a Church of the Brethren pastor in 1974, and he's been working on it ever since. How many of you have seen it?" A few members of the congregation raised their hands. Harley felt himself regaining his focus and reconnecting with his congregation. "No, I'm not talking about a physical ark—instead, a spiritual ark. Riverside Methodist Church is a spiritual ark for us, one that shelters us from the worst storms of life and keeps us sailing in the direction that God wants us to go. We are in this ark together, and that's a good thing, since the maintenance and sailing of this ark can never be an individual pursuit. I can't do it by myself, and neither can you. It requires the participation of everyone in the church, a group that wants to get through the flood and find safety on the other side. Within this church we can support each other, hold each other accountable, and gently correct each other when we go off course." Once again, Harley found himself making eye contact with Paul, but this time no unwanted words assaulted him.

"The best thing about our spiritual ark is that Jesus is at the helm. Look again at the image behind me. Jesus saved his disciples from a storm on the sea. He showed his power over chaos by actually walking on water. That's amazing, isn't it? Walking on water. Jesus rescued Peter when he was about to sink beneath the waves. He healed the sick, raised the dead, and cast out demons . . . yes, cast out demons." Mentioning demons, Harley feared that the spinning loop of "ancient foe" and "devils filled" would begin again, but it did not. Instead, he heard another phrase from the hymn, one that shifted his thoughts to the witches of Occoquan. *"The Prince of Darkness grim / we tremble not for him." Yes, that's right,* he realized, *even if the witches serve the Prince of Darkness, we tremble not for him . . . or for them.* Feeling a rush of bravado, he pondered the line again, *"The Prince of Darkness grim / we tremble not for him." Who is the Prince of Darkness in the face of Jesus, the Light of the World? Who are his minions against the people of God?* Harley's mind was spinning again, but this time with exuberance. "Jesus has overcome the power of chaos," he proclaimed to the congregation. "He can give us peace in stormy times, and healing of body, mind and spirit. He is the Light of the World, more powerful than the Prince of Darkness!"

Harley's words did not uplift the congregation, as he hoped they would. *Prince of Darkness,* they wondered, looking mystified, *where did that come from?* Harley's sermons were usually logically constructed, sometimes to a fault, but this line came out of the blue. Seeing the bewildered faces, Harley realized that he had allowed his internal ruminations to enter the sermon. He felt embarrassed, and quickly pivoted back to the idea of Jesus being at the helm of a spiritual ark. Then he brought the sermon in for a safe landing by asking the people to join him in prayer. Disaster averted.

∼

After the service, Harley felt angry with himself. How could he lose control like that? He hated that he had been swamped by unwanted thoughts and crazy ruminations: Devils . . . ancient foes . . . the Prince of Darkness. *How could I be so weak, so undisciplined, so easily thrown off course?* He hated it when preachers made their messages all about themselves and their issues, spilling their guts about their internal tensions and spiritual struggles. His job, he believed, was to deliver a solid biblical message to the congregation, one that focused on *their* issues, not his. Preaching was not supposed to be a personal therapy session or a TED Talk, but look what he had done—he had let his internal craziness break through his prepared words, bringing his grief and fear to the surface. What a muddled mess he had dumped on his congregation. Harley felt ashamed of his performance and swore that it would never happen again. *Keep God at the center,* he said to himself, *not devils. Focus on Jesus, not the Prince of Darkness.* And yet, even as he made these promises to himself, he felt that his madness was still there, bubbling beneath the surface. He realized that he couldn't wipe it out by a sheer act of will, so he changed his clothes and took a brisk walk.

Strolling westward along Mill Street, he looked at the soggy carpets and ruined furniture piled on the sidewalk. *As big a mess as my sermon*, he thought to himself. The candle shop was still a trail of debris that stretched from the street to the edge of the river, with a few remnants of police tape flapping in the afternoon breeze. Then, looking up, he let himself take in the unexpected splendor of the light blue sky, cloudless and radiant on that late September day. It filled his head and heart and body with a sense of serenity and well-being. At ground level, his view of Occoquan was nothing but mud and destruction and chaos. But above the treetops, everything was clear and orderly and peaceful—a window to the heavens. Seeing a white heron swoop over the river with wings spread wide, Harley longed to leave the earth and see the world from the perspective of that soaring bird.

Continuing his walk into River Mill Park, he saw a slender woman stretching her long legs against the railing that prevented pedestrians from falling onto the rocks in the water below. She looked well-conditioned and strong, but he sensed that she was vulnerable. *Where did that impression come from? Crazy thoughts*. With temperatures in the seventies, it was a perfect afternoon for a run, and the woman was dressed in a sleeveless running shirt and form-fitting short pants. Her face was turned away from him, but he was drawn to her river of reddish-brown hair, her well-toned arms, and legs that were as muscular as the haunches of a lioness. *This is the kind of distraction I need*, he thought to himself, enjoying the sight as he strolled toward her along the sidewalk. But then the woman shifted to stretch her other side and turned toward him, catching him in the act of staring at her. "Hello there," she said. *Oh no*—he was busted. It was the witch.

"Uh, yes," said Harley, averting his eyes. "Hello." *This world, with devils filled, will threaten to undo us.*

She stopped stretching and stood up straight. "I'm Kelly."

"Yes, that's right. We met."

"And you're Harley. The pastor."

"Correct," he said. "Good memory." But unwanted words returned to his brain: *Ancient foe. Seek to work us woe.* "How are you?"

"Not bad," she said. "Just about to go for a run."

"Nice day for it."

"So how are you doing?" she asked. "After the flood?" Harley had noticed her piercings and her pale white skin on their first meeting, but he now saw how really lovely she was. There didn't seem to be any grim Prince of Darkness in her. She had bright green eyes and sharp angles in her face that revealed a very fine bone structure. Out of nowhere, he found himself wondering if she had ever been a model, and then his mind began to spin again. *Come on, Harley, focus. Don't let craziness control you.*

"I'm okay," he replied. "My house is fine, and the church will recover. Water in the social hall and a broken steeple."

"Yes," she said. "I saw that the cross came down." He thought he saw the hint of a smile as she said that. *There it is, ancient foe.*

"We'll fix it," Harley added. "Steeple rot."

At that, she broke into full grin. "Steeple rot?" she said. "I like that."

What was she trying to do to him? She wasn't vulnerable at all. He closed his eyes for a moment, and when he opened them her slender face was a serpent's head with fiery eyes and needle-sharp fangs. Her muscular body coiled and then struck, again and again and again—attacking a man on the ground between them, a man with a crude tattoo on his back. Horrified, Harley closed his eyes hard, and when he opened them, she was a woman again. *First sounds, now sights?* Not wanting to reveal his shock and disorientation, he swallowed hard and tried to compose himself. She gave him time, her green eyes trained on him. After what seemed like an eternity, he asked her, "How about you?"

"Our apartment building is fine, and so are we."

"That's good."

"But the candle shop is a crime scene, and we've had to answer a lot of questions."

"Terrible about the death."

"Yes. We don't know the man."

Was this the truth? Hard to say. As Jefferson said, Satan is the father of lies. Harley paused to see if she would say any more, but she just stood there. "I guess the police are working on it," he added.

She nodded, and seemed to be gathering her thoughts. Then she said, "I'm guessing that you are wondering about me. And my religion."

How did she know that? "Yes, I am." *Devils filled.*

"We believe in balance," she said, standing even straighter and pulling back her shoulders. *God, she's beautiful.* "Balance in everything. Darkness and light. Earth and heaven. Good and evil." She turned her face toward the churning river and said, "We try to live in harmony with the world around us. Birds. Fish. Snakes. Deer. We don't kill, except for food. And unlike Christians, we accept the insights of science."

Harley bristled and said, "Well, unlike *some* Christians." He had to take a stand if he wasn't going to lose all control. "We Methodists are not anti-science."

"We will not attack someone unless we are attacked," she said. "Have you ever heard of Patrick Stewart?"

"The actor?" asked Harley, confused.

"No, the serviceman who was killed in Afghanistan. He was the first Wiccan to die in combat. His helicopter was hit by a rocket-propelled grenade, back in 2006."

"That's too bad."

"He was awarded the Purple Heart and the Bronze Star. Wiccans will serve their country and will attack if they are attacked. We will curse someone, but only if we are cursed." Kelly stared at him with her deep green eyes, giving him a long, probing look. "Unfortunately," she said, "we are being attacked and cursed."

"I don't support that," said Harley, wondering who or what she was referencing. *Beau Harper? New Life Community Church?* And then the thought popped into his mind that most of the nations of the world were closely aligned with Wiccan theology—attack if attacked, curse if cursed.

"We will restore the balance," Kelly said with determination. "We have the power. You can share that with all of your Christian friends." Then she put her hands on her hips and did a swiveling stretching motion, causing the muscles in her legs to ripple. "And now, pastor," she said, "I need to get started on my run. Enjoy this beautiful afternoon."

Harley felt a rush of blood to his face as she took off down the path, and a voice in his head—*was it hers?*—saying, "Enjoy this beautiful body." Fright. Arousal. Dread. Attraction. Feelings rolled like a flood, churning and mixing. Wasn't it the apostle Paul who said that Satan could be transformed into an angel of light? He didn't know if Kelly was threatening him or giving him a message, but in either case he found it hard to resist her. Although he really didn't believe in spells, he was getting a sense of what one must feel like. Looking up into the branches of a tree near the river, he saw four black vultures with hideous skull-like heads, looking down at him. And then, across the river, he caught sight of movement in the bushes by the riverbank. A large figure, moving through the brush. *A bear? No, not around here.* Then a head popped above the foliage, and Harley recognized him: John Jonas. *But what is he doing?* Harley stood at the railing and watched for a minute. John dragged something heavy through the bushes and threw it into the river. *A body? No, a log!* Then he disappeared again, appearing a few moments later with a handful of branches. These also went into the river. Then he vanished.

That night, Harley watched a baseball game on television while sipping a couple of beers. When he had first gone to Honduras, the beer *Salva Vida* had been his lifesaver after a hot day on the archaeological site. But as he drifted off to sleep, he realized that there were no beers in the world that had the power to save him. He needed more powerful spirits.

6

Monday morning, the spell seemed to be broken. Harley drove to the neighboring city of Woodbridge for a monthly clergy breakfast at the Bob Evans restaurant, his confusion replaced by a surge of confidence and determination. He thanked God that his car had not been destroyed by the flood, despite a couple feet of water flowing through his carport and leaving an inch of mud on the concrete floor. Yes, the waters had risen high enough to soak the car's carpets, and he had to leave the doors open and run a couple of fans for several days to dry the interior, but the engine had fired right up after the flood passed. As he expertly negotiated the turns that took him left and right from his home to the restaurant, he became convinced that he was being equipped by the Lord to do battle with demons and devils and darkness—something that Harley had never experienced in his first three decades as a pastor.

Arriving at the restaurant, he found that the standard table for ten had been set up, and the group was beginning to gather, half in clergy collars and half in the casual attire so favored by trendy evangelical pastors. Harley was the odd man out in his tie and blue blazer, but at age fifty-eight he felt comfortable in his skin and wasn't about to change his ministerial uniform. He greeted Jim Black, the pastor of Sacred Heart Catholic Church in Woodbridge, with whom he had worked on some immigration issues, as well as Tony White, the pastor of New Life Community Church in Lake Ridge. "Terrible what happened to your church member Beau Harper," said Harley as they sat down. "Just awful."

"There's some real evil in Occoquan," said White as he opened his menu. "No offense to you, Harley."

"None taken," Harley replied.

"The flood that hit Occoquan is a sign that our country has turned away from God," White continued. "He is going to bring judgment."

"Really?" interrupted Father Black. "You don't see the flood as connected to climate change?"

"No," said White, shaking his head. "I don't believe that."

"Believe it or not, science says that rising temperatures lead to more severe storms. Don't let my collar fool you," said the priest. "Before I entered seminary, I was an atmospheric researcher."

"Really?" said White, genuinely surprised.

"Damn right. Worked for NOAA."

"On the ark?" interjected Harley, smiling.

"Not that Noah," said Black. "National Oceanic and Atmospheric Administration."

"Didn't know you had a science background," said White.

"Global temperature has risen over the past century," explained the priest, "and the warmer the air is, the more water it can hold. That's why rainfall is getting heavier and storms are getting worse."

"Welcome, gentlemen!" boomed an African-American pastor from the head of the table, calling the group to order. His greeting stopped the chatting that had been going on among the clergy, including the conversation about climate change. Looking around, Harley noticed that there still weren't any women in the group, which was quite unusual for a suburban clergy group in the year 2018. At one point, he had thought about inviting a Methodist clergywoman to join the group, but that no longer seemed important to him—spiritual warfare, he sensed, required true warriors, mighty men of God. "Put on the whole armor of God," says the apostle Paul to the Ephesians, using masculine, militaristic imagery, "so that you may be able to stand against the wiles of the devil." Then another black man in a dark blue suit entered the room, and the pastor at the head of the table introduced him. "Gentlemen, I'd like you to meet Kwaku Yeboah, the new pastor of the Ghanaian Presbyterian Church in Dumfries."

"Good to meet you, brother!" said Tony White, always energetic, but a little too eager to make a connection.

"Blessed to have this chance to fellowship with you," said Kwaku Yeboah with a slight bow.

Breakfast orders were given to the waitress, and Father Black offered an opening prayer that gave thanks for the food that would nourish them to be strong in the Lord and in the strength of his power. "Amen," said Harley, "good prayer."

Since Black had been asked to be the moderator of the group for that particular year, he invited the men to go around the table and introduce themselves to Pastor Yeboah, who then took a few minutes to tell the story of the rapid growth of his church through the recent arrival of Ghanaian immigrants. Harley could see concerned expressions on the faces of some of the African American pastors, who wondered why these newcomers were not joining black churches, and a disappointed look on the face of the one Presbyterian at the table, who no doubt wished he could attract these immigrants to his own congregation. But in the end, everyone gave Yeboah a warm welcome and one of the African Americans said that the church's growth was clearly "the Spirit at work, praise God."

Then, as the breakfasts arrived, Father Black asked the members of the group to give their attention to a request he had received from a man named John Jonas, representing a religious group in Occoquan. Pulling out a piece of paper, he read the printout of an email that Jonas had written to him, introducing himself and asking if he could join the breakfast group. He said that members of his Wiccan congregation wanted to work with other faith groups on shared concerns, especially on issues related to the environment. "Do you know him?" Father Black asked Harley.

"Yes, I've met him," he replied.

"They're devil-worshipers," said Tony White. "You know what Psalm 5 says, 'God is not pleased with wickedness.'"

"'For still our ancient foe,'" said Harley, "'doth seek to work us woe.'" White was surprised that Harley had said this, but he seemed to be pleased.

"Evil people are not welcome," added White. "That's what the Bible says. Again: Psalm 5."

"This does pose a challenge for the group," Father Black admitted as he sipped his coffee. "On the one hand, we want to be inclusive. On the other hand, hospitality has its limits." Clergy around the table began to share what they knew about Wiccans in general, and the members of the Occoquan coven in particular. One man reported that one-and-a-half million Americans now identify as either Wiccan or Pagan. Another described the Halloween celebration that had been held in Occoquan the year before, an event that Harley had missed. White told about the protests that his church had been staging and spoke of what had happened to his member Beau Harper. An Episcopal priest said he would be open to having Jews and Muslims in the group, since they worship God, but would draw the line at those who are not theists.

"Although I am new," said Kwaku Yeboah, "I am a little surprised that you would even consider including witches. Why would you want to invite evil spirits into your group?"

A number of men around the table nodded, and Tony White added, "Since the Evil One is the father of lies, the coven cannot be trusted."

As moderator of the group, Father Black encouraged them to make a decision based on theology, not on fear of evil spirits or personal concerns about the group's trustworthiness. The Episcopal priest made a motion to limit the group to faith leaders who are theists and believe in what he called "the one true God." There were more nods around the table, and when the motion was seconded and voted on, Harley's hand shot up in support.

∽

"Beautiful sunset, don't you think?" The sky was a fiery red and orange on that cool Monday evening, making it look as though River Mill Park was shooting plumes of fire from earth to sky. Leah Silverman asked Harley the question as they walked westward along Mill Street, heading toward dinner at the new pizza place that had just opened near the park. Leah had finished her day at the Woodbridge Health Clinic, a non-profit serving low-income residents, where she worked as CEO. She looked comfortable and stylish in khaki capris and a Navy-blue top, her silver hair was cut in a trendy bob, and she was holding on to her summer tan by continuing to play tennis into the fall. She still had the quick smile that had charmed Harley when they were on an archaeological dig together in the 1980s, as well as the ability to tease him when he was getting too serious about himself and his ministry. Because she had known him in his student days, she always saw him as Harley—never Pastor Camden—and that was a perspective that was held by no one else in town. The two had renewed their friendship when they discovered that they were neighbors in Occoquan, and over the past year they had met for dinner almost every week, at one of their homes or a local restaurant. But tonight, Harley wasn't seeing beauty when he looked at her or at the sky. Instead, his mind went to the flames that he had seen dancing out of the top of the steel drum in the park. "Looks like hellfire," he replied, looking up at the sunset.

"Well, aren't you a delight?" she said, giving him a punch on the arm. "Bet you lifted a lot of spirits today."

"I'm just not seeing the beauty," he replied. "Looks apocalyptic. You know, fire and brimstone." But then he thought that maybe she wouldn't see it, given that she was Jewish.

"Eye of the beholder," Leah remarked, opening the door to the pizza restaurant that occupied the first floor of an old stone building that looked like something out of a Charles Dickens novel. She loved how the structures of Occoquan were constantly being renovated and repurposed for new tenants, instead of being torn down and replaced. The people of the town had so far avoided the lure of glass, steel, and reinforced concrete, preferring instead to live and work in renovated wood, brick, and stone.

After being shown to a table, Leah ordered a glass of Malbec and Harley a mug of a local IPA. "Nice place," said Leah, looking at the menu. "How about if we get a couple of these gourmet personal pizzas?"

"Fine with me," said Harley, not showing much interest in the food. He was feeling as if someone were looking over his shoulder, maybe a ghost or an evil spirit? They were sitting across the street from the apartment building where the witches lived, so maybe they were watching him.

"I like the way they have exposed the stone walls from the original structure," Leah said, looking around. "I'll bet this building goes back to the 1700s."

"Probably," Harley nodded, returning his eyes to the menu. "Don't know." He sensed an ancient foe, working him woe. But why he was feeling it here, he had no idea. Maybe he was being spied on, in advance of the first attack.

They each ordered a pizza, and then Leah asked Harley about his upcoming mission trip. "You seem kind of stressed," she said. "Are you concerned about the trip?"

"Not really," he replied, sipping his beer. "Bill Stanford has things well planned. There's just a lot going on right now in the church . . . and in the town."

"Oh really," she asked. "Anything you want to talk about?"

Devils, he thought to himself, but bit his lip. Instead, he took another drink and then replied, "No, not really." The fact was, he really did want to talk about spiritual warfare and the forces of good and evil that he saw gathering on the horizon. But he knew very well that Leah and he had never talked about such things, and probably never would. She was a Jew, a lesbian, and a progressive Democrat. If he started talking about evil witches and the Prince of Darkness, she would think he had lost his mind. So, Harley changed the subject: "How about you?"

"Well, I've been trying to organize the annual river clean-up," she said after taking a drink of wine. "But the storm has really done a number on the riverbank."

"You can say that again."

"I don't know if I told you, but I've been attending meetings of the Creation Care Council."

"What's that?" asked Harley.

"It's an interfaith environmental group: Jews, Christians, Muslims . . . a few Hindus and Buddhists, as well. They are working on issues such as recycling, energy efficiency, solar panels, community gardens. I went to a meeting to recruit for the river clean-up and got hooked."

"Doesn't sound very spiritual," said Harley.

"Well, that depends," Leah said. "You read the same Book of Genesis that I do. It says to 'have dominion' over the earth." She had been a religion major at Duke, so she knew her Bible. "What does that mean to you?"

"Control, I guess. Mastery."

"Yes, but also responsibility," she said. "Good stewardship. For years, 'have dominion' was understood as endorsement of environmental exploitation. But now, most people of faith support efforts to be good stewards of natural resources."

To Harley, Leah had always been a sexy nerd, and he loved to watch her get worked up about a topic. But tonight, he wasn't being charmed by her passion. "Well, you studied a lot of Bible in college," he admitted. "I guess you're right."

"Darn right I'm right," she said, emphatically. "A survey just revealed widespread support for stricter environmental laws among religious people. We Jews were at the top—yay!— followed by Buddhists, Muslims, Hindus, and mainline Protestants like you."

"Well, good for you," said Harley, raising his beer mug in a toast.

"Know who was at the bottom?" Leah asked.

"Satanists?" said Harley, sarcastically.

"No, evangelical Christians," said Leah. "But even some of them are getting on board. After all, conservatives should be conservers, right?"

"Guess so."

"At our last meeting, I heard about the pastor of a 27,000-member Baptist church in Texas. How big is your church, Harley?"

"A little bit smaller," he admitted, doing a quick calculation in his head. "One hundred times smaller."

"Anyway, this pastor has come to believe that Christians should not abuse the earth. He recently led them through an energy audit that resulted in savings of one million dollars in one year."

"Not bad," said Harley, taking another drink. "But how many souls were saved?"

"I'm not talking about saving souls, Harley. This is about saving the earth."

At this point, Harley was really losing interest. For him, the battle was good versus evil, Christians against the Prince of Darkness. *In a world full of devils, is a pastor really supposed to be doing an energy audit?*

"There is a lot you could do at Riverside," said Leah: "Installing compact fluorescent lamps, using conservation landscaping, purchasing organic coffee." All Harley heard was blah, blah, blah. Then he was startled by a shout in the street and jerked his head toward the front window. He heard a name, a curse, a car door slamming. It was nothing, he quickly realized—just two teenagers getting rowdy. But the commotion reminded him of another struggle for the hearts and minds of Occoquan residents, one which had taken place right behind the pizza place, not far from where he was sitting, on the lawn of the Rockledge Mansion. There had been a lot of shouting back then, as residents lined up to do battle in the Civil War. *That struggle*, thought Harley, *was about something bigger than Leah's conservation landscaping.*

Although Prince William County was strongly pro-slavery in the years before the war, Occoquan was an abolitionist stronghold. In the 1860 Presidential election, Abraham Lincoln received only FIFTY-FIVE votes from the whole county, and they all came from Occoquan. Tie-dye Tim had told Harley that on July 4, 1860, supporters of Lincoln raised a Liberty Pole on the grounds of the Rockledge Mansion, a pole that flew both the American flag and Lincoln's campaign banner. But it didn't last. Within a few weeks, the Prince William militia rode into Occoquan from Brentsville, the county seat, chopped down the Liberty Pole and rode off with the offensive banners. It was a small struggle, for sure, but a foretaste of the massive destruction to come, one that quickly became as theological as it was political: *Mine eyes have seen the glory of the coming of the Lord / he is trampling out the vintage where the grapes of wrath are stored.* Once again, Harley felt that battle lines were being drawn. *Let the Hero, born of woman, crush the serpent with his heel / since God is marching on . . .* And now the words of a hymn were once again intruding on his thinking. *Glory, glory, Hallelujah! Glory, glory, Hallelujah!*

The pizza arrived, and the two of them began to eat. But Leah was on a roll, and Harley's lack of interest in her topic of creation care was not going to slow her down a bit. Wiping pizza sauce off the corner of her mouth with a napkin, she said, "You want this environmental stuff to be more spiritual? Well, listen to this. The Creation Care Council had a guest speaker last month, from the Sierra Club. She was a young woman raised in a religious and politically conservative home in eastern Tennessee. One day, she found out about a low-income community outside Knoxville where the water supply had been contaminated—totally fouled by the illegal dumping of lead, arsenic, diesel fuel, and PCBs. Horrible, horrible pollution."

Harley chewed his pizza and nodded. Although he had been thinking about the Civil War and crushing the serpent, *Glory, glory, Hallelujah*, he heard something about PCBs and pollution, which sounded bad. "That's terrible," he responded, but his words lacked conviction.

"So, here's what she did," Leah continued, eyes sparkling. "She joined a coalition that demanded clean water for the neighborhood. In the course of that effort, she made a discovery: Caring for creation is part of loving our neighbors."

"Huh?" said Harley, realizing that his mind had wandered again. *Glory, glory, Hallelujah!* "Say that again." Leah had been one of the witches at the cauldron in his dream, and he didn't like the image. "Caring for creation is . . . what?"

"Part of loving our neighbors," said Leah. "That's the spiritual part: Caring for creation is part of loving our neighbors."

Harley grasped what she was saying but wasn't moved by it. It just didn't seem to be important to him. After all, if a pastor is doing spiritual battle with a coven and a serpent, is he actually going to put time and effort into finding the best organic coffee? "I hear what you are saying," he said, "but I don't see this as a priority for me. Or my church."

"Really?" said Leah, looking disappointed. "Saving the planet is not a priority for you? Saving *God's* planet?" She shook her head, causing Harley to feel a pang of regret. After all, he had always been drawn to her, and usually wanted to please her. Since the summer they had worked side by side, digging under a blazing sun in the dirt of Israel, he had loved to talk with her, joke with her, and make her smile. But today he was preparing for battle, so he couldn't be distracted by the soft words of a woman, even one he adored.

"I'm sorry," he said. "We've got an ancient foe. And it's not PCBs." *His truth is marching on!*

～

That Friday afternoon, Harley received a group email, sent to him and the other clergy who had been at the breakfast. The subject line read "Clergy breakfast decision" and the body of the email said, "Attacks and curses will be met with attacks and curses." From the email address, he could tell that it came from Kelly Westbrook, but the message itself was signed "Fire Dolphin," her Wiccan name.

So it begins, thought Harley. Reading and rereading the message, the words "ancient foe" and "devils filled" began to pound in his head like a drumbeat, but this time he was not afraid of what he was hearing. Instead, the words evoked anger and indignation, and they steeled him to face whatever evil lay ahead. *Let the Hero, born of woman, crush the serpent with his heel / since God is marching on . . . .*

Early the next morning, as he boarded the plane for his flight to Honduras, he prayed repeatedly that God would make him the warrior that he was supposed to be. His rocky road would not be a Honduran highway, but the challenging path of living by every single word that came from the mouth of God.

7

As the airplane dipped beneath the clouds on its approach to San Pedro Sula, Harley stared out the window at the lush vegetation beneath him. Green on green, *verde en todas partes*, as far as the eye could see. Never before had he seen such a succulent landscape, stretching across the valley floor and rising up the slopes in the distance. He wondered what the crops were, irrigated by muddy rivers and rooted in black soil that was no doubt teeming with slithering worms and ravenous beetles. As he looked down at the verdant carpet rolling out beneath him, he heard the clicking and crunching of life and death on the ground—stalks growing, worms burrowing, insects eating, flowers blooming, dead leaves decaying, poor farmers toiling, and rich landowners exploiting. He felt thrilled that he would soon be immersed in a land of such dynamic vitality, with the struggle between light and darkness being revealed in every encounter.

"You can really see it, can't you?" Harley asked his seatmate, pointing out the window.

"See what?" said Bill Stanford, craning his neck to look.

"The struggle," said Harley. "The struggle between life and death."

"Uh, yeah . . . sure." The dentist nodded, but looked at Harley with concern. The pastor had been making bizarre comments since they took off from Washington. At first Bill thought that Harley was joking around, but now he was beginning to wonder.

"It's exciting," said Harley. "I'm glad I'm here."

"Yes, me too," said the trip organizer.

Looking around the plane, Bill took stock of the other participants in the mission trip. He realized that he might need some help if Harley continued to behave in an erratic way. Andy Stackhouse, the retired Navy officer, was right behind them, reading a paperback thriller. Gretchen Bennett, a nurse, was across the aisle, organizing little caps to give to newborns in the health clinic. Juan Erazo had construction experience, but was especially valuable to the mission because he was bilingual and could act as Bill's translator. All three were members of Riverside, and they knew Harley well enough to talk with him and assist him if needed. The other six were not part of the congregation, but were dentists and dental assistants that Bill knew professionally.

To an outsider, Harley looked normal, although his eyes were unusually bright as he took in the sights from the plane window. On past mission trips, Bill had seen people experience unexpected reactions to the work, from crippling anxiety to deep sadness over the plight of the Hondurans they served. But he had never seen anyone become completely out of touch with reality.

"What medications have you taken today, Harley?" the dentist asked, fishing for answers.

"Nothing," said the pastor.

"Nothing at all?"

"Well, an allergy tablet this morning," he added. "But I don't have any prescription meds."

"How about your anti-malarial medicine?"

"My Melial?" Harley asked. "Three days ago, and again this morning."

"And you're not on anything else?"

"Nope," said the pastor. "Bill, you know I'm a healthy guy. I run three days a week, sometimes more."

"Yeah, you do seem pretty fit for an old man."

"Who you calling old?" joked Harley, knowing that the dentist was just a year or two younger.

Bill hoped that he was overreacting to Harley's behavior, but he couldn't help but be concerned. Since he was going to be coordinating the care of a long line of dental patients through the week, he couldn't spend time holding the hand of a troubled volunteer. Bill liked Harley and had certainly been glad that he wanted to be part of the trip, but at this point he was beginning to wonder if his pastor was going to be an asset or a liability. Already, the other volunteers were giving Harley odd looks, and the pastor wasn't saying or doing anything to send the message that he was a regular guy.

A wave of hot, wet, air washed over the group when they stepped outside the airport and began to load their bags onto a fifteen-passenger van from the medical clinic. Those who had been wearing sweatshirts on the airplane immediately stripped them off, and a couple of men ducked into the bathroom to change from long pants to shorts. Bill had been busy shepherding the group through baggage claim and customs, so he hadn't been paying much attention to Harley. But when they started down the long and curving road to La Entrada, he noticed that the pastor was alone in the back of the van, keeping to himself. When Bill walked back to check on him, he could see that Harley had tears streaming down his face.

"What's up, man?" asked the dentist.

"The poverty," whispered Harley. "I had forgotten."

Bill looked out the window and saw what was so upsetting to him. Two thin boys were playing on the side of the road, kicking a scuffed soccer ball along the shoulder. A black-haired girl clutched a dirty doll to her chest and whispered in its ear. Impossibly skinny dogs ran in and out of the road, looking for scraps of food, and a grizzled old man in a cowboy hat carried a huge bundle of sticks to his home for the cook fire. Adobe huts with tin roofs had been built by squatters along the highway, and in their open-air kitchens Bill could see women making tortillas for the evening meal. Behind the huts were piles of trash being burned by teenage boys, adding to the air pollution and respiratory problems being experienced by so many of the residents.

"Yes, it's really bad," agreed the dentist. "But that's why we come here."

Harley sat silently in his seat, with tears continuing to run down his face. Bill would have been glad to have a conversation about the goals of the mission team, but he sensed that Harley was in a different frame of mind. He plopped down in a seat next to his pastor and let him have some time to watch the impoverished world go by. Looking inward, Bill wondered if he were too focused on dental care, with not enough emotional involvement in the needs of the Honduran people. He remembered a guest preacher at Riverside Methodist once saying that Americans love the expression, "Don't just sit there, do something." Americans love to take action. But in other parts of the world, where empathetic connections are valued more highly, the opposite is preferred, "Don't just do something, sit there." He tried to remember this when he came to Honduras, where so many of the locals want to develop a connection and discover that their North American neighbors really do care for them as individuals.

After a few minutes, Harley turned to Bill, let out a sigh, and said, "'Blessed are the poor, for theirs is the kingdom of God.'"

"Yes, that's what Jesus said," the dentist agreed.

"They are a window to heaven."

Bill sat and thought about that for a few seconds, then asked, "What do you mean by that?"

"They help me to see paradise."

Bill looked out the window and tried to figure out what Harley was talking about. The malnourished children, the impoverished adults, the substandard housing, the smoky cook fires, and the endless meals of beans and rice, beans and rice, beans and rice. Where was his pastor seeing paradise? "I'm sorry, Harley," he finally said, "but I don't see it."

"They have nothing, so nothing distracts them," the pastor said. "When you have nothing but God, you find that you need nothing but God. God is no thing, you know, so having no thing helps you to see God. I trust the poor to help me experience the kingdom, God's kingdom."

Bill nodded, but only half-heartedly. He was getting a sense of what Harley was saying—the whole idea that wealth and possessions can distract us from the things of God. But Bill did not see the poverty of the Honduran people as a glimpse of paradise. If anything, it was a clear vision of the hell that is created by corrupt politicians and violent gang leaders and greedy businesspeople, all of whom make life miserable for the struggling families who make up most of the country's population. Every time Bill looked into a mouth full of rotten teeth, he saw problems to be solved and pain to be eliminated, not heavenly visions. He knew that dental problems prevented people from being productive citizens, so by pulling bad teeth he believed that he was actually helping entire communities. Small interventions had big results, in his mind—what some called "the butterfly effect," in which the flapping of a butterfly's wings could alter the path of a tornado. Bill came to Honduras to ease the suffering of its people, not to spiritualize their poverty. Finally, he said, "Harley, I just don't know."

The pastor smiled and said, "That's okay. Knowing is overrated." Then he asked Bill if he could have a little quiet time to pray. The dentist went back to his seat at the front of the van, more worried than before.

∽

Dinner was served that night in the dining room of the hotel in La Entrada de Copán, a bustling crossroads city in southwestern Honduras. Harley had told Bill that he stayed in the very same hotel in the 1980s, when he traveled to the country to do archaeological work at Copán Ruinas, and it was in the hotel bar that he had enjoyed his first *Salva Vida* beer. "I liked beer," said Harley; "I still like beer!" Knowing that history, Bill was anxious to buy one for Harley and get him to tell some stories about his summer at the ruins. He wanted the other members of the mission team—especially his colleagues in the dental world—to see the pastor as something other than an emotional eccentric. But when the dinner hour came, Harley was nowhere to be found.

Bill bought a round of *Salva Vidas* for the members of the team and made a toast to a successful week. He sent Andy Stackhouse to Harley's room, but the Navy guy came back with the message that it was empty. "Bags in place," he reported, "but no pastor." Thinking that Harley had run an errand, Bill delayed dinner for as long as he could, but finally they had to sit down. The group enjoyed generous helpings of grilled chicken, vegetables, beans, and tortillas, all washed down with beer and bottled water—essential in a country where the water from the tap is undrinkable. Everyone enjoyed the dinner and conversation except for Bill, who was silently stewing about Harley and his disappearance. *Where could he be*, Bill fumed, *and why is he doing this to me?*

"He'll be all right," Gretchen Bennett said at the end of the meal, putting her hand on Bill's arm. "He's been here before." She had a kind, round face, a pointy nose, and brown eyes. Her hair was also brown, but the color came from a bottle, no doubt—maybe it was an attempt to match her eyes. She radiated warmth, and clearly wanted to be supportive of Bill without being dismissive of Harley.

"I just can't believe he would walk off like that," said the dentist.

"He hasn't been himself," she said. "We've all seen it."

"I just don't know if I can lead this team while also babysitting him."

"It's not what you were expecting," she acknowledged. "But don't worry—we'll work together on this."

At that point, the rest of the group got up from the table to go to their rooms and get unpacked. Gretchen asked Bill if he wanted her to stay with him, but he declined. Then he wandered out of the front door of the hotel and looked around. The sun was beginning to set in the direction of the Mayan ruins, and the merchants who sold belts and hats and fruit along the street were beginning to break down their stalls. Tractor-trailers downshifted as they rolled through the dusty city center, and laborers in the backs of pick-up trucks called out to their friends as they rode home from work, dirty and exhausted. After ten mission trips to La Entrada, Bill had developed an affection for the city and its people, but he still would not feel safe walking the streets after dark. There was a reason that the guard at the front door of the hotel carried a forty-four Magnum.

And then, as he was about to go inside, he spotted Harley strolling toward him. "Harley, where the hell have you been?" Bill growled, unable to control his frustration.

"Did you know that I needed to be doing my Father's work?" Harley replied, unfazed by the dentist's tone of voice.

"What are you talking about?" Bill barked. "We had dinner, and you missed it."

"I needed some Honduran baleadas," he explained. "If I am going to do God's work in this place, I need to eat with the people."

"Harley, you are part of this mission team. You needed to eat with us."

"That's a human reaction, Bill. I understand. But Jesus wants me to get close to the land and break bread with the poor. I'm anointed."

"You are what?"

"Anointed. In the Bible, prophets are anointed with olive oil. Jesus is the Messiah, which means 'anointed one.' It's a sign of God's presence and power."

"Anointed or not, you upset me, Harley. You wandered off and I was scared. You are not respecting me or this team."

"Bill, I hear you. I'm not trying to upset you. But I have been given a window to heaven. I must open it."

"Are you sure you are not having a drug reaction?" the dentist asked him. "You are not acting like yourself. You only took your Melial and an allergy pill?"

"That's it."

"Has anything else happened in the last few days? Any accidents, any head trauma?"

"No, not really. Although I did get a strange email last night. It came from one of the witches in Occoquan, Fire Dolphin."

"What did it say?"

"She threatened me with attacks and curses."

"Okay, that's weird."

"She didn't like what the pastors and I did, excluding her group."

"Maybe she put a spell on you, Harley."

"I don't believe she has the power."

"Neither do I," admitted Bill, a scientist at heart. Then, realizing that it wouldn't help to stay mad at Harley, he invited him to come inside the hotel for safety.

"I am always safe with God," said the pastor.

"Not even God walks in La Entrada after dark," Bill said as he grabbed Harley by the shoulder, pulled him inside, and pushed him toward the staircase.

Harley smiled and said, "I appreciate your concern, Bill."

As they were climbing the stairs, Bill asked, "So where did you get your baleadas?"

"On the street, at a stand."

"*What?*" said Bill. "You ate street food?"

"And drank a cup of cool water."

"Bottled water, right?"

"No, out of the vendor's thermos."

"Harley, you are going to be so sorry you did that."

"The Lord is my shepherd, I shall not want," said the pastor as he went into his hotel room. "He leads me beside the still waters. He prepares a table before me."

"Goodnight, Harley," said Bill, shaking his head.

∽

Sure enough, the pastor became violently ill the next afternoon. The day started uneventfully, with Harley volunteering in the waiting room of the dental clinic and using his rudimentary Spanish to help the patients to get checked in. He seemed to be thinking a little more clearly than he had the day before, and Bill was beginning to believe that Harley's strange behavior was due to the stress of travel. But then, mid-afternoon, he overheard Harley giving multiple blessings to the people in the waiting room—*muchas bendiciones*—and realized that his pastor was still seeing the world through a hyper-spiritualized lens. Fortunately, the bacteria of Honduras brought him down to earth with a bout of explosive diarrhea. Harley ran for the *baños* and didn't come out for an hour. When he did, he was completely wiped out.

Back at the hotel, Bill helped Harley to get into bed, and Gretchen brought him some Gatorade to try to rehydrate him. He looked like a dead man, with hardly enough energy to lift his head off the pillow. Bill rooted through Harley's bag until he found his Cipro, and then gave him a pill, promising him that the antibiotic would kill the bugs in his system, although it would take a few days. Harley took a pill, sipped a little more Gatorade, and then asked for help in getting to the bathroom—one more time. He had another gut-wrenching experience, one that left him unable to stand. Bill helped him back to bed, Gretchen wiped the perspiration off his face, and they promised they'd check on him in the morning. "*Muchas gracias*," he said to them as they turned off the light and let him get some sleep.

The work at the dental clinic went smoothly with Harley out of the picture, which left Bill feeling an uncomfortable mixture of satisfaction and guilt. Gretchen brought crackers and broth to Harley's room, and slowly he got to the point where he could go a few hours without a trip to the bathroom. On the third day, he rose from the dead and actually joined the group for breakfast. Andy Stackhouse said that he was glad that Harley had regained his strength, and Juan Erazo slapped him on the back, saying that he could use his help with the Spanish translations. The dentists and dental assistants held back and kept quiet, still trying to figure out who this strange pastor was. But then Harley surprised everyone by announcing that he wouldn't be coming back to the clinic. "God has other plans for me," he said, quite cryptically.

Bill Stanford took a long sip of coffee, and then said, "Would you like to share them, Harley?"

"No," he said, taking a bite of dry toast. "You all do what you need to do, and I'll do what I need to do."

Bill nodded and said, "Okay." He was concerned about Harley, but also relieved that he wouldn't be causing problems for the clinic operation. "Do your thing and we'll see you at dinner."

That was the plan, but it didn't work out. Harley left the hotel at the same time as the rest of them, but he didn't return in the evening. He wasn't back by sunset, and by ten o'clock Bill and Gretchen were becoming deeply concerned. They talked with the hotel desk clerk about whether he had received any messages from Harley—no—and whether the Honduran police could handle a missing person's investigation—not very well. Then, as they were feeling panic set in, the phone at the desk rang. A priest from the Catholic Church in the town of Copán Ruinas had Harley at his rectory, and he wasn't sure what to do with him.

The desk clerk had limited ability to translate Spanish into English, so Gretchen fetched Juan to tell them what the priest was saying. "This man, Harley Camden, showed up at our church this afternoon, after spending the morning at the Mayan Ruins. He prayed in our church until we closed at eight o'clock, and then asked if he could pray all night. We said no and asked what he was doing there. He said that he had been in the archaeological park, praying for an end to human suffering, for the coming of God's new heaven and new earth, for the arrival of the New Jerusalem." Bill and Gretchen shook their heads as Juan provided this translation, wondering what had possessed Harley to go on this bizarre quest.

"He was hungry, so we fed him," said the priest. "Now, what do you want us to do with him?" Juan said that they really wanted to get Harley back to La Entrada, but he wouldn't be able to drive the van to Copán Ruinas until the morning. The priest offered to keep him in the rectory, give him breakfast, and allow him to pray in the church until Juan arrived.

"Thank you," said Juan, while Bill and Gretchen shared their appreciation as well. "Just one more question, Father: How did Harley get to you?"

"He hitchhiked," said the priest. "Over sixty kilometers. I don't know how he did it, but he did. He's a man on a mission."

"Indeed, he is," said Bill to Gretchen. "Just not the mission that the rest of us are on."

8

Harley climbed the giant steps one by one, making slow upward progress on a windless summer day. Never had the sky been so clear and blue, nor the sun so powerfully bright, a blazing diamond in the heavens. He remembered a line from the prophet Isaiah, "the Lord has laid on him the iniquity of us all." Although the day was brutally hot, a chill went through him, and he stopped. He realized that he had been chosen—he was the sacrifice designed to repair a shattered relationship and build a bridge between earth and heaven. *But why me? And why here? Why was the prophecy coming true on the steps of a Mayan temple?* Looking down and then out over the plaza, he saw a sea of faces looking up at him in wonderment and expectation. *My father, if it is possible, let this cup pass from me.* Realizing that he couldn't scramble down and escape though the crowd, he pulled himself up and over the final stone on the temple staircase. There, he saw a group of Mayan priests in feathery headdresses, with bright face paint that only intensified and accentuated their grim expressions.

Two strong young men immediately grabbed him, ripped off his jacket, tie, and shirt, and threw him backwards over a rounded stone. He looked like a plucked and basted chicken, his pale, hairless chest glistening from the perspiration of his climb. When they tied his hands with thick cords to the base of the stone, he was forced to look at the blazing sun above him, burning his eyes. Grooves had been cut in the stone, spiraling down from the top to the bottom, to act as channels for the flow of blood. Harley knew that the blood of Mayan sacrifices was burned as an offering to the gods.

Suddenly, the sun was blocked by the silhouette of a figure. A chief priest in an expansive headdress leaned over Harley's bare chest and raised a large black obsidian knife. "'Out of his anguish he shall see light,'" said the priest, quoting Isaiah; "'he shall find satisfaction through his knowledge.'"

But what knowledge, wondered Harley in a panic, *and what satisfaction?* The only light he saw was the fierce sun behind the obsidian knife, and he could not grasp the possibility of any satisfaction or knowledge.

Then he heard his name. Turning his head toward the group of priests, he saw that behind them was a crowd of spectators. Between two priestly headdresses, Harley spotted the face of Leah, contorted in pain, crying out, "Harley! Harley! . . ."

And then the chief priest gave a shout and plunged his knife into Harley's chest. A searing pain radiated through his body as a geyser of blood shot toward the sky. But the cries of his name continued.

"Harley! Harley!" said Leah, shaking him roughly. He awoke with a start, unaware of where he was. "You were dreaming," she said to him gently. "Must have been a bad one." The chief priest in the headdress was gone, and in his place was his silver-haired friend. Harley sat up and grabbed his chest. There was no wound, no pain, no spurting flow of blood.

"Where am I?" he asked.

"In Occoquan. In my condo."

"How did I get here?"

"Bill Stanford dropped you off," she said, stroking his back. "He didn't think you should stay alone. Since I was your emergency contact, he called me when your plane stopped in Atlanta. You arrived here late last night, and I put you right to bed."

"I don't remember any of that." Harley was in a fog, and he shook his head to try to clear the confusion.

"I'm not surprised," said Leah. "You've been . . . kind of . . . out of it."

Harley stroked his chin, which had stubble from several days without shaving. "I know I was on the mission trip, but I don't remember much of it."

"Yeah, they told me that you weren't acting like yourself."

"I remember wanting to get very close to the people," recalled Harley. "I got sick to my stomach. I ended up in a church. But it is all very fuzzy."

"Do you think you had a drug interaction?" asked Leah, opening his suitcase.

"No, I don't think so."

"What are you taking?" She rooted around and pulled out his toiletry bag.

"Just an anti-malarial," said Harley, pointing. "There it is: Melial."

"Well, they are all gone," she said, shaking an empty bottle.

"Oh," recalled Harley, remembering another medication. "I think Bill also gave me some Cipro when I got sick."

Finding the Cipro bottle, Leah said, "They're gone too."

"Well, at least they worked." Harley remembered his days of explosive diarrhea but not much else—just random recollections that were like the scattered images of a fever dream. He was frightened by the fact that he had no memory of flying all the way home from Honduras. *How can I not remember passing through the Atlanta airport?*

Taking his hands in hers, Leah sat on the edge of the bed and said, "Harley, I'm worried about you." She looked at him with affection, and this transported him back to the summer of 1985, when they had met in the Galilee region of Israel. She was an undergraduate at Duke while he was a seminarian at the divinity school, and they quickly bonded while working together in the same square of an archaeological dig. Harley was drawn to her athletic physique, dark brown hair, olive complexion, and quick smile, and he immediately fell in love with her. Now, seeing the deep concern in her eyes, those feelings came rushing back.

"Thanks, Leah," he said, squeezing her hands. "I'm worried too."

"Do you think you had a psychotic break?" she asked, as tenderly as she could.

"Maybe," he said. "Although it would be a first."

"How about a stroke?"

"Don't know. I'm fifty-eight, so it's possible, but I've never had any problems like that."

Leah sat in silence, thinking, and then said, "Don't mean to interrogate you." Stroking his arm, she explained, "I just want to help you. Running a health clinic, I like to solve problems."

Harley's thinking was still sluggish, but he saw her face clearly and was comforted by her smile. She is real, he thought to himself, really real. Feeling the warmth of her hands around his, he realized that he had not been touched so tenderly by a woman since his wife died two years earlier. He didn't know what had been going on in his heart or his head over the past few weeks, but he was beginning to see, with absolute clarity, that Leah loved him. "Thank you, Leah," he said.

"You are truly one of the best people I know," she said, squeezing his arm.

"You must not know many people," Harley replied, trying to lighten things up.

"I'm serious," she continued. "You were such a good friend to me on the Galilee dig. Other guys were always hitting on me, but you were a total gentleman."

"Oh, I *wanted* to hit on you," said Harley, smiling.

"But you didn't," she said. "That was such a tough time for me, figuring out who I was, and what kind of relationships I wanted." Harley remembered

Leah holding hands with a Muslim girl at the dig site, which had been so confusing to him. "I didn't come out for years," she recalled, "but you were great for me in a time of real confusion, real searching."

"Well, I loved you," Harley admitted.

"And I loved you," she said, looking deep into his eyes. "I still do." He knew that she was talking about a love much deeper than erotic love, a love that always seeks the welfare of the other person. Harley knew that Leah loved him in this way, and that knowledge made him feel less shattered and confused.

"Leah," he asked, "do you believe in spells? In curses?" The image of her standing at a cauldron popped into his head, unwanted, and he tried to push it aside.

"You mean, like, witch's spells?"

"Yeah," said Harley. "Curses that hurt people. And maybe even change events."

She pondered for a second, and then said, "No, not really. I tend to see things scientifically. People get sick—physically and mentally—and good medicine can often make them well."

"But you studied religion," said Harley. "How about the world of the spirit?"

"Well, sure," she admitted. "I do believe in God. God is a spirit. God is the creator of all that is. But God made a world that runs in an orderly, cause-and-effect sort of way."

"So, you don't believe in spiritual power?"

"Yes, spiritual power . . . to love. To forgive. To change things for the better. I do believe that we each have spirits, and that our spirits can connect with God's spirit."

Harley pulled his hands away from Leah's and sat back in the bed. He rubbed the back of his neck and tried to clarify his thoughts. He wasn't processing things as clearly as he had before he disappeared into the events of the last few weeks. *It all started*, he thought, *with his focus on devils in the worship service at Riverside, his encounter with Kelly Westbrook in the park, and the decision of the clergy group to shun the Wiccans.* The craziness continued with his contentious pizza dinner with Leah, followed by the threatening email from Kelly. And then, in Honduras, he acted strangely and everything went completely to hell. *So, what was the common thread in all this? The Wiccans and their desire to do him harm.* "But what if people use their spiritual power to hate?" he asked Leah.

"Well, that's possible," she admitted. "I've seen some patients really screwed up by the power of hate. But I don't believe in magical thinking."

"What do you mean by that?"

"When you simply think that something will happen and then it does. When you make a connection between your thoughts and what happens in the world. You know, hoping that someone will fall down and then, *bam*, they fall down."

"I get it," said Harley. "A thought cannot cause a physical event."

"I don't think so."

"But a hateful thought can still mess with a person's mind, right?"

"Absolutely," said Leah. "The families I see in my clinic, with children abused by their parents—it's awful. Parents don't have to hit their kids to hurt them. They can mess them up by insulting them, belittling them, criticizing them, ignoring them . . . ."

"Cursing them?" asked Harley.

"Yes, cursing them," said Leah. "The way they abuse their kids, they are really cursing them. That's a good word for it."

Feeling a need to stretch, Harley got up, walked around the room, and looked at a calendar on the wall. "What day is it?" he asked, feeling a sudden rush of panic.

"Sunday," replied Leah.

"Shouldn't I be preaching?" he asked, the blood draining out of his face.

"Bill told me you had arranged a guest preacher before you left," she said. "Guess you didn't want to have to worry about missing the service with flight delays."

"I have no recollection," said Harley, shaking his head. "Absolutely no recollection. I guess I'm still not myself."

Leah put her arm around him and said, "Harley, you'll get through this. I believe in you." She held him tightly, like the blonde woman that had been embracing the tall Native American in the window across from his house. "Look, let me make a pot of coffee and then we can take a walk. Clear your head."

Harley thanked her and said that he would get cleaned up and change his clothes. As she stepped toward the door, he asked her, "I passed through Atlanta?" She nodded. "I have no memory of that. But you know what they say about the airport, don't you? Whether you go to heaven or hell, you have to change planes in Atlanta."

She smiled. *Maybe he is going to be okay.*

∽

Orange, yellow, and red leaves swirled around them in little whirlpools of breeze as they left Leah's condo, which sat on the top of a hill overlooking downtown Occoquan. "I'm not in Honduras anymore," said Harley as he looked up at the trees and zipped his jacket. "Looks like the fall colors are reaching their peak."

"I do love it up here," said Leah, gazing out over the town, the river, and the rocky ridge on the other side. "I get a panorama of the changing seasons."

The two of them headed down a wooden staircase that connected Leah's condominium community to the downtown area, walking a series of switchbacks that zigged and zagged along the hillside. The temperature had dropped into the forties, a stiff breeze was blowing, and clouds were moving quickly across the sky. At one spot, the two looked toward Riverside Methodist and could see worshipers getting out of their cars and heading into church. "Glad I'm not preaching," said Harley, smiling crookedly at Leah. "They don't need crazy in the pulpit." At another point, they spotted a group of children kicking a soccer ball in River Mill Park. The chill of the air whipping through the trees sent the clear message that the season of playing ball in the park was coming to an end.

In a few minutes, they made it down to Rockledge Mansion on the western edge of the town, and from there they walked past the park entrance to the pedestrian bridge. A couple of fishermen were standing on rocks under the bridge, casting their lines into the river, and Leah asked Harley what they were hoping to catch. "No idea," he said, shaking his head.

At the center of the span, they paused and looked toward the concrete bridge that carried traffic over the river on the east side of town. "Is this where he was?" Leah asked.

"Yes," said Harley, "right here." Harley's friend and parishioner Dirk Carter had climbed over the railing and threatened to kill himself with a handgun, expecting that his body would tumble into the river below.

"You talked him down," Leah said. "That was some good work."

As Harley looked across the water, the sun broke through the clouds and caused the river to sparkle. A fish jumped, flipped sideways, and then splashed into the water. Harley suddenly remembered what he had been focusing on while he was in the archaeological park at the Mayan ruins: The tree of life, *el árbol de la vida*, and the river of the water of life, *el río del agua de la vida*. He had hitchhiked to the ruins because he felt compelled to pray in that ancient and sacred place and ask for God's will to be done, his kingdom to come. There, he begged and pleaded with God to bring about a new heaven and new earth, the New Jerusalem of peace and eternal life, a place in which there is no more poverty or pain, illness or dying, suffering or crying. Standing on the top of the Mayan temple, Harley saw the river of the water of life stretched out in front of him, bright as crystal, flowing from the throne of Christ the Lamb. On both sides of the river were the tree of life with its twelve kinds of fruit and its lush green leaves with healing powers, with its roots drawing life from the water. The river of the water of life was running through the center of the New Jerusalem, and the people who drank from the river and ate from the tree were able to live in serenity and security forever and ever. *Thy kingdom come,* he prayed, *thy will be done.*

"Leah," he said, turning toward his friend, "I'm remembering my time in the ruins. Suddenly, it is crystal clear. I saw a holy river, and a grove of sacred trees."

"A real river?"

"Well, the Copán River runs nearby. But I think I was seeing something else."

"A hallucination?"

"Maybe a vision. I saw trees that grew fruit for food. The water for the trees flowed from the throne of Jesus. Their fruit was for food, and their leaves for healing."

"Sounds kind of like Ezekiel," said Leah.

"Ezekiel?" said Harley. "I was thinking the Book of Revelation."

"I did my senior thesis on Ezekiel," Leah said. "It's been a long, long time. Haven't thought about it for years. I remember that Ezekiel had a vision of a river with trees on the banks. The leaves and fruit of the trees were nourished by the river. Ezekiel said that the fruit would be for food and the leaves for healing."

"That was my vision," said Harley, looking back over the glistening sunlight on the Occoquan River. "That's what I saw in the ruins, near the Copán River and the ceiba trees."

"Well," Leah said, "That's a weird vision, Harley. I won't deny it. But Ezekiel wasn't crazy, so maybe you're not crazy either."

Harley looked back at her and saw that she was smiling. He realized that she wasn't just talking when she said she loved him. She believed in him. With her help, he would somehow find his way. The gift of Leah's friendship was more powerful than any Wiccan curse. "Thanks, Leah," he said. "I do appreciate it." Then, when a stiff breeze blew past them, he asked, "Want to walk me home?"

She nodded, and the two of them headed back across the pedestrian bridge to Mill Street, which ran parallel to the river. They strolled past the new pizza place and the witches' apartment building, and surveyed the vacant lot where the candle shop once stood. "Looks like they have cleaned up pretty well," noted Leah.

"Yeah," said Harley. "Jefferson Jones wants to get started on his redevelopment."

"He doesn't mess around," she added.

When they reached Harley's townhouse, they climbed the wrought-iron stairs on the side of the building and entered the kitchen. Everything seemed normal except for a number of opened packages of basil on the counter. "What's all this?" Leah asked. "Making a ton of caprese salad?"

"I have no idea," Harley said, scratching his head. "No memory at all."

They went upstairs to Harley's bedroom, where some clothes were strewn around on the bed. "I guess this is left over from my packing for the trip," he said.

Leah wandered into his bathroom and saw a huge mess in his bathtub: Green leaves were clogging the drain and floating in what was left of the bathwater. "Here is where the basil ended up," she said. "But what were you doing?"

Harley walked in behind her and looked at the bathtub, mystified. "Leah, I really don't remember doing this."

"Well, someone took a weird kind of bath."

"What's this?" said Harley, seeing a printout of a website on the bathroom counter. "Cure for Black Magic Spells: Bathe in Salt and Basil."

"You can find anything on the Internet, can't you? Guess you were fighting a spell," Leah said. "But I don't think it worked."

9

The afternoon sun streamed through Harley's bedroom turret windows, waking him from a deep sleep. Rolling to one side, he looked at his alarm clock: Six o'clock. He groaned and pulled his pillow over his head, wishing he had been able to sleep longer, since his waking reality was more bizarre than the strangest of dreams. Earlier that afternoon, Leah had cleaned out his tub, straightened up his kitchen, and then run back to her condominium to pick up his suitcase from the Honduras trip. She had helped him get unpacked, and then offered to stay with him and talk about what he was feeling and what he was going through. But Harley had declined, encouraging her to go home and get ready for her week at work.

The truth was that he was deeply embarrassed by his erratic behavior, and ashamed of the burden he had become to Leah and to everyone around him. As a Methodist pastor, he had always been proud of his ability to live a professional Christian life that made sense to the average person, one that did not require speaking in tongues or performing miraculous healings or handling serpents. He took the Bible seriously but not literally, focusing more on earthly challenges than on heavenly dreams. But that professional veneer had proved to be a fragile shell, easily shattered and providing no defense at all against the chaotic forces that threatened to consume him. He knew that he had been acting like a maniac in recent days, fighting spells with salt and basil, eating street food in Honduras, and running off to pray for the apocalypse in the Mayan ruins. Unable to understand and explain himself, he had climbed into bed after Leah left and said a short prayer, asking God to help him escape into unconsciousness.

Harley's prayer had been answered, but only by a three-hour nap. Now he was lying in bed, fully dressed, watching the sun begin to turn the sky a fiery orange and red. He wondered what had been said about him in church that morning, and what kinds of reports had been made by members of the mission team at coffee hour. Would tall Bill Stanford lean down to whisper stories of Harley's disappearance into the ears of the ladies in the sewing group? Or would Gretchen Bennett tell her Bible study classmates about the report they got from the Roman Catholic priest at Copán Ruinas? Harley imagined Juan Erazo trying to be diplomatic, but then shaking his head and saying that he suspected that their pastor was *muy loco*. And Harley also feared that Andy Stackhouse, using his authority as a retired Navy officer, would quickly organize a task force to go to the bishop and have her remove him from his position. Two years ago, Harley had felt his life coming to an end with the deaths of his wife and daughter, followed by his forced relocation from Sterling to Occoquan. But at least he had his health. No longer. Maybe this really was the end.

A chilly breeze sliced through the small opening in the turret window, fluttering the white curtains that were being turned into burnt sienna by the sun. Harley gave a sigh and told himself to stop ruminating and obsessing over things he could not control. The truth was, he didn't know what had been said that morning—if anything. People could have been cruel—or kind. There was no concerted effort to remove him from his pulpit—yet. All he could do was try to get his own life back on track. Knowing that he always felt better when he was moving around, he rolled out of bed and went to the bathroom to wash his face. He looked in the mirror and saw his features clearly, maybe for the first time in several weeks. *That's weird*. He had certainly looked in the mirror in recent days, but he hadn't registered what he was seeing. *Now, I see myself—unshaven, haggard, stressed—but clearly myself.* Then he returned to his bedroom, grabbed a sweatshirt, and laced up some sneakers for a walk.

Ever since Harley had become serious about exercising, physical fitness had been a key to his spiritual fitness. And it had all started with walking. At his fortieth birthday party, a Catholic priest friend challenged him to run the Marine Corps Marathon. The goal seemed crazy, since Harley had no experience as a runner, and the prospect of running twenty-six miles was daunting.

But Harley needed a midlife challenge. His priest friend had run several marathons, so he gave him some tips and turned him loose. The first time Harley hit the road, he ran for three minutes and had to stop, gasping for breath. But after walking for seven minutes, he was able to run for another three, and then he walked another seven and ran three. Over several weeks, his running increased and his walking decreased until he could run for an hour. And then he ran two hours. "If you can run two hours, you can run four hours," the priest said to him. "If you can run four hours, you can do a marathon."

The priest was right. Six months after beginning his training, Harley finished the Marine Corps Marathon in a respectable four hours and twelve minutes. He felt as if he'd been through boot camp, but his wobbly elation at the finish line made the pain worthwhile. Marathon training quickly became a meditation for him, an opportunity to think, dream, pray, and problem-solve. He came to appreciate how exercise cuts through the clutter of life and gives the gift of simplicity for a few hours each week. In a career dominated by phone calls, emails, meetings, counseling sessions, and sermon preparation, Harley found that it was calming to spend time focused only on the path ahead. Walking and running became the very best way for him to keep body and soul together.

Now, on that autumn day, he realized that he needed to begin to walk himself back to health. The sun was nearing the horizon as Harley headed west on Mill Street, and as he strolled along, he peered into the windows of shops that were now closed for the evening. He looked at hand-crafted pottery, rustic furniture, jigsaw puzzles, even bridesmaids' dresses—anything to take his mind off of his troubles. A stiff wind rustled the trees, and autumn leaves drifted down and did pirouettes at his feet. Since it was late on a Sunday, there was not a single vehicle in motion. The unexpected beauty and peace of the October evening was doing its best to cool the fever in Harley's brain.

Then, a block ahead of him, he saw a young woman in a white headscarf coming his way. She spotted him and waved, and he quickly realized who she was: Sarah Bayati, the twenty-five-year-old daughter of Muhammad and Fatima Bayati, owners of the Riverview Bakery. As she walked closer, he saw her round face and flashing eyes, which matched the brightness of her flowing green and gold dress.

"Pastor Camden," she called out, "I've missed you!"

"Hello, Sarah," he said, "I've been away." He hoped that she had heard nothing about his recent troubles.

"Really?" she said, stopping to chat in front of the brew pub. "Where have you been?"

"Honduras. I went on a mission trip to help in a medical clinic."

"Oh, that's good," she said. "That will earn you much *hasanat*." Harley knew that she was talking about credit for good deeds, tied to the Muslim belief that after death, God weighs your bad deeds against your good deeds. If the balance tips toward good deeds, you enter heaven. "You are a good man," she said with a smile.

"'No one is good except God,'" said Harley, quoting Jesus.

"Well, then, you share God's goodness."

Harley shrugged, not knowing how to respond, and then asked, "How is your family doing?"

"Omar is continuing to study at George Mason, but has switched his major to law enforcement. Father is working on getting some new ovens for the bakery, and is having to bring in electricians to do some rewiring. Mother works hard every day and tries to be cheerful, but she is still grieving." Harley understood, since it had been just a little over a year since Sarah's sister, twenty-seven-year-old Norah, had been murdered in her bed. "We all are," added Sarah.

Harley knew the ache of losing a loved one to violence, but his head was not clear enough to go any deeper with Sarah. Having made such a fool of himself with his church members, he didn't want to get a reputation with his neighbors—especially a family that respected him for the help he had given them after Norah's death. Instead, he kept things light and asked, "What are you doing this afternoon?"

"The bakery closed at one," she said, "then I did some clean-up and preparation for tomorrow. At three o'clock we had a big Sunday dinner, one of our traditions."

"Sounds nice," said Harley, remembering the lazy Sunday dinners that he used to have with his own family, after a hectic morning at church. His wife Karen had been such an adventurous cook, trying new recipes every week from her ever-expanding library of cookbooks, and she always filled the house with surprising, savory aromas. When Harley walked through the door and took a deep breath, the eyes of his daughter Jessica would sparkle and she would say to him, "You'll *never* guess what mom is making!" In fact, he couldn't ever guess. But he was never disappointed.

Now, the aromas were gone. As were Karen and Jessica. And Norah Bayati as well. Sunday dinners would never be the same.

"I needed a walk after eating so much food," said Sarah, "so I have been walking all around town. Father always discouraged Norah and me from going out alone, but this is Occoquan in daylight. As soon as the sun sets, I'll go home and do the Maghrib prayer."

"Maghrib? What's that?"

"The sunset prayer. It begins when the sun sets and lasts until the red light has left the sky. It takes about twenty minutes."

"Do you use your own words?"

"No, the words are set," said Sarah. "The prayer is in Arabic, and begins with '*Allah-hoo Akbar*,' which means 'Allah is Great.'"

"Yes, that sounds familiar," Harley said.

"It goes on to give glory to Allah, and to praise Allah for his perfection. We also ask for forgiveness. There is a lot of repetition."

"Does it ever get boring, being repetitive?"

"No," said Sarah. "The repetition gets us out of our heads. It connects us to God."

Out of our heads, thought Harley. What a phrase. For weeks, he had been out of his mind—from a curse, a stroke, a psychotic break—who knew *what* it was? But maybe the way back to health was to get out of his head and reconnected to God. He had clearly been living too much *in* his head, worried about witches and Hondurans and the coming of a new heaven and a new earth. But if he got *out* of his head, maybe he could find some peace and healing and hope. "Thank you, Sarah," he said, after a few moments. "That's helpful."

Glancing west, Sarah noticed that the sun was about to drop below the horizon. "I better go home," she said. "It's almost time for Maghrib."

"*Salaam alaikum*," said Harley, using the only Arabic he knew, a phrase which meant "peace be upon you."

"*Salaam alaikum*," Sarah responded with a bow.

Harley continued his walk by crossing the pedestrian bridge and strolling up the road which ran along the river on the northern bank. The sun had set, but there was still enough light to illuminate the charcoal gray outcroppings of rock that rose up from the edge of the river and undergirded the road along the ridge. Harley knew that the rocks were old, formed about three hundred million years ago, in the era in which the North American and African land masses slowly plowed into each other and created a supercontinent called Pangaea. When the supercontinent began to separate into the continents we know today, it left behind the shelves of rock that stand on either side of the Occoquan River. *These ancient formations have been around forever*, thought Harley. Putting his hands on a rock by the roadside, one with a flat top around three feet high and six feet wide, he knew that he was making a connection with something much bigger than himself.

Sitting down on the rock, he had the strange sensation that his center of gravity was moving out of his head. It moved down, down, down . . . past his shoulders and chest and waist, and deep into the stone beneath him. *What*, he wondered, *had this massive rock witnessed as it looked over the Town of Occoquan?* Native Americans and settlers, Revolutionary soldiers and Redcoats, slave-owners and abolitionists, blacks and whites, and now an odd collection of witches and Jews and Christians and Muslims. The rocks had seen it all, standing silently above the fading light on the Occoquan River. Pulling out his smartphone, Harley called up a psalm, number eighteen, "The Lord is my rock, my fortress, and my deliverer, my God, my rock in whom I take refuge." Harley read it, and then repeated it. *Get outside your head*, he thought to himself, *let yourself rest in the Lord of the rock*. This is what is really real, he realized, a fortress that can stand strong against any assault. Lean on this, rely on this—the rock in which you can take refuge. "The Lord is my rock, my fortress, and my deliverer," Harley repeated to himself, over and over again. The line became his own Maghrib prayer.

With eyes closed, he began to hear other words being spoken all around him. "In the beginning was the Word," rumbled the outcropping of rock beneath him, "and the Word was with God, and the Word was God. He was in the beginning with God. All things came into being through him, and without him not one thing came into being."

"But who, who, who, who"—asked an owl in a tall tree behind him—"who is this Word, this Word, this Word?"

"He is the image of the invisible God, the firstborn of all creation," said the river, lapping gently against the rocky shoreline; "for in him all things in heaven and on earth were created, things visible and invisible, whether thrones or dominions or rulers or powers—all things have been created through him and for him."

The Word, the image of the invisible God, the firstborn of all creation—Harley knew that these ancient truths were all connected to Jesus, the Word of God. He had heard the lines first in the words of Scripture, and now he was hearing them in the sounds of nature. "He himself is before all things," said a voice from deep within the rock, "and in him all things hold together."

A stick snapped behind him, causing Harley to open his eyes and turn around. He saw a Grizzly bear—tall, powerful, rising up on its haunches with jaws open and claws out. Harley screamed as he jumped up, and immediately tripped over a root and fell on his side. He rolled one time and heard the creature coming toward him. *Lord, be my rock!* Struggling to his knees, he looked up in a panic. *Please—deliver me!* But there was nothing there. Nothing but a man in his early forties, with a bushy brown beard and dark eyes. "You okay?" asked the man.

With his heart pounding, Harley pushed himself back and sat against a tree. He looked left and right, and realized that the bear was gone, really gone. Closing his eyes, he tried to calm himself and get his breathing under control. Then he slowly opened his eyes and stared at the man in front of him. He was tall, dressed in a broad-brimmed hat and hiking clothes, and in his right hand he carried a large hand-carved walking stick with a skull at the end. Although the light was fading, Harley recognized him as John Jonas—the witch who went by the name Earth Eagle.

"John," said Harley, in a voice as calm as he could muster. He didn't want to show his vulnerability or admit his panic. "Did you see that?"

"See what?"

"The bear."

"No," said John. "I only saw you."

"No bear?"

"No bear," he said, shaking his head. "What were you doing here?"

"Sitting," replied the pastor. "And praying." With his heartbeat returning to normal, he assured himself that he had made a connection to the one who was his rock, his fortress, and his deliverer. The serenity had been real and he had found a firm foundation. *Right up until the appearance of the bear.*

"It's beautiful here," said John, looking around. "A good place to pray. But I didn't think you people prayed in the woods."

"Oh, sure," Harley nodded. "We do. We see God in creation."

"You wouldn't know it," said the witch.

"Why's that?"

"By the way you Christians treat the Earth."

Harley put the palms of his hands on the ground, and leaned back against the tree, thinking for a moment. *He's trying to hook me. Don't take the bait.* He tried to change the subject by saying, "I think I saw you on the riverbank a few weeks ago. What were you doing?"

John seemed to be surprised that Harley had noticed him. He paused for a moment before saying, "Clearing debris."

Harley nodded. "That makes sense, after the flood."

"I do a lot of trail maintenance," said John. "There is a path along the river that was totally covered in logs, branches, and trash."

"I bet."

"Took me several days to get it all clear. It's part of my commitment to the environment."

Harley nodded. "Thank you for doing that."

John tapped the tip of his walking stick on to the road a few times, and then said, "I'm just finishing a hike through the Occoquan Regional Park. Have you been there?"

"No, I haven't. I've seen it from the river but haven't hiked it."

"Interesting place," said John. "Used to be a prison, you know."

"Yes, I have seen the old buildings on top the hill, the ones turned into the arts center."

"Well, that's just part of it. You know, down on the river, the dock on the northern bank? That is where prisoners used to be dropped off, after being transported by boat from DC. Hard to escape from a boat in the middle of a river."

"Huh," said Harley. He had cruised past the dock many times but didn't know its history. "I guess that's where you get the expression, 'sent up the river.'"

"Exactly. And the prison is where suffragettes were imprisoned, after they protested for the right to vote."

"Right here?" asked Harley. "Didn't know that."

"Some were even beaten."

"Really?"

"Yes. When they were first taken to the workhouse, they were clubbed. One was thrown into a dark cell and she hit her head, which knocked her out. Her cellmate thought she was dead."

"Unbelievable," said Harley, shaking his head.

"They called it the 'Night of Terror,'" said John, "and it galvanized support for the cause."

"That makes sense," Harley said, thinking of Civil Rights workers being beaten and thrown in jail in the 1960s. "Sometimes a great injustice can advance the cause of justice."

"But the suffering continued," said John. "Rats ran in and out their cells. The women had no privacy. It was like they were being kept in a zoo, with U.S. Marines standing guard."

"All because they wanted the right to vote."

"Which they got," John said, "three years after the Night of Terror. It's amazing how people are imprisoned in one generation for something that seems so noble in another."

This witch is thoughtful, Harley realized. *More reflective than I expected him to be.* "You're right," Harley said.

"May I join you?" John asked, pointing to the rock.

"Okay," said Harley, getting up from the ground, brushing himself off, and taking a seat on the rock again, a few feet from the witch. *I wonder what this guy is up to?*

John sat down but kept his walking stick propped between his legs, holding it with his massive hands. The two men looked out over the Occoquan River, as the last flickers of light danced on the water. "We do most of our services outside," said John.

"That was my impression."

"There is so much power in nature," John said, "so much energy. We believe that the spiritual world and the physical world are totally interconnected, and that every single thing has a spirit."

Harley believed that Christ was the firstborn of all creation, and that all things were created through him. But he kept this to himself.

"In our services, we tap into this power," John continued, "and we embrace it all—earth, wind, water, fire, sky."

"Earth, wind, *and* fire?" asked Harley. For some reason, he felt he could take a chance on humor. "Like the music group?"

"Yeah," nodded John, smiling, "just like them. But I'm serious about everything having power. We embrace it all. You Christians get all holier-than-thou and pretend that you are such a force for good, but you are not. You do as much evil as anyone, but you deny it. We have no problem with pride and personal freedom and individualism."

"We are certainly sinners," admitted Harley. "None of us is all good."

"We embrace the evil *and* the good," John continued. Using his walking stick as a pointer, he swept it across the scene in front of them. "Nature is a fierce and violent system. Hawks use their talons to pluck fish out of the river, snakeheads eat frogs, coyotes attack chickens. Humans are violent, too, and always have been. It is part of our nature. We don't deny it. But everything should be kept in balance, whether the system is a river or a forest or a town or a city. Even if the system is two people, or two groups of people, or two nations—balance is the goal, through violence if necessary."

Harley looked at him and asked, "But is violence the best tool?" Gazing into his dark eyes, Harley sensed that John would not hesitate to use violence if it suited him.

"Not the best tool," he admitted, "but one tool of many. Violence and non-violence. Hate and love. Aggression and gentleness. All are forces that can be used and should be used. The name I have taken in the coven, Earth Eagle, is a reflection of this balance."

"Same for Fire Dolphin?" asked Harley.

John nodded. "All of these forces are seen in the physical world, and they exist in the spiritual world as well. They are as real as electricity or x-rays or radio waves. They cross time and space and shape the world we see."

"Give me an example," said the pastor, feeling skeptical.

"Have you seen the Indian?" asked John.

"The Indian?" he asked.

"Yes," said John. "Across the street from your house. He appears in the second-floor window."

Harley felt a cold shiver. "You mean, he's not a real person?"

"Well, yes, he's real. But not living."

"What are you saying?" asked Harley, wondering if his craziness was returning.

"He's a ghost," said the witch. "The building was once the Occoquan Lodge, built in the early 1800s. For a while, the Dogue Indians and white people lived together peacefully, but eventually the Indians moved west, except for one man. He was tall with long black hair, and he fell in love with the beautiful blond-haired wife of the lodge's owner. The husband came back from a trip one night, caught the Indian coming down the stairs from a second-floor bedroom, and shot him dead. The husband was trying to right a wrong and restore a sense of balance. But in this case, the love of the Indian and the wife was too strong. That's why you still see them. Their energy was not destroyed."

Harley was having a hard time absorbing what John was saying. All he could say in response was, "I've seen him . . . I've seen them both. I assumed they were real."

"Well, they *are* real," said John. "Spiritually real. Embodiments of an invisible power. And we believe that these powers can be controlled. That's what we do when we gather."

"So, you cast spells?" asked Harley.

"Sometimes."

"You make curses?"

John said, "We do." Harley felt a rush of fear, but also curiosity.

"Watch this," said John. "See those moths?" There were dozens of moths fluttering around them in the gloaming, the growing dark of the woods. Harley might not have noticed them unless they had been pointed out, but once he saw them, he realized they were all around, dancing in playful spirals and loops among the trees. John pulled his car keys out of his pocket, made a guttural sound, and shook the keys at the insects. The moths fell to the ground, as lifeless as stones.

"Curses," said John.

"Curses," repeated Harley, stunned by what he had seen. "I got one from Kelly. It was an email that said, 'Attacks and curses will be met with attacks and curses.'"

"Yes," John nodded, "I knew about that. But that's more of a threat than a curse."

"What do you mean?"

"We didn't actually curse you, we threatened to curse you. That email was more of . . . an intimidation technique."

"Why did you send it?"

"To put you guys on the defensive," explained John, staring at him with his dark eyes. "To get you to respect our power, maybe even realize that you had made a mistake."

The pastor swallowed hard.

"But don't take it personally, Harley. It was sent to the whole group."

"So, you didn't curse me?" he asked.

"No," said John, shaking his head. "If we cursed you, you'd know it."

10

"Why didn't you tell me about the Indian?" snapped Harley, frustrated with the man sitting in a Town of Occoquan golf cart at eight o'clock on a Monday morning.

"Good morning to you as well," said Tie-dye Tim. His outfit was an assault on the eyes: A red and green plaid jacket over a tie-dye t-shirt, topped off by a wide-brimmed orange hat with a leather chinstrap. He had absolutely no fashion sense, but he didn't seem to care. Some people thought he was odd but harmless, others ignored him because he did such menial work, and still others kept their distance because he had showed inappropriate interest in an Occoquan teen, back when he was in his thirties. To Harley, Tim was an underappreciated public servant, one who had been consistently good to the pastor since he arrived in town. Now, looking through the steam that was rising out of his coffee into the cool air, Tim smiled and asked, "What Indian?"

"The ghost," said Harley, pointing to the apartment across Mill Street.

"Oh, you mean Tayac."

"Have you seen him?" Harley asked.

"No," Tim responded, shaking his head. "But plenty of people say they have."

"Do you believe them?"

"Sure. Why not?"

Harley wasn't sure if Tim was being serious or not. "What did you call him?" he asked.

"Tayac. That's the Dogue Indian name for chief. Don't know if he was really a chief or not, but that's what people call him."

"John Jonas told me that he was shot dead by a jealous husband."

"Yes, that's the story," said Tim. "Tayac was having an affair with the innkeeper's wife and was killed on the staircase. Folks say that their love affair continues today. But why are you asking? Have you seen them?"

Harley hesitated, still worried about what people were thinking about him. But if he couldn't confide in Tim, who could he? "Maybe," he said, very quietly.

"Don't worry about it, Harley," said Tim with a smile. "Lots of people say they have seen Tayac and Sadie—that's her name, by the way—standing in the window. There's a lot going on in this town, just below the surface."

"What do you mean by that?"

"Hidden things," said the maintenance man. "Stuff that bubbles up."

"You mean like Paul Ranger and his erotica?"

"Yeah, that," said Tim, laughing, "but stranger things as well. Sounds come from deep within the earth, across the river, wailing sounds. I've heard them myself, and they are very creepy, like they come from another world. Some say that they are the cries of people who were killed in the massacre."

"What massacre?" Harley couldn't believe he had never heard any of this.

Tim leaned back in his golf cart seat and took a long drink of coffee. "Back in the 1600s, the Dogue Indians had their main settlement east of here, at the mouth of the Occoquan River. They were river people and were closely linked to the Piscataway Indians across the Potomac. When English settlers arrived, they found ways to trade with them, offering fish from the river in exchange for iron tools and decorative glass."

"So why did the settlers massacre them?"

"They didn't," said Tim. "There were power struggles but no open warfare. Instead, another tribe became jealous of the growing power of the Dogues. You've heard of the Susquehanna River, right?"

"Yes, up near Baltimore."

"There was a tribe from that area called the Susquehannocks, and they advanced on the Dogues from the north. Came down in serious numbers and crossed the Potomac by canoe, although not before they were spotted by the Piscataway Indians over in Maryland. The Piscataway scouts warned the Dogues, who went to the settlers and asked for help. Those Indians weren't fools—they knew all about the power of English firearms."

"Technology always wins," said Harley.

"Not necessarily. The English had a tiny little settlement just across the river, near the dock in the park. When they heard about the Susquehannocks, they circled their buildings with large carts and armed themselves to the teeth. But they refused to venture out to the Dogue village to offer assistance. The settlers were going to defend themselves, but *only* themselves."

"Selfish," muttered Harley, shaking his head.

"There was a fierce battle in the Dogue village," said Tim. "Many Indians from both sides were killed, and a number of homes were set on fire. The settlers could see a glow on the horizon as the village burned. And then, silhouetted against the flames, they saw canoes coming towards them. They pointed their muskets at the canoes but held their fire until they could see who was in them."

"The Susquehannocks?"

"No. Dogue women and children. They were fleeing the fighting, terrified. They beached their canoes and ran toward the settlement, crying out for help and shelter. But the settlers pointed their muskets at them, blocked them from entering, and drove them away."

"Oh no," said Harley, feeling an unexpected rush of shame. *My people.*

"It gets worse," said Tim, looking across the Occoquan to the bank on the other side. "See those caves? The Dogues ran along the bank until they found them, and then went inside. Dozens of women and children hid in the rocks, hoping that they could avoid the invaders. But soon the Susquehannocks arrived, searching for surviving Dogues. The English settlers feared that they were outnumbered, so they took a gamble and pointed the Susquehannocks toward the caves, hoping that they would take the Dogues and leave them alone. The gamble worked—although the slaughter in the caves was sickening. The invaders took the best of the young women as slaves and killed the rest."

Harley was stunned and dropped his head. "What evil," he said.

"Indeed," said Tim. "You learn that history, and you can understand why cries still come out of those caves."

"And I thought that the witches were bad."

"Nowhere near as bad," said Tim. "When it comes to evil, they still have a lot to learn."

Harley hadn't expected his day to begin with the opening of a window to hell. He looked out over the Occoquan River, its shimmering surface reflecting the red and yellow of the fall leaves, and he felt an impulse to plunge into it and go down to its silent depths, to a place where his mind could be still and he could find peace. Enough of witches' curses, visions of ghosts, and stories of massacres—his mind needed healing. He wanted to die and rise in the watery depths; to experience a deep-water baptism and a fresh start. The shimmering of the water captivated him, and he felt lured by its promise of cleansing. But looking at the river and then back at Tim, he knew these were crazy thoughts. He would never take the plunge, no matter how good it would feel. With his reputation already frayed, what would a leap into the Occoquan River do to his remaining respectability? *Funny how that it is*, he thought to himself: *If I were to invite church members to join me at the river for baptism, I'd be seen as a bold and innovative pastor. But if I jump into the river to cleanse myself, I'm a lunatic.*

Glancing at his watch, Harley realized that he had an appointment at the church, one that had been made before the mission trip. "Better get rolling," he said.

"Me too," said the maintenance man. "Still a lot of debris from the storm, down under the bridge."

∽

Walking toward the church, Harley could see Juan Erazo waiting for him on the landing at the top of the wooden steps that led to his office. Harley felt a knot in his stomach, wondering what Juan would say about the mission trip, since Juan had been an eye-witness to Harley's erratic behavior and the translator of the Catholic priest's report. But what could Harley do? He was powerless to change the past. *Better get it over with*, he thought to himself as he climbed the steps. He could not alter a single fact about the week in Honduras.

"*Buenos días, mi pastor!*" said Juan with enthusiasm. He was a short, dark-skinned man with salt-and-pepper hair and a big toothy grin. That morning, he was dressed in blue jeans and a t-shirt from the local high school, Lake Ridge.

"*Cómo está?*" asked Harley.

"*Muy bien gracias. Y usted?*"

"*Bien, gracias.*" Opening the door, Harley said, "Come on in, Juan."

The two entered the pastor's office, and Harley asked if Juan wanted any coffee. "Honduran?" asked the man as he sat down.

"No, not today," said Harley. "I should have bought some while we were down there." He carefully measured some grounds into a coffee filter, and then added water. As the coffee started to perk, he added, "I just didn't think about it. I wasn't quite myself."

Juan nodded, acknowledging what Harley was saying, and then said, "I'm sorry for what you went through."

"I'm not sure what caused it. But I seem to be doing better now."

"You have a tough job," said Juan. "Lots of stress. That can have an effect. You've been through a lot—the stress of losing your wife and daughter, the stress of a new church, the stress of a mission trip."

Harley wasn't sure if stress was the cause of his problem, but he appreciated the kindness and said, "Thanks, Juan."

"I had a cousin who came to the US and became so stressed that he went crazy. *Un loco*. Would sit around his house in his underwear, doing nothing all day except picking on his guitar. We sent him back to Honduras, and guess what? He was fine. So, pastor, I think you'll be fine now that you're home."

"I sure hope so," said Harley. Juan's understanding and acceptance felt like a gift, unexpected and unearned. What the Bible called grace.

"The Christian life is stressful for all of us," Juan went on to say. "It's hard to know how tight to be, and how loose."

Harley was confused but curious. "What do you mean by that?"

"Tight, loose. Like turning a bolt," he explained. "You know I like to work on cars, don't you?"

"Yeah, I heard that."

"Well, you have to be careful when you tighten a bolt. Too much and it will strip or get stuck, too little and it will fall off. Same with being a Christian. Try too hard and become prideful, try too little and sin. Christians can be too tight or too loose, just like bolts."

"Interesting," said Harley, never having thought about Christianity in this way.

"So maybe you got too tight," suggested Juan. "Too stressed. Your threads got stripped."

"Could be."

"But God is a fixer," Juan added. "The master mechanic. He'll retool you."

"That's good," said Harley, smiling. "I feel like I had a screw loose."

"You'll be fine," said Juan, waving off his comment. "But let me share one other thought. You don't mind, do you?"

"Not at all," said Harley, appreciating his insights. Auto repair had not been on the curriculum at divinity school, but maybe it should have been.

"Don't assume that your actions have the effect you think they have."

"Huh?"

"Cause and effect is not always clear."

"Okay, Juan. You are going to have to say more."

"I just fixed my brake lights, so this is fresh in my mind. You know how when you press the brake pedal, the brake lights come on?"

"Sure."

"Well, what you might not know is that when you press the pedal, you don't press a switch, you *release* a switch."

"What do you mean by that?"

Using his hands to demonstrate, Juan said, "Here is your foot pushing down. Here is the switch, above your foot. When you press down, the switch opens up, causing the brake lights to come on. The switch doesn't close, it opens. Your action doesn't have the effect you think it has."

"I didn't know that," said Harley. "I assumed the opposite: You hit the brake and depress the switch."

"The point is: Sometimes we push down hard, thinking that we are making something happen. We think the harder we work, the more effect we will have. But when it comes to your brake lights, it doesn't matter how hard you push. The lights will come on whenever the switch is released."

"So, I shouldn't slam on my brakes?" asked Harley.

"Just a tap will activate your brake lights. Same with life: Don't work so hard. Don't stress yourself out. Tap your brakes and let God do the rest."

"Good thoughts," said Harley, pouring them each a cup of coffee. Juan's words were cleansing him. "*Gracias, amigo*," he said as he handed the cup to the Honduran. Harley had been amazed over the years at how seriously his church members took their faith, and how they connected it so deeply and naturally to their daily lives. "I'm going to remember about your bolts and brake lights."

"But I didn't come here to talk auto mechanics," said Juan, putting a heap of sugar into his coffee, Honduran-style. "I wanted to talk with you about some volunteer work I'm doing at Lake Ridge High School."

"Go on," said Harley, drinking his coffee black.

"When I retired from construction work, I got bored," he explained. "I decided to become a substitute teacher at the high school."

"Very brave!" Harley volunteered. "*Qué bélico*."

"I liked it," said Juan. "I enjoyed the kids and their energy." Harley had done enough youth work to know what he was talking about. "While I was there, I got connected with the Latino Students Association, and became a volunteer advisor. Eventually, I quit the subbing but continued the advising. It's just one day a week."

"So, what do you do?" asked Harley.

"I sit in on their meetings. Help with fundraising. Keep them connected to the administration. But mostly just get to know the kids."

"I bet they look up to you."

"Most of them," Juan nodded. "They call me *abuelo*, grandfather. A lot are recent immigrants, and they have tough lives. Their parents are working hard to make ends meet, so they need someone who will just sit and listen to them."

"Sounds like a great service."

"I do my best," said Juan. "But the longer I worked with them, the more they opened up to me. And what they told me was very disturbing."

"What do you mean?"

"The MS-13 gang has become strong in the county, and its members have started recruiting at the high school."

"I've heard of MS-13," said Harley, "but don't know much about it."

"The full name is *Mara Salvatrucha*. It started in LA in the 1980s. When it became strong in the nineties, thousands of gang members were deported to El Salvador, Guatemala, and Honduras. Then, about ten years ago, it returned with a vengeance. Ever since, the kids at the high school have been running scared. Same for the teachers—they worry about being targeted."

"What does the gang do?"

"Drug dealing, illegal immigration, human trafficking, robbery," said Juan. "But what they do best is violence. They are one of the fiercest gangs in the world, killing people for snitching or wearing the colors of a rival gang. One innocent family was gunned down because they had a traffic dispute with a gang member."

"Unbelievable," said Harley, shaking his head.

"You know the number thirteen in MS-13? It comes from the thirteen seconds of beating that is inflicted on anyone who joins the gang. These guys are incredibly violent, I tell you, and they are here."

Harley felt his blood run cold. "What do you mean by 'here'?"

"Occoquan," said Juan.

"Really?" asked Harley. "Where?"

"You know that body that was found after the flood? The young Latino with tattoos? He had Satan's claws carved into his back. That's an MS-13 gang sign called *la garra*, the claw."

"Was he MS-13?"

"Probably not. His tattoos seem to be signs for another Latino gang, *Los Gatos*. But the carving looks like the work of *Mara Salvatrucha*."

"So maybe he crossed MS-13."

"Could be," said Juan. "All I know is that my kids at the high school are terrified. They tell me that the dead man's name was Enrique, and that he was a leader of *Los Gatos*. They feel his death will escalate the violence. Last week, in Prince William County Park, another body was found. The victim had been stabbed one hundred times, decapitated, and dismembered."

"I didn't hear about that," said Harley.

"It happened while we were in Honduras. Even more grisly is the fact that the victim's heart had been cut out and put on a big rock. Like a sacrifice." Harley's mind flashed back to his dream about the Mayan temple and the priest with the obsidian knife. "People are calling it a satanic murder," said Juan. "The rumor is that MS-13 members often kill people to honor *la Bestia*, the beast."

La Bestia, thought Harley. Why did he keep coming around? Harley had thought more about Satan in the past month than he had in his decades of ministry, and he was anxious to change the subject. But Juan was visibly troubled, and Harley wanted to help the man who had been so compassionate and understanding toward him. "What can I do," he asked him, "to help you and these kids?"

"Just be aware," said Juan. "Keep your eyes open. The rumor is that some drug dealing is being done around here, maybe in the abandoned house across the river. The castle. What my kids call *el Castillo.*"

11

Every day for a week, Harley passed the abandoned house. Some mornings, he ran his standard figure-eight route and saw the house on his left as he was coming down the hill on the north side of the river. Other days he took a walk at lunchtime, from his church to the pedestrian bridge, across the river, up the hill, and then back to Occoquan across the big concrete bridge, looking at the house on his right. Some evenings, he would stroll the big bridge as the sun was going down, and he would look westward at the colors of the sunset shimmering on the river. Then he would gaze down at the house along the shoreline and give it a close inspection from above, as he walked the length of the bridge.

El Castillo.

Whenever he passed it, the house was empty. Built out of large gray stones to look like a medieval castle, it had turrets in all four corners and a series of arrow slits in the walls, which Harley assumed were purely decorative. Its large wooden front door had forged iron hardware, and seemed to be strong enough to repel an attack. The second floor of the house was smaller than the first and set back from the stone walls, giving the impression that the upper level was rising like a castle tower out of the first floor. This sturdy but whimsical structure sat at the end of a curving driveway that snaked downhill from the road, and the only deviation from the medieval motif was a series of large plate-glass windows that faced the river. *Even if you're obsessed with castles,* Harley mused, *you're not going to waste a good river view.*

Although the walls of the house were moldy and in need of a good power-washing, the place wasn't as derelict as you would expect an empty house to be. *Someone must be maintaining it,* Harley thought as he looked down on the lot from the concrete bridge. There were leaves in the driveway, but that was no surprise for the month of October, and the small amount of grass around the house looked like it had been cut in the past month. None of the windows was broken and the massive front door had a single padlock on it, with no signs that anyone had tried to break in. In short, it was a surprisingly well-kept empty house.

Who had lived there, and where did they go? Harley wondered what secrets the abandoned structure held, and on Friday evening he paused on the concrete bridge long enough to ruminate. *Was it built by a married couple, scrimping and saving to put a down payment on their dream house, and then filling it with their hopes and dreams and fears? Did they make love in that house, conceive a child, scream at each other, drink themselves to sleep? Why the castle motif—was that the husband's choice, or the wife's? Did their child drive a Big Wheel in the driveway, and have a play house in the side yard? Was it a boy or a girl?* He imagined a little girl like his Jessica, content to play by herself and talk to her imaginary friends on the series of stone terraces that separated the house from the water. What a magical place that riverfront castle would have been.

But then Harley looked at the river and felt a chill blow through him, like a message from another world. The child had ventured too close to the river and had fallen in, being swept away before her father even realized she was in trouble. He searched frantically for her up and down the rocky bank, and then called the police. The Occoquan sheriff and deputy responded immediately, and quickly radioed the river patrol of the Prince William County Police Department, who sent boats up and down the river, searching the water and the shoreline. The man phoned his wife but could hardly form any words, and when she raced home and saw her husband's face in the pulsing blue police lights, she flew into a rage. She screamed and began to hit him in the face, so violently that the sheriff had to pull them apart and send the wife into the house with the deputy. In their panic and fear there was no way that they could comfort each other, so they stayed apart until the news came over the police radio that their daughter's body had been found in the river, down by the Dogue Indian caves. The couple left the house that night and never returned, quickly divorcing and moving as far from each other as they possibly could.

Harley looked away from the house, up toward the setting sun and tried to break the spell of the story. Why had he allowed himself to be taken to such a dark place? *Where did this horror story even come from?* He had no evidence that the owners of the house had suffered a tragedy. There was no sign that a child had ever died there. Yes, he knew that archaeologists always try to make sense of the objects and structures they uncover, and as they do this they extrapolate wildly from very small clues. Harley saw an empty castle and a shoreline, and jumped to the conclusion that the place had been abandoned because the owners suffered the loss of a child in the river. He was acting like the diggers in Honduras who see otherworldly hieroglyphics and deduce that the Mayans had contact with a group of aliens who revealed the secrets of the cosmos. *Wouldn't it be more plausible for a house on a river to be abandoned because of repeated flooding? Doesn't it make more sense for hieroglyphics to be pictures of actual Mayan kings?* Sure, pastors are drawn to the supernatural, but that doesn't mean that every structure is a window to heaven or hell. Not even *el Castillo*.

After watching the sun dip below the horizon, Harley turned to walk back across the concrete bridge to Occoquan. But as he started moving, a light from the northern side of the river caught the corner of his eye. He turned back toward the empty house and saw the headlights of a vehicle moving slowly down the hill on the winding driveway toward the house. He leaned over the railing to get a better look and saw that the vehicle stopped in front, illuminating the large front door. A man emerged from the car, walked to the front door, and opened the padlock. Then he returned to the car, shut off the engine, and extinguished the lights. Using a flashlight, he returned to the door, opened it, and entered the house. The lot was now in complete darkness, but Harley could see the beam of the flashlight cutting like a sword through the empty house. Then it disappeared. Harley stood in the gloom for another fifteen minutes, staring at the house, but he saw no light or movement. It was as though the visitor to the house had vanished.

The next morning, Harley's morning run took him past the house again. The vehicle was gone and the padlock was back on the door. But this time he saw the terraces between the house and river in a new light: They were like a giant yardstick marking the elevation of the house above the water. He slowed to a walk and counted the terraces . . . one, two, three, four, five. It looked like each one was about five feet tall. Although he had thought of the castle as being on the river, it was really twenty-five feet above it. And this meant that the house was really in no danger of flooding, except in the most extreme and unlikely of storms. In fact, it was high enough to have a basement, which may have been why the man with the flashlight disappeared the night before. Clearly, there was more to this place than met the eye.

∽

"You know the little castle across the river?" The question caught Jefferson Jones off guard when Harley asked it in the basement of Riverside

Methodist Church. The businessman clearly had his mind on other matters when the two men crossed paths in the mopped up and dried out social hall on the morning of Saturday, October 20. Jefferson had just directed one of his nephews to set up another banquet table for the platters and bowls of food that were coming through the doors, carried by Joneses of every age and shape and size from throughout the Mid-Atlantic region.

"Bertie!" Jefferson said to a large woman in a floral print dress and matching hat. "Let me introduce you to Pastor Harley Camden, our host here at the church."

"Thank you so much for your hospitality," said the woman with a broad smile. "You are so kind to open your church to us."

"It's your church, as you know," said Harley with a slight bow. He was happy to be mixing with a group of people who had no knowledge of his erratic behavior before and after his Honduras trip. Sometimes, it was liberating to be anonymous.

"Daddy, you shouldn't be doing all this," said Tawnya, appearing out of nowhere. She looked gorgeous, as usual, casually elegant with perfect braids and makeup. "Shoo, shoo, sit down with Pastor Camden. I'll get things set up."

Jefferson liked to be in charge, but seemed to be grateful for Tawnya's intervention. He had lost weight since the last time Harley saw him, and he looked weary—even though it was only eleven in the morning. Tawnya led them to a couple of chairs in the corner of the room, where Jefferson could see everything from the sidelines.

"Sorry to distract you from your family," said Harley, as they sat down.

"Not at all," Jefferson replied. "I'll have lots of time to get caught up with everyone." Harley noticed that the older man had a cane in his right hand, which he had not been using before. "I'm just glad that you could stop by this morning and give everyone a formal welcome."

"My pleasure," said the pastor. "This is going to be quite an event."

"We do everything big," said Jefferson, grinning.

An enormous young man with long dreadlocks came striding across the room, arms spread wide. *Talk about big.* "Uncle Jeff!" he said, leaning over to give the old man a hug.

"Oowee," said Jefferson as he squeezed the man's forearm. "You are a rock, young man." Then turning to Harley, he said, "My great-nephew Charles plays for Rutgers. Offensive line."

"Nice to meet you," said the pastor. "How's your season going?"

"Okay, till I got hurt. But hey, it freed me up to come to the reunion."

"That's a blessing to us," Jefferson nodded. "Bad things happen, but God uses them for good."

"Nice to see you, Uncle Jeff. Hope you feel better soon."

"Me too, son."

When the young man moved on to greet a cousin, Jefferson turned to Harley and said, "Now, about that house."

"Yes, I'm just wondering about it. I pass it almost every day, and never see anyone in it." He was bending the truth, slightly, but eventually he'd talk about the man with the flashlight.

"It's on the market," said Jefferson, "and I'm handling the listing. It's going to take a while to sell. It's what I'd call a 'unique property.'"

"What do you mean by that?"

"Not for everyone," said the real estate man. "It's a castle, after all! They say that a man's home is his castle, but who wants a castle, really? It sits all by itself, next to the bridge. Nice view of the river, but no neighborhood to speak of."

"Who built it?" asked Harley. He wanted to find out if he had been given a supernatural message about the couple with the lost child.

"A wine merchant from Lorton. The stone house you see today was built by him in the late seventies, when interest in wine was just picking up. He may have fallen in love with castles while he was visiting wineries in Europe. I don't know. What I *do* know is that he was attracted to the site because of the large basement carved out of rock."

So, there *is* a basement, Harley thought to himself. "What was that about?"

"It was the cellar of the ferryman's house, back in the 1700s. There was no bridge over the river in those days, so a ferry had to take people across. The ferryman lived in a house on that site, and his basement was used as a prison during the Revolutionary War."

"No kidding," said Harley. "How long did that house survive?"

"I'm not sure," admitted Jefferson. "But you don't want to abandon a perfectly good basement carved out of rock. There were probably several houses built on top of it over the years. When I was a small child, it was a Craftsman style house used by a DC lawyer as a weekend getaway. That was replaced by a Cape Cod, built by one of the top guys at the Lorton Reformatory. He lived there with his family."

"Was that what the wine guy bought and tore down?"

"Exactly," said Jefferson. "The Cape Cod was removed and replaced by the little castle you see today. He loved the rock basement, which was always a consistent fifty-five degrees for the storage of his wine."

"So why did he move?"

"Personal issues," Jefferson said. "His wife was never happy there."

"Did they have any children?" Harley asked. He was wondering about his vision of the drowned little girl.

"No, never did. Not while they lived there."

"So, why was she unhappy?" Harley probed.

"I don't really like to talk about it," Jefferson admitted, "since I am trying to sell the place. People get spooked."

"Spooked?" asked Harley. Every day, he was peeling back another layer of Occoquan's hidden history.

"Yes, they do," said the businessman. He looked at Harley in silence for a minute, his hands crossed on top of the cane between his legs. "But you keep things confidential. Right, pastor?"

"Of course," said Harley.

Dropping his voice to a hoarse whisper, Jefferson said, "The basement is carved out of rock, but the walls are not solid. There are ancient cracks and fissures that open it up to the caves that line the banks of the Occoquan. You know about the caves, right?"

"Yes," said Harley, nodding.

"None of the cracks are big enough to pose any structural problems, but they do allow some air to pass through. And . . . according to some people . . . voices."

"Voices?"

"I've never heard them myself," said Jefferson. "But the word on the street is that the wine merchant's wife heard voices in the walls, and even worse than voices . . . screaming. She went to the basement one night for a bottle of wine and heard something that caused her to drop the bottle and run out of the house. Said she would never return."

"So, that's when the couple put the house on the market."

"Yes, they tried to sell it, but they couldn't. As I said, it's a unique property. Eventually, my company stepped in and bought it for a very good price. We've been trying to flip it ever since."

"You have someone maintaining it?" asked Harley, wanting to learn about the man he saw in the house.

"Sort of," said Jefferson. "Just the bare minimum. We're trying to control our costs, since the sale is taking longer than we expected."

"Who is doing it?"

Jefferson looked surprised at the question, and Harley realized that he had crossed a line. *But what did it matter, really? The house was being maintained, so who cares about the identity of the caretaker?* Harley felt embarrassed by his question, but he didn't want to retract it. "I just saw someone going into the house the other night," he confessed. "My curiosity got the best of me."

The businessman gave a slight smile, appreciating Harley's honesty. "I guess there's no harm in telling you. I think you know him: Paul Ranger."

"Sure do," said Harley. *Why wouldn't a collector of vintage erotica want to work in a castle with a solid rock basement? Creepy guy, creepy house.*

"He does a little work for me—cuts the grass, rakes the leaves." Jefferson had no idea why Paul was going into the house at night, but he figured that he would bring that question directly to his employee. "Anyway, the house needs all the help that it can get, especially in this market."

"What do you mean by that?" Harley asked.

"The flood has done a number on us," Jefferson explained. "As you can imagine, 'Occoquan Riverfront' is not the hottest real estate listing right now."

"I hear you," said the pastor. "Recovery from the storm is going to take a very long time."

At that point, Bertie Jones in the floral print dress reappeared and told Jefferson that the time had come for them to get started. "You're right," said the patriarch of the family. "Pastor Camden and I were just getting caught up. Talking about the flood."

"Such a terrible thing," said the cousin. "I was surprised by the destruction. All due to those witches."

"The witches?" asked Harley.

"Yes, the witches," said the woman with conviction. "They didn't like Jefferson's plans to redevelop their apartment building, so they put a curse on him and on the town. They are the cause of the flood."

"Now, Bertie," said Jefferson. "You don't know that." Harley was intrigued, but stayed out of their conversation.

"It's the only thing that makes sense," she added. "You've lived here your whole life, Jefferson, and there has never been a flood . . ."

"Well," said the businessman, "there *was* Hurricane Agnes."

"But that was a huge storm," Bertie insisted. "Did terrible damage all up and down the East Coast. I was a counselor at Girl Scout Camp when it hit, and I thought we were going to be washed away. Unlike Agnes, this flood came out of nowhere. I blame the witches."

"It did surprise us," admitted Jefferson. "No one expected this particular storm to do so much damage."

"It was a curse," said Bertie. "No doubt about it."

"You could be right, but I don't know," said the old man. "Some of the witches may want to hurt the town, but not all. I've had dealings with a few, and they are reasonable people. Harley, you know John Jonas, right?"

"Yes, I do."

"He has some contacts in the police department, and was helpful to the Bayatis after the death of their daughter."

"I didn't know that," said Harley. As close as he was to the Bayatis, he didn't know they had contact with the witch.

Wanting to change the subject, Jefferson then said, "Pastor, we need a blessing. If you would, please welcome the Jones family to your church—to our church—and bless this reunion."

"It would be my pleasure," said Harley. Occoquan was in need of blessings, not curses.

12

"Modela Negra, Harley?" asked the large woman behind the bar of La Casa Blanca in Lorton, a Mexican restaurant with strings of fiesta lights hanging from the ceiling and sombreros nailed to the fake adobe walls.

"You know it, Miranda. Set me up." Harley was happy to be where he could drink a few beers and eat enchiladas in peace. He always ate at the bar and was waited on by Miranda Weiss, a woman in her late thirties who was working hard to raise two teenagers on her own, while her husband served time in prison for multiple drug offenses. She was the only one in the joint who knew that Harley was a pastor, and he tipped her very well to keep that information to herself, knowing that patrons at a bar can get annoyingly theological when they learn that they are drinking next to a clergyman. As it was, La Casa Blanca was a safe place for Harley to be a regular guy, and he was quite sure that no one in that particular community had heard about his erratic behavior in Honduras.

"Happy Halloween to you," she said, wiping the bar with a rag and setting a frosty bottle in front of him. "What are you dressing up as this year?"

"Bitter, middle-aged, white guy," he said, putting the beer to his lips.

"You nailed it," she quipped, pulling on the lapel of his blue blazer. "Your costume is great."

"How about your kids? Still trick-or-treating?"

"Turning tricks? Hope not," she said with a sigh. "My daughter has grown up way too fast."

"Hold on to her," said Harley. "You don't want to lose her." *That was morose*, he realized, but the loss of his daughter Jessica still snuck up on him in surprising ways. Even now, he found himself looking at the front door, expecting her to walk in, flip her hair, flash him a smile, and give him a hug.

The death of his wife had been wrenching, but the loss of his daughter? Still inconceivable.

"So, what will you be eating? Enchiladas verdes?" Miranda knew his order.

"Of course. What else? But you've got to tell me what makes them so good."

"Wish I knew," said Miranda. "Ana keeps the recipe secret. Says it's a family recipe from Mexico City."

"She won't share it with gringos?"

"Guess not. Can you blame her?"

"No. Just bring me a plate full."

"You got it, Harley."

Miranda was heavier than Harley's wife had been, but she had some attractive qualities—bright blue eyes, a quick smile, and long brown hair which she usually kept pulled back in a ponytail. Harley knew she struggled with her weight, but she had nice curves and was surprisingly nimble as she danced around the restaurant and took care of her customers. Harley liked it when she brushed against him as she passed him at the bar, and he would sometimes call her on it: "You hitting on me?"

"Maybe. What's it to you?"

Although Miranda did not fit his image of an attractive woman, he had to admit that she stirred feelings deep within him. In fact, she often appeared to him in his dreams and popped up in his sexual fantasies. He didn't understand this at all. With his wife Karen gone, he assumed that he would be drawn to another woman like her—but no, here was Miranda. In terms of a romantic checklist, he still wanted slender Karen, not overweight Miranda. Pearly-smile Karen, not crooked-teeth Miranda. Salon-cut Karen, not ponytail Miranda. College-educated Karen, not dropout Miranda. *What was going on here?* Miranda made no sense to Harley as a romantic or sexual partner, but she evoked deep longing. Maybe it was her kindness, her honesty, or her vulnerability. Or perhaps it was something more physical. Maybe her large breasts and wide hips were awakening a longing that was far more reptilian—namely, Harley's desire to spread his seed and procreate after losing his wife and only child. *The biological imperative.*

On slow nights, the two of them would talk while Harley ate and Miranda dried glasses behind the bar. She would talk about the problems her kids were having at school and the trouble they were causing at home, and Harley would listen and try not to think about sex. He always made appropriate comments, often shared stories from his own parenting, and had even referred her to a counselor who was particularly good with teenagers. Since she felt overwhelmed by the challenges the kids were throwing at her, he knew she needed reassurance and hope. He never revealed what was stirring inside him.

"Harley," she asked when she walked past him, "what do you know about Halloween?"

"Not much," he admitted. "Literally, it is All Hallows' Eve, the day before All Hallows' Day, All Saints' Day." That information didn't seem helpful to her.

"Have you met my son?" She pulled out her smartphone and showed Harley a picture of a skinny teen with pale skin, acne, and long, straight, greasy, brown hair. "Jason. He says he is now a pagan, and that he is going to celebrate something called 'Samhain.'"

"Yeah," said Harley, nodding. "I've heard of that. Some kind of a harvest festival."

"He says that the physical and spiritual worlds are very close on Samhain," said Miranda. "Magical things can happen."

"That fits with what I know," said Harley, taking a sip of his beer. "Traditionally, the souls of the dead were thought to wander the earth until All Hallows' Day. Halloween—All Hallows' Eve—is the last chance for angry ghosts to get even with their enemies."

"I don't know if my son believes in ghosts," said Miranda. "But he gets the anger part."

"Are you worried he is going to get violent?"

"Not towards me," she said. "Maybe just raise some hell."

"That may not be the worst thing."

"What do you mean?" asked Miranda, surprised.

"Kids are under so much pressure—school, home, social lives. There seems to be no escape. Halloween can be a pressure valve."

"I'm not following."

"It's a harvest festival, right?" Harley's beer had gone to his head, and he was a bit fuzzy. "Change of seasons. Turning point. Whether you call it Halloween or All Hallows' Eve or Samhain, it is a time to see new possibilities."

"Maybe," said Miranda. "I get the need for relief and release."

"Look at the costumes," said Harley. "They come from the time when people put on masks to disguise themselves from angry ghosts. Now, kids dress up as princesses and pirates."

"I don't think my son wants to be a pirate."

"No, not at his age. But still, this is the day to look beyond the stresses of the world. Imagine new possibilities. Halloween reminds us that the spiritual world is real, and very close."

"I think that he and his pagan buddies are going to build a bonfire. Drink some beer. Howl at the moon."

"As I said," said Harley, raising his beer, "may not be the worst thing."

Miranda saw a customer signaling to her, made a quick apology to Harley, and dashed off. The pastor turned on his barstool and faced the restaurant, his beer in his lap. He was feeling the effect of the alcohol, having been so busy at church that he skipped lunch. The restaurant was getting crowded, and Harley enjoyed sitting anonymously on his stool, sipping his drink, and watching the people. A hundred years ago, it would have been a scandal for a Methodist pastor to be spotted at a bar. The church had been strong in the temperance movement and had expected its pastors to abstain from alcohol—even the communion wine was grape juice. Today, most pastors could drink socially without losing their jobs, but Harley still felt more at ease in an out-of-town restaurant.

His sizzling enchiladas verdes were delivered by one of the kitchen staff, a young Mexican woman who could see how busy Miranda was on the restaurant floor. She didn't speak much English, so she pointed to Harley's beer as a way of asking if he wanted another one. He nodded yes, and she brought him a second Modela as he began to eat. Out of the corner of his eye, he watched for Miranda, but she was busier than usual—probably covering for another waitress. She snuck up on him once and touched his shoulder, asking how his dinner was, but she hardly waited for a reply—a customer across the room called for her, and she was gone. Harley saw that she wouldn't have time that night to sit and talk with him, and the realization made him sad. *She's not into me,* he thought. *A mother of teenagers with a Methodist pastor? Not going to happen! Nor should it! She's married!* Finishing his enchiladas, Harley paid the Mexican woman for his dinner and tucked a twenty under his plate for Miranda. Then he waved to her from across the room and headed out.

∽

Back in Occoquan, Harley walked toward River Mill Park to stretch his legs and digest his dinner. He wished he could see the leaves on the trees, which had hit their peak in an explosion of yellows, reds, and oranges, but the sun had set. Gas streetlights were flickering, and the half-full moon gave off a little light, just enough to allow the trick-or-treaters to see where they were going. Mill Street was swarming with costumed children, followed closely by their parents, along with young adults in masks popping in and out of bars as part of a Halloween pub crawl. As Harley strolled westward, he could see a crowd of people in the cul-de-sac at the end of the street, standing under the streetlights at the edge of the park. Unlike the trick-or-treaters and pub crawlers, this crowd was not going anywhere. Instead, they were milling around with their backs to the town, looking into the darkness of the park.

As he got closer, Harley realized that they were protesters. Some held hand-lettered signs that said, "Fly Away, Witches" and "No Coven in Our County." The hair on his neck began to stand up. *Who were they?* He couldn't identify anyone from behind. The group was interracial—mostly whites and blacks—and seemed to be middle-aged. He could hear some of them chanting, but he couldn't make out what they were saying. He heard a shout or two, but all their words were being directed toward the park. Then, when Harley was within a few yards of the group, two men suddenly turned around: Beau Harper and pastor Tony White.

"Tony!" said Harley, taken by surprise.

"Harley?" replied the pastor, having trouble seeing him clearly.

"What are you doing?" asked Harley.

"Protesting the witches," answered Beau.

"This is a God-fearing community," said Tony. "New Life Church doesn't think this is the place for devil-worshipers."

"They have cursed our town," added Beau.

Harley looked around, trying to get a sense of who else was there and what they were doing. He had heard about protests before, but had always pictured small picket lines. This was an angry mob. "Why are you here tonight?" he asked.

"It's Halloween," Tony said. "Their high holy day."

"And where are they?" asked Harley.

"In the park," said Beau, pointing. "Doing their hellish ceremony."

Harley stood on the tips of his toes but couldn't see over the crowd. "Are they dancing?" he asked, remembering the scene he had stumbled upon in September. "Around a fire?"

"They definitely have a fire," said Tony. "But I don't know what they are doing. We don't want to get too close."

"They almost killed me, as you know," Beau added. Harley nodded, having seen his house in shambles.

"You may be right," Tony said to his church member. "They have definitely been directing evil toward you. Whether they brought the flood or not, God only knows."

"But if their curse didn't do it," said Beau, "what did?"

A shout went up from the crowd, perhaps in response to something that the witches were doing. The three men tried to figure out what was going on, but they couldn't see over the people in front of them. Tony returned to the conversation and said, "It could have been God himself."

"What do you mean by that?" asked Beau, annoyed. Harley sensed tension between the two, and got the feeling that the conversation was about to become theological.

"I'm not saying that God wanted to destroy your house," said Tony. "But you might have been collateral damage."

"An unintended consequence?" asked Harley.

"Exactly," said Tony. "God is not pleased with what is happening in the world today: Terrorism, abortion, homosexuality, devil worship. God himself may have sent that flood as a warning."

Beau pondered this for a moment, and then said, "Maybe a sign of the end times. The loss of my house could have been birth-pangs."

"Could be," Tony said, putting his hand on Beau's shoulder. "God works in mysterious ways."

At that moment, the crowd began to roar in anger at something going on in the park. Terry Stone, the sheriff of Occoquan, came up behind Harley and asked him to step aside. He pushed through the crowd, followed by his deputy Sharon Madison. The two of them were determined to get between the crowd of protesters and whoever was in the park. Realizing that his only chance of understanding the situation was to follow the officers, Harley fell in behind them.

Once on the other side of the crowd, he could see that the witches were walking toward the protesters, slowly and deliberately. Their Halloween ceremony appeared to be over, and they were moving toward the entrance of the park, wearing robes and carrying torches in an otherworldly procession. *If the coven is trying to fit into the community*, thought Harley, *this is not the way to do it.*

"No damned witches in Occoquan!" shouted a protester at the front of the crowd. "Take your fire back to hell!" screamed another. Part of that phrase turned into a chant, which immediately spread throughout the crowd: "Back to hell! Back to hell! Back to hell!"

The coven was a small group, roughly twenty-five people, and they were dwarfed by the crowd of protesters, which seemed to approach one hundred. When the witches came close enough for their faces to be seen under their hoods, Harley discovered that the group was being led by Kelly and John. They looked fierce and determined: Fire Dolphin and Earth Eagle.

Pulling back his hood, John said to the sheriff, "We are finished here, and are ready to leave the park. Let us pass."

"Let them pass," shouted Sheriff Stone, using his nightstick to part the protesters. Deputy Madison also drew her stick and tried to help him make an opening. "Step aside," she ordered the protesters, who reluctantly complied. Although they continued to chant the line about wanting the witches to go back to hell, the group moved enough to create a narrow passageway.

John and Kelly led the coven through the crowd, quietly cursing the protesters. Two-by-two they walked through the mob; hoods drawn over their heads to protect them from the spit that was flying through the air. It appeared that they were going to make it through safely, but then one of the witches at the end of the line hurled himself at a protester, grabbing the man by the neck. The two of them knocked over several people and then tumbled to the ground, punching and clawing at each other while the crowd screamed and shouted. The sheriff and the deputy tried to get to them to break up the fight, but the crowd was too thick. All of a sudden, a gunshot split the air, a man wailed, and the protesters scattered. The witch writhed on the ground, with blood on his robe. The protester struggled to his feet, with a small gun in his hand.

"Freeze!" shouted Sheriff Stone, pointing his own weapon at the man. Deputy Madison quickly disarmed the protester, and Stone called for an ambulance.

The witch was lying on his back, face exposed, crying out in agony. Harley recognized the face: Miranda's teenage son Jason.

13

All Saints' Day was clear and uncommonly warm for the first day of November. Harley began his day on the grounds of Arlington National Cemetery, standing in the bright sunshine and gazing out over the rows of white marble headstones that stood like silent soldiers in formation. He was there to lead a graveside service for Arvin Natwick, the war veteran who had participated in the clean-up of the church after the flood. Although he was ninety-three years old—and very few people get out of their nineties alive—his death had come suddenly and unexpectedly. One day, this veteran of fierce battles in the Pacific was gently applying a fresh coat of paint to the baseboards in the Sanctuary; the next, he was dead in his kitchen, the victim of a massive stroke. Harley had marveled at his consistent good humor and his boundless willingness to serve, even when his strength was waning. Arvin was a member of "the Greatest Generation," but Harley considered him to be more than just great. He was closer to holy—upbeat, big-hearted, and seemingly ready to lay down his life for his friends, not just in war but in peace. As Harley stood on the sacred and silent grounds of Arlington Cemetery, he sensed that the darkness of Halloween had been vanquished, replaced by the light of the saints on a cloudless fall day.

"'If there is a physical body, there is also a spiritual body,'" said Harley, reading from Paul's first letter to the Corinthians. "'For this perishable body must put on imperishability, and this mortal body must put on immortality.'" Looking around the small group of family members and friends at the graveside, Harley wondered how they were responding internally to these words, if at all. *Spiritual body? What's that?* From years of conversations with church members, he knew that most people did not associate the afterlife with "spiritual bodies." Many imagined their souls leaving their bodies after death, and maybe flying up to heaven. Some believed in ghosts, understanding them to be spirits that continued to move among the living, haunting them or playing tricks. For most of his life, Harley had waved off ghosts as silly superstitions, figments of overactive imaginations, but then he moved to Occoquan. The sight of the Indian in the window had rattled him, causing him to rethink his casual certainty about the line between this world and the next.

Do these folks believe that Arvin has received a spiritual body? Harley sensed that they were listening to his reading from the apostle Paul, but he had no idea whether they were really paying attention. If they were, they would be surprised to learn that Paul had no interest in souls flying up to heaven or ghosts continuing to move among the living. No, the apostle believed that bodies were important, both in heaven and on earth. In his view, souls and bodies were united, so it made no sense for a soul to leave a body. Instead, when a person's physical body died, it was replaced by a spiritual body, so that soul and body could remain together. This was made possible by resurrection, according to Paul, seen most clearly in the resurrection of Jesus. "Where, O death, is your victory? Where, O death, is your sting?" asked Harley, reciting the last verses of the passage from First Corinthians. "Thanks be to God, who gives us the victory through our Lord Jesus Christ."

Three volleys from seven rifles followed Harley's reading from scripture, loud shots that echoed across the rolling hills of the cemetery. A member of the honor guard presented a folded American flag to Arvin's daughter, and then a bugler played taps. The military chaplain who was overseeing the ceremony announced that the service was concluded, and said that the attendees could return to their cars. As Harley walked with the family across the lush grass to their vehicles, a slender girl with long brown hair came alongside him and introduced herself as one of the great-grandchildren. Harley guessed that she was a high-schooler.

"I have a question," she said.

"Sure," Harley replied. "I'll do my best to answer."

"When my great-grandfather gets his spiritual body, what will it look like?"

Harley smiled at her, pleased that she had been paying attention. He sensed that she was not playing a trick on him, but was asking an honest question. "I cannot say for sure," he replied, "since I've never been to heaven. But I'm guessing it will look like a body."

"With a head and arms and legs?"

"I think so. We will recognize each other in heaven, and make the same kinds of connections we make in this life."

"So, we won't be spirits?" she asked, pushing her hair out of her eyes.

"Not in the sense of floating around," he responded, shaking his head. "Our bodies won't be flesh and blood in heaven, but they'll still be bodies—spiritual bodies."

"Why?" she probed.

"Because God wants us to have bodies. They are part of the goodness of what God has made. Our souls and bodies are together in this life, and God wants them to be together in heaven as well."

"But wouldn't it be easier to be a spirit?"

"Maybe," Harley admitted. "But easier isn't always better." He remembered a line from the cadet prayer at West Point that an Army officer had taught him: "Make us to choose the harder right instead of the easier wrong."

She thought about this for a second, and then asked, "So will my great-grandfather's spiritual body be old or young?"

"Good question," Harley answered. "I have often wondered the same thing. Will he be like he was in the war? Or middle-aged? Or old? What do you think?"

"I'd like to see him young, like he was before the war."

"Then maybe that's the spiritual body you will see," Harley suggested. "Maybe each of us, in heaven, will see the person at the age most important to us."

At that point, the girl reached her car and her father opened the door for her. Harley thanked her for her questions and said good-bye. Then the military chaplain tugged on his sleeve and asked, "You want to see something?"

Harley nodded. "Sure."

"Come over here," she said. The chaplain was dressed in a crisp dress uniform, and she had been solemn and professional throughout the funeral, clearly taking her job very seriously. But when she gave him a sly smile, Harley sensed that she had a playful streak. People who spend a lot of time around death—such as funeral directors—often do. The two of them walked toward a row of headstones beyond the line of family cars.

"Check this out," she said, pointing to a headstone with two symbols: A cross and five-pointed star in a circle.

"What's that?" asked Harley, mystified. He had seen a Star of David on a tombstone, but that Jewish star had six points, not five.

"A Wiccan pentacle," explained the chaplain. "The first at Arlington Cemetery. Dedicated on July 4, 2007."

"Huh," said Harley. And then he read the inscription out loud: "Jan Deanna O'Rourke. Who was she?"

"She was a businesswoman, I'm told," said the chaplain. "She's buried here because she was married to Captain William O'Rourke."

"But what's with the star?" asked Harley. "The ... *what* did you call it?"

"Pentacle. She was a Wiccan priestess, which is why there is a pentacle on her side of the gravestone. But I guess she was what you would call a 'good witch.' People say she was active in the interfaith community, trying to build bridges between people of different religions."

"And her husband?"

"A Christian," said the chaplain. "That's why his side has a cross."

"Interesting," Harley nodded, thinking about the witches of Occoquan.

"Witchcraft is definitely on the rise," said the chaplain. "Attractive to people who feel marginalized, I've heard. Over the years, when people get frustrated with the normal channels, they turn to the occult."

"Really?" asked Harley. "I didn't know that."

"Oh yeah. Witches are protesting the Trump administration now, but this is nothing new. Same thing happened after the Civil War and before the Russian Revolution. When society is in turmoil, people want to tap into unseen powers and change the world by casting spells."

"You seem to know a lot about witchcraft," Harley said.

"I've got to," said the chaplain, smiling. "The military is very diverse: Racially, culturally, spiritually. You never know what kind of religion a service member is going to practice."

"Guess that's right," Harley said. "You've got to be ready for pagans fighting right alongside Christians."

The chaplain nodded, and then looked out over the rows of gleaming tombstones. "Used to be mostly crosses, but we'll see more variety in the years to come."

"True in my town as well," said Harley.

"Anyway, I thought you'd want to see it," she said as they turned to go to their cars. "It's historic: The first VA-issued headstone with both a cross and a pentacle."

On his way home from Arlington Cemetery, Harley pulled off the interstate highway to make a visit at Saint Brigid's Hospital in Lorton. The glass and steel structure housed one of the finest medical care facilities in the region, but its current incarnation revealed little about the deep and earthy roots of the institution. Saint Brigid's had been founded in the 1800s by an order of nuns to provide care for the inmates and staff of the Lorton Reformatory, including the suffragettes who had been imprisoned there for daring to demand the right to vote. These nuns took seriously the words of

Jesus in the Gospel of Matthew, exhortations to care for the sick and visit people in prison, and they did this sacred work for decades in a set of small brick buildings outside the reformatory walls. Now, with the prison closed and the region booming with housing subdivisions, the hospital had grown into a gleaming, high-tech wonder. And since it was just across the river from the Town of Occoquan, many of Harley's parishioners and neighbors considered it to be their preferred facility for all kinds of medical care.

Postmistress Mary Ranger had told Harley that Doris King was experiencing congestive heart failure, and would appreciate a visit. He had a complicated history with red-haired Doris, one of the owners of the Yarn Shop in Occoquan, and she never failed to intimidate him. Always the pit bull, she had been one of the first to defend the Muslim Bayati family when their bakery tent was attacked by hoodlums, an assault that Harley had witnessed in a voyeuristic and cowardly way. This had caused him to feel ashamed in Doris's presence, and he didn't know where he stood with her. Later, he was surprised when she stood by his side in front of the Bayati bakery, after a second attack. So, were they on the same side or not? Hard to say. In his recent dream, she had been one of the witches chanting around the cauldron.

"Hello, Doris," Harley said, as he poked his head into her hospital room. In pastoral ministry, you have to visit people in need, whether they are allies or opponents.

"Pastor!" she responded with a smile, motioning him toward her bed. "Pull up a chair."

"How are you feeling?" he asked as he sat down, taking her left hand in his. His three decades in the ministry had taught him exactly what to do in a hospital room.

"Not great. I'm short of breath, tired, and I've got a rapid heartbeat. That's why they put me in here."

"I'm so sorry," he said, squeezing her hand.

"And look at these legs," she said, pulling the covers aside. "Swollen legs. Swollen feet." *Oh, please! No underwear? I don't need to see that.* Harley had witnessed a lot of nakedness in hospital rooms, an occupational hazard for sure.

"Awful," he said, shaking his head. "Can they do anything to help you?"

"They tell me to lose weight, cut down on sodium," she said with a wry smile. "But I've always been a big woman, and I like to eat."

"But worth trying," Harley suggested.

"Easy for you to say, Mr. Running Man," she said, poking his arm. "But look, I'm not looking for you to give me medical advice. I've got plenty of docs and PAs and nurses here at Saint Brigid's."

"So, what can I do for you?"

"Will you do my funeral, Harley?"

He didn't see that coming. Doris was not a member of his church, and he really didn't know what she thought of him. "Why me?" he asked, failing to come up with anything more profound.

"You're a decent man," she said, squeezing his hand. "I like the stand you took in front of the Bayati bakery. Mary says nice things about you at the post office—and she's not keen on everyone, as you probably know. You are a good neighbor to the Yarn Shop. And for God's sake, you're our only pastor in Occoquan!"

"Okay," Harley nodded. "That makes sense. But you're not dying soon, are you?"

"Not that I know of. But look, I need to prepare. This heart condition is probably going to get me eventually."

"So, tell me a little about yourself," said the pastor, letting go of her hand and taking a small notebook out of his jacket pocket. "Did you ever go to church?"

"As a kid, yes. Down in Durham."

"North Carolina?"

"Yeah," she said. "Ransom Methodist Church."

"Ransom? Are you kidding?"

"Not at all," said Doris. "Do you know it?"

"Sure do. That was my student assignment when I was at Duke Divinity School." Harley was shocked that he and Doris had spent time at the same small church. "My supervisor was a pastor named Cornbluff."

"Don't know him," she said, shaking her head. "I was a teenager there in the 1960s. Pastor was a guy named Wimpey."

"Wimpey?" asked Harley. "Name rings a bell, but he was gone by the time I arrived."

"Yeah, he was wimpy," Doris said. "The name fit."

"Why do you say that?"

"Well, my dad was a drunk. A mean drunk. After a day of work at the cigarette factory, he would tie one on and go after my mom, screaming and yelling. The stupidest things would set him off."

"Rough," said Harley, shaking his head.

"I would go to my room, put on a record, and turn up the volume."

"Sorry you had to deal with that."

"By the time I got to high school, he was deep into alcoholism. He started pushing my mom around and one night he knocked her to the kitchen floor. When I heard her scream, I ran out of my room and told him I was calling the cops."

Harley was impressed. Even as a pup, Doris was a pit bull.

"That scared my dad. You see, under all of his bluster, he was a coward. I grabbed the phone and was about to make the call. Then my mother intervened."

"Your mother?"

"Yes, my mother. She begged me not to call the police. Said that the two of them would get some counseling."

Harley was amazed by how vivid the story was, fifty years after the fact. "How did you respond to that?"

"I wasn't happy, but I loved my mother. I didn't want to disrespect her. So, I hung up the phone, walked up to my dad, put my finger in his chest, and said, 'Do it.'"

"Wow," said Harley. "Brave."

"I don't know where it came from," admitted Doris. "But I was bigger than him at that point. And I was serious. He looked scared, and didn't say a word. He just nodded."

"So, did they do it?"

"Yes, they did," said Doris, shifting her weight in the bed, in an attempt to get comfortable. "They made an appointment to see Rev. Wimpey at Ransom. Saw him the very next Saturday morning. And after they came back, I left the church, never to return."

"Really?" said Harley. "Why?"

"I was a hot-head," she said, pointing to her bright red hair. "Always have been. But what caused me to leave the church was the pathetic advice that Wimpey gave them. 'Forgive him,' he told my mom. Can you believe that? Forgive that violent, abusive, unrepentant alcoholic."

"Bet you wanted him held accountable," Harley said.

"Wimpey even gave them a Bible story. Told them that when Peter asked Jesus how often he should forgive, Jesus said, 'Not seven times, but, I tell you, seventy-seven times.'"

"Not the advice I would give."

"I hope not," said Doris with disgust. "Anyway, I told my parents that Wimpey was a wimp, and that I would never go back to Ransom Methodist Church. And I never did."

Harley sat in silence, absorbing her words. He wanted to say something about the value Jesus put on justice and reconciliation and the healing of broken relationships, but he realized that it was not the right moment for a sermon. After a pause, he asked, "What happened to your parents?"

"My dad crawled farther into the bottle, but he never hit my mom again. I think he was afraid of me . . . and the cops. By the time I was a senior in high school, his liver shut down and he died. I didn't shed a tear."

"And your mom?"

"She continued to live in our house in Durham, but got lonely. Eventually she headed for Florida and moved in with her sister."

"Did she keep going to church?"

"Yes, off and on. I admit that I didn't make it easy for her. I started calling the church 'Rancid,' because it made me sick. I would ask her what the Wimp was preaching on. Not very nice of me."

"Well, Wimpey didn't serve your family well."

Doris looked out the window and sighed. "I suppose I should have given the church another chance. Forgiveness has never been my strong suit. But Wimpey is long gone and Rancid is ancient history. In any case, pastor, I consider myself a Christian—'do unto others' and all that good stuff—and I'd like you to do my funeral."

"Yes, Doris. I can do that. I'd be honored."

"By the way, have you met Kelly Westbrook?"

"The witch?"

"Yes. She is also a product of Ransom."

"What?" said Harley, shocked again. "How is that possible?" *The world is way too small.*

Doris gave a crooked smile, one that was wickedly gleeful. Harley remembered her face in his dream, illuminated by the fire under the cauldron. "Kelly and I were talking in front of the post office one day," she told him, "and we discovered that we were both from Durham. Of course, we never crossed paths there—the two of us are thirty years apart. Anyway, we started talking schools and neighborhoods, and found out that we grew up just a few miles apart. And then, when I said I went to Ransom Methodist as a child, her face went white."

"Really?" said Harley.

"Yes, white as a ghost. She whispered, 'Me too,' but she clearly didn't want to talk about it. I tried to lighten the mood by calling it Rancid, but it didn't help. We moved on to other topics."

"Why do you think she reacted that way?" asked Harley. "Her Wiccan religion?"

"Don't think so," said Doris. "Her reaction was raw, emotional. She could have said that she didn't believe in Christianity anymore—that's what some of the witches have said to me. But she was shocked, really shocked, when I said Ransom."

Harley did some calculating in his head and realized that Kelly was a child when he worked at Ransom. He might have even seen her in the pews. Cornbluff was the pastor in the 1980s, and Harley knew that he remained in that position for many years. "What do you think happened to her?"

Doris looked Harley deep in the eyes and said, "Something traumatic."

14

The elevator to the lobby of Saint Brigid's was slow, with stops on every floor. Medical personnel came and went, as did patients and visitors, giving Harley time to think about Kelly Westbrook and the trauma that could have turned her into a witch. As a pastor, he always had an eye on patterns of church growth, and he was seeing that Wicca was one of the fastest-growing religions in the country. In fact, he had read a report on religious trends that very morning, one that popped up on his smartphone while he was eating a bowl of cereal. Research from Trinity College in Connecticut revealed that there were now one-and-a-half million Americans who identified as Wiccan or Pagan. Wicca had seen a forty-fold increase in the number of adherents between 1990 and 2008. *Forty-fold!* Harley would have loved that kind of church growth. *So, what had transformed Kelly from a Methodist to a Wiccan?*

When the elevator doors opened at the lobby level, Harley was surprised to see Miranda Weiss, looking better than ever.

"Harley!" she blurted out, equally caught off guard.

"Hello, Miranda," he said. For a second, they did a little dance, with Harley getting off the elevator and Miranda getting on. But then he motioned for her to follow him into the lobby, and she did. "Good to see you," he said, wondering what was different about her.

"So funny to run into you," she replied. Although she had dark circles under her eyes, her big smile revealed that she was happy to see him. *But what was different?* Her teeth were still crooked and her face was as round as ever. But then Harley realized why she looked so good: Her hair was no longer pulled back in a ponytail, and she was not dressed in a polyester waitress's uniform. Instead, her long hair spilled in curls around her face, and she was wearing a form-fitting sweater and a pleated skirt. Unlike so many people, she had actually dressed up for her visit to the hospital. "I'm here to see Jason," she explained. "Or, should I say, 'Trauma Bilbey.'"

"Huh?" said Harley, confused. "Trauma Bilbey?" If Miranda was trying to be funny, he couldn't imagine why.

"Here at Saint Brigid's, they give all the trauma patients a code name. Since so many gunshot patients are victims of gang violence, they give them code names to protect them. The doctors wouldn't want a rival gang member to come for a visit and finish the job."

"Trauma Bilbey," repeated Harley, pondering the need for such protection. "I've never heard of such a thing." From nowhere, an image flashed into his mind: A gang of Christians entering the hospital to finish off the young witch. *Bang, bang, bang*—right in the hospital room! He quickly dismissed the thought. "Want to sit down?" Harley asked, leading her to two padded chairs on the edge of the lobby. After sitting down, he asked, "So, how is he doing?"

"He'll be fine," she said. "Thank God."

"Yes, thank God."

"He was shot in the shoulder, but the bullet missed his major blood vessels and only nicked a bone. He was lucky."

"Indeed. Still, it must be painful."

"Oh yes. They've got him on some strong pain-killers."

"What happened to the shooter?"

"Not sure. He told the police he was acting in self-defense. Said Jason attacked him and choked him."

"I would have hoped for a different response from a Christian," said Harley. "You know what Jesus says, don't you?"

"No," she said. "Not exactly."

"If anyone strikes you on the right cheek, turn the other also," Harley said, quoting the words of Jesus in the Sermon on the Mount. "Love your enemies and pray for those who persecute you."

"Guess the shooter didn't know that passage."

"Or didn't *want* to know it," said Harley. "Some people prefer to live by the words, 'If anyone strikes you, pull a gun on them.'"

"Hate your enemies," added Miranda, "and shoot those who persecute you."

"I'm so sorry," he said. "As a church leader, I feel terrible about what happened."

"I appreciate that, Harley. But look, Jason is no saint. He was going out to raise some hell, and he got some hell back at him."

"Still, he didn't deserve to get shot."

"You're right," she nodded. "I'm just glad he's alive. I'll be having a conference with the doctors this afternoon, and I think I'll be able to take him home before too long."

"How is his mood?"

"Well, he was in tremendous pain when they brought him in here. After they doped him up and operated, he slept for a long time. I stayed with him all night, getting a little sleep in a chair in his room, and then we talked before I went home to get cleaned up. He is feeling a lot of anger."

"What did he say?" asked Harley.

"He cursed the guy who shot him, not that I can blame him. He is furious at the whole group. He says that the church is full of hate; judgmental of him and his friends. A lot of his friends are gays and goths, and he doesn't feel that any of them would be accepted in a church."

"He may be right," admitted Harley. "Sadly."

"I'm just not sure what to do," Miranda said, her eyes filling with tears. "I don't want him to get hurt. I don't want him to be filled with such anger."

Harley took her hands in his, and kept silent for a moment. "Just keep loving him, Miranda."

She sniffed and said, "That's all I can do."

"Love is more powerful than you think," he said, squeezing her hands. Then he asked, "Would Jason like it if I visited him?"

Miranda pondered the offer, but said, "I don't think so. I appreciate it, Harley, but a visit from you might make him angrier. He's really got no use for the church right now."

Harley nodded, feeling deep sadness. He had built his entire ministry on one foundation—the love of Jesus. In his mind, this love could break through any barrier and heal any wound. But now this love was being poisoned by the attitudes and actions of a few of his fellow Christians, making it toxic to those who needed it the most. Harley wanted so badly to communicate to Jason that he was loved by God and by Jesus, but such a message could not be delivered. At least not now. "I understand," he said to Miranda.

"I'm glad we could talk," said Miranda, removing her hands from Harley's grasp. "I'd better head upstairs to see Jason and the doctors."

"Hope to see you again soon," he said, unable to mask the sadness in his voice. And then, as he watched her walk across the lobby, looking so attractive in her stylish clothes, he was struck by a wave of guilt. He realized that it was wrong for him to have longings for Miranda. Yes, it was natural to have a hunger for companionship and a desire for an intimate connection. His God-given body was going to be attracted to another God-given body. Miranda's kindness and honesty, combined with her vulnerability—these qualities pulled him toward her, no doubt about it. *But my sexual fantasies?*

My mental pictures of her breasts and hips? My kinky obsession with her crooked teeth?

In an instant, Harley knew that he had to let it go. For the sake of Miranda and her son Jason, he had to redirect his heart and mind. The challenge for Harley was true repentance, turning himself around and moving in a radically different direction. In particular, he saw that he had to make a determined effort to stop lusting after Miranda. *Lust, Gluttony, Greed, Sloth, Wrath, Envy, Pride—the Seven Deadly Sins.* Harley knew that if he was feeling lust toward Miranda, then he was really no better than the shooter who had directed his wrath toward Jason. In order to be better than the shooter, and to be a person who could speak of Jesus with credibility, Harley had to get rid of his lust.

But what would love for Miranda look like? Harley had loved his wife Karen, and that love had included a bodily, sexual dimension. His love for Miranda could never include such intimacy, not as long as he wanted to offer Jason an example of authentic Christianity. *So how can I show this kind of love?* At that moment, Harley realized that he could begin by leaving her alone. As doctors say: First, do no harm.

Getting up from the soft chair in the hospital lobby, Harley decided to head for the gym. He needed a workout, and he knew that one of the best ways to address questions of body and spirit was to stress the body. Over the years, many of his greatest theological insights had popped into his head while running on a treadmill or swimming in a pool.

∽

When the weather had turned cold a few weeks earlier, Harley had joined a gym in Lorton—the same one in which Kelly Westbrook worked. It was a large, high-tech facility called Fitness Triad, with a focus on what they called the "triad" of good health: Endurance exercise, strength training, and good nutrition. When he walked into the place for the first time, Harley didn't know if he was entering an amusement park or a megachurch. The place was well-lighted, colorful, and spotless—filled with staff members who were consistently cheerful and welcoming. High-def video screens were hanging in all of the exercise areas, and a funky beat pounded in a variety of fitness studios. Patrons sat on stools and enjoyed healthy smoothies in a comfortable café, while their children played in a child care center with a ball room and padded jungle gym. The facility had an indoor pool, abundant treadmills, and a seemingly endless row of stationary bicycles, which enabled Harley to do the swimming, running, and cycling that kept him in decent shape over the cold winter months. The only thing that bothered Harley about Fitness Triad was the evangelical zeal of the staff members—it seemed to him that they were pushing a kind of salvation through workouts. The fact that they had a Triad instead of a Trinity made his uneasiness even worse.

Although he had not seen Kelly on previous visits, she was visible when he entered on that first day in November. *Oh great—I've been struggling with lust, and here's another object of desire.* Kelly was on full display in one of the fitness studios, wearing tight-fitting exercise clothes that showed off her lean and muscular body. *First, full-figured Miranda; now, slender Kelly. God, what are you doing to me?*

Kelly was teaching a class of people on machines that looked like a cross between an exercise bike and a weightlifting machine. Called Strength-Cycles, they enabled patrons to experience an hour workout that included both endurance exercise and strength training. When Harley arrived, the participants were pedaling hard and getting their aerobic exercise. Individual statistics were projected on a large screen, and Kelly was urging them to pass each other and establish their own personal records. *Hey, isn't that Tony White? What's an evangelical pastor doing in a witch's class?* By the time Harley had changed into his exercise clothes, the class members were still on their bikes but were doing their anaerobic weightlifting, using exercise bands that were attached to their bikes. Kelly was giving them instructions as she modeled for them the proper techniques, through lifts that caused her arms to ripple. Harley intentionally selected a treadmill that was facing away from the studio, so that he wouldn't have to look at her. *Custodia occulorum,* said Harley to himself: "Custody of the eyes." He knew that controlling what he was looking at was one way to combat lust. He didn't want to end up in Dante's second circle of hell.

As he started to run on the treadmill, he felt proud of himself for changing his focus. *But isn't pride a sin?* Given that it is one of the Seven Deadly Sins, he thought he shouldn't let himself go in that direction. *No matter.* He looked up at the television screens that were mounted around the gym and tried to focus on the news.

Unfortunately, Kelly was speaking into a headset in the StrengthCycle studio, and her voice was amplified through that section of the gym. "Find your breath," she said to them in a calm and soothing tone. "Breathe deep. Take your breath all the way into your belly. Your life is in your breath." *Sounds like mindfulness training,* thought Harley. *Part of the Fitness Triad cult.*

"There is no yesterday," continued Kelly. "There is no tomorrow. There is only this moment. There is only your breath. Focus on your breath." Harley realized that Kelly was, in fact, a religious leader, just as she said she was.

"Do not hold your breath when you use the bands," she cautioned. "Exhale as you pull the band. Inhale as you lower the band. Exhale. Inhale." Harley listened as she repeated these instructions, and he continued to absorb her words as she transitioned into a gentle patter about everyone creating their own best self through endurance exercise, strength training, and proper nutrition. Harley found her smooth words to be very seductive, and he felt as if she were casting a spell on the class. *Exhale, inhale. Focus on your breath.*

Harley's own breath was rapid and labored as he jogged on the treadmill, since he was determined to run hard for a half hour before he showered and drove to the church office. But after about fifteen minutes he started to feel pain in his chest, so he slowed to a walk. The pain was not severe—more like a feeling of pressure—making him wonder if he was experiencing heartburn. But then he was overcome by shortness of breath, which he knew should not be happening at a walking pace. Something was going on, and this realization threw him into a panic. He began to feel light-headed and dizzy, and he broke into a cold sweat.

Harley stepped off the treadmill and immediately fell to the floor. A woman on the next treadmill called for help, and then jumped off and knelt down beside him. "What's happening?" she asked, dripping sweat on his face.

"Don't know," Harley croaked, gripping his chest and closing his eyes. "It hurts." The pain moved beyond his chest to his shoulders, back, and arms.

"We're getting help," said the woman.

When Harley opened his eyes, he saw Kelly Westbrook standing above him, silhouetted against the fluorescent lights like a Mayan priest against the sun.

The pressure in his chest was so overwhelming that he would have welcomed the sharp point of an obsidian knife—anything to stop the pain.

It hurt so bad.

He had never felt anything so intense.

God, he prayed, *make it stop.*

Into your hands . . .

But instead of a black knife, he saw a white light. And out of the light he heard a voice, "Harley, it's Peter."

"Saint Peter?"

"No, Peter Pann."

Huh? It took a moment for Harley to identify the voice. Peter Pann was not the character from the children's story, but was a fellow pastor from Duke Divinity School—energetic, adventurous, charismatic. Harley hadn't seen him in years, but he had heard that Peter had gone mountain climbing and had frozen to death in the Rockies. Yes, he had died, but he hadn't stayed dead—Peter had returned to life in what is called a near-death experience.

"Harley, look around." Harley could hear Peter, but he couldn't see him. As Harley turned his head, he began to make out features in the light. Around him was a city, and flowing through the city was a river, bright as crystal, pouring down from a heavenly throne. On either side of the river was the tree of life—*el árbol de la vida*. There was no darkness in this city, for God provided all the light that anyone would ever need. The light was illuminating, but also purifying.

"Harley, you are about to feel all of the pain that you have caused others," said Peter. "It will be burned out of you by a refining fire."

Harley wondered how this could be happening. *What was he seeing and what was he hearing? Was this heaven, or a window to heaven? How could Peter be talking to him as though he were standing at his side?* Peter wasn't dead, or at least he wasn't dead at that moment. Maybe in the afterlife there is no time, but everything that has happened is present in the same heavenly moment. *Maybe we live our earthly lives day after day after day,* thought Harley, *but not so in heaven. One day is like a million years, and million years are like one day . . . endless time in a single second . . . an eternal now.* And in that same divine moment the flames hit, burning out his impurities like a refiner's fire. It was simultaneously the most excruciating and liberating wave of emotion he had ever felt.

At that very instant, Kelly administered CPR and brought Harley back to life.

15

Harley stood silently in the archaeological park in Copán, Honduras. The sky was clear and blue, and the sun was powerfully bright, a blazing diamond in the heavens. He and a group of students were touring the ruins and inspecting the hieroglyphic writings.

Professor Larry Baker asked them to examine one carving very carefully and make a guess as to what it meant: Coronation, military victory, harvest celebration, sacrifice to the gods, birth of a prince? Harley knew that the temples of Copán had traditionally been thought of as a center for religious ceremonies, with only priests living in the city center. The figures depicted in the art were linked to gods and priests, and the hieroglyphic writing was connected to astrological observations and a system of prophecy. But Baker thought that there may be another way to understand what was going on in Copán.

"What if this is not a god or a priest?" he asked the group. "What if it is a carving of an actual ruler of Copán, remembered in art in the same way that the pharaohs of Egypt were memorialized?"

The group stood in silence, reflecting on his question. A Guacamaya extended its wings and cried out from a nearby tree. "What if this is the picture of the president," said Baker, "on the front page of *The New York Times?*"

For too long, thought Harley, *we have made distinctions between religion and history, heaven and earth, faith and science, spirit and body. But what if the truth requires both?*

"Both what?" asked Kelly Westbrook, standing beside Harley's bed.

Harley opened his eyes slowly, and her pale skin, silver piercings, auburn hair, and bright green eyes came into focus.

"You were talking in your sleep," she said.

"Where am I," he asked, "and what are you doing here?"

"Is that any way to talk to your savior?"

"My savior?"

"Yes, I saved your life," said Kelly. "You had a heart attack."

"I did?" Harley's memory was clouded by his visit to the Mayan ruins and his vision of a gleaming city. So many images were jumbled in his mind. Fortunately, the pain of the refining fire was gone, along with the excruciating pressure in his chest. "When?"

"Yesterday. You collapsed on a treadmill, and fortunately I was able to bring you back with CPR. You're getting treated here at Saint Brigid's."

Harley felt a rush of embarrassment, knowing that patients at hospitals often unwittingly exposed themselves to their visitors. But looking down, he saw that his body was completely covered by a blanket. He pushed his head back into the pillow and relaxed. "Thank you," he said hoarsely. "Thank you for saving me."

"You're welcome," said Kelly.

Harley closed his eyes and thought for a minute. His life had been turned completely upside down since his visits with Doris and Miranda in the very same hospital, going from a pastor to a patient in twenty-four hours. Now he was lying helpless in a hospital bed, being visited by a witch who should have opposed him at every opportunity. Opening his eyes, he blurted out, "Why did you save me?"

Kelly smiled. "It's my job," she said. "I'm good at what I do."

"You could have let me die," said Harley. "No one would have blamed you."

"No one?" she replied. "That's not right. *I* would have blamed me."

"Why? You're a witch. You're not supposed to help a pastor."

"Harley, you're a human being," said Kelly. "Your health is important to me. So is your life."

"But what about your beliefs? I thought Wiccans hated Christians."

"Some Christians, sure. People who attack and curse are going to get attacks and curses right back. But you've not wronged me."

Harley felt ashamed for the decision he had made at the clergy breakfast, excluding the coven because they did not believe in "one true God." *What would have been the harm of including them?* Harley had always believed that his church should be solid at the center, focused on worshiping God the Father, the Son, and the Holy Spirit. But at the very same time, he thought that the church should also be soft at the edges, willing to work with all kinds of groups on issues that can improve the community. *Environmental issues? Why not?* For years, members of his previous church had partnered with Muslims to feed and shelter the homeless on cold winter nights, even though Muslims don't agree with Methodists about the divinity of Jesus. *Why did I make such a rash decision about the witches? I assumed they meant harm, but maybe they don't. Or maybe they do. I don't know!* Harley was feeling torn between his beliefs and his experiences, between his convictions and his connections. All he could say to her in that moment was, "Jesus would want me to be kind."

Kelly looked at him. Her green eyes shimmered like reflections of trees in the Occoquan River. "Remember what I said about balance?"

"A little," said Harley.

"Darkness and light. Earth and heaven. Good and evil. Body and spirit. In my religion, we try to live in balance, in harmony with ourselves and the world around us. I want to be in harmony with you."

"I appreciate that," he said. "I guess."

"You don't know it," said Kelly, "but I've been watching you. I see you jogging around Occoquan. I knew that you had joined the gym. You value health and fitness, and so do I. You are trying to achieve the same sort of balance—body and spirit—that is important to me."

Harley nodded. "It's important to keep body and spirit in harmony."

"So, when I saw you lying on the gym floor, I wanted to help you."

"I really am grateful to you. Truly."

"I'm happy to have saved you," said Kelly.

Your savior. Saved your life. At that point, Harley recalled her words to him as he was waking up. He felt he needed to make one thing clear: "But you know you're not my true Savior."

"I know," she said, smiling. "I said that to mess with you."

At that moment, a doctor walked into the room. "Mr. Camden?" he asked. "I'm Dr. Gupta, the cardiologist assigned to your case." He was an Indian-American, dark and Hollywood handsome, in his mid-thirties. "How are you feeling?"

"Not bad," said Harley. "No more pain."

"That's good." Then, looking to Kelly, he asked, "Are you family?"

Kelly shook her head, and Harley said, "I'm single, with no family. This is Kelly Westbrook, the fitness instructor who gave me CPR."

"Good work," said the doctor.

"Would you like me to step out?" Kelly asked Harley.

"No need to," he said. "In fact, it's good to have an extra set of ears, listening to the doctor. Please stay."

Dr. Gupta nodded, and then announced that the electrocardiogram revealed that Harley had suffered a mild heart attack, but they would need to do further tests to assess the damage. He hoped that Harley could be treated with medications, but there was a chance that surgery would be required. Overall, he said that Harley was in good physical shape, so he didn't foresee any complications.

"How long will I be in?" asked Harley.

"Three to five days," said the doctor, "depending on how much needs to be done. But you are through the worst of it." Then, after asking if Harley had any other questions, he vanished.

"Sounds like good news," said Kelly.

"I think so. Would be great to avoid surgery."

"Whatever it takes."

"And I hope I can get back to exercise soon," said Harley. "I need it for my mental health, not just my physical health."

"I hear you," she said. "I was a collegiate swimmer, and I never felt better than when I was spending long hours in the pool. Talk about balance: Skimming the surface, half in and half out, suspended perfectly between the water and the air. In the pool, I had power, independence, control, peace."

Harley smiled and said, "For me, swimming has never been that serene. I do a lot of thrashing around."

"My goal is always harmony," Kelly added. "Earth, air, water. I believe in balance, connecting with all of the energies that are in me and around me." Harley imagined her moving powerfully through the water, doing graceful flip-turns at the end of each lap, and suddenly he understood why she called herself Fire Dolphin. "I'm responsible for my own reality," she continued, "using nothing but my own body and mind and energy. If I want a good life, I have to create it."

"I get it," said Harley, "and I know the peace that can come from being out in nature, running, walking, moving around."

"Our bodies are so important," Kelly continued. "That's something I never heard in church."

There it is, thought Harley, *church*. "Really?" he said.

"When I was a kid, I heard Christians talking about the spirit being good and the body being bad. The focus was always on being spiritual. But at the same time people were stuffing their faces with junk food, and having sex in ways that made them feel dirty and shameful."

Harley's heart began to pound, which was probably not good in light of his heart attack. But he wanted to find out about Kelly's church background, so he took a chance and got specific. "I know what you mean," he said. "When I was in seminary, I worked for a pastor who trained me in premarital counseling. He told me that in his very first session with a couple, he would ask the bride, 'What would you do if your husband went off to a professional conference and had an affair?'"

"That's bizarre," said Kelly. "In a first session of premarital counseling?"

"Yeah. It really was strange and inappropriate, but I didn't know it at the time. I was a student and had never been married. I realized later that he was talking about his own life, and about his own history of inappropriate sex. He considered himself a very spiritual guy, but his sex life was shameful."

"I saw a lot of that in the church," said Kelly. "That's why I left."

"His name was Cornbluff," said Harley, and Kelly jerked back as if touched by a live wire. The blood drained out of her face, and Harley felt a wave of shame.

"Cornbluff," she said, after a moment of silence. "I knew a Cornbluff."

"I'm sorry," said Harley. "I didn't mean to startle you." *Yes, I did! Liar!* Harley wished he could take back his words. *I knew this would hurt her, and I did it anyway.* He hated himself for inflicting pain on the person who had just saved his life.

"Was he at Ransom Methodist Church?" she asked.

"Yes."

"In Durham?"

"Yes."

Kelly spent another moment in silence, then she surprised him by asking, "What does the name 'Ransom' mean, anyway? That's a weird name for a church."

Harley was relieved by the change in subject. "I think it comes from Jesus being a ransom. The Bible says that he offered his life as a ransom—a ransom for the people of the world. It means that we are captives to our sins and Jesus ransoms us."

"Huh," she said, shaking her head. "That figures. People like Cornbluff do whatever the hell they want, and then Jesus ransoms them. Let's them off the hook."

Harley nodded. "Jesus makes forgiveness possible."

"Well, that's why I stopped being a Christian. That's not right. There needs to be accountability. There needs to be balance—not just in heaven, but on earth."

A nurse popped her head in the door and asked if Harley wanted to get out of bed and take a walk. "Just a short one," she cautioned. And then, turning to Kelly, the nurse said, "Would you be willing to walk with him?"

"Sure," said Kelly, looking up at the wall clock. "I need to leave soon, but a walk would be good."

The nurse removed Harley's blanket, swung his legs over the side of the bed, and helped him to put on a robe. Then, when he was standing by the bed, she turned him over to Kelly, who steadied him as he began to walk. Even one day in bed had led to a decrease in his muscle tone.

Walking next to Kelly, closer than he had ever been before, he could count the number of silver studs she had along the edge of her right ear. He also noticed a small tattoo of a Celtic cross on her shoulder. "That's an interesting cross," he said as they moved slowly down the hall.

"Yes, a lot of pagans wear it."

"It's a Celtic cross," said Harley, "part of the Christian tradition of Saint Brigid."

Kelly looked surprised. "I didn't know that."

"Yes, Brigid was Irish, and the Celtic cross was popular in Ireland and Scotland."

"So, tell me about Brigid," said Kelly as they made their way toward the window at the end of the hall.

"Her name was Brigid of Kildare, and she was a Celtic nun in Ireland, well known for her healing work. That's why this hospital is named after her. She followed in the footsteps of Jesus, who was a healer as well. Brigid's feast day was originally a pagan festival, and she is sometimes associated with a goddess named Brigid. I guess that's why she has both Christian and pagan connections."

"You know a lot about Brigid," said Kelly. "I wouldn't expect that from a Methodist pastor."

"I appreciate Celtic Christianity," Harley told her. "It is an approach that comes from the early Middle Ages. I've studied it a lot, since I think it provides an important balance to other styles of Christianity."

"Tell me more," said Kelly, helping Harley to make the turn at the window.

"Take a look at your tattoo," he said. "It has the cross of Christ, which tells us that Jesus died to free us from our sins. But it also has a circle, which represents the sun. These symbols, together, capture the heart of Celtic spirituality—the sacrifice of Christ on the cross, and the glory of God in creation."

"I still don't like Jesus letting sinners off the hook," said Kelly.

"I understand," Harley said. "But this a Christian attempt at balance. Jesus should be honored for his many sacrifices, not just on the cross. The Bible tells us that Jesus came to earth to serve others, and to help people with their struggles. This life of sacrifice is balanced by the glory of God that is found everywhere in the world: Sun, moon, air, water, earth."

"I guess that's why pagans like the Celtic cross."

"No doubt," said Harley. "Celtic Christianity is not anti-earth or anti-body. It celebrates all of the good gifts of life in this world: Eating, drinking, playing, loving. In fact, there are some Celtic wedding vows that I have used with couples. I like them so much that I have memorized them."

At this point, the two stopped walking and Kelly stood to face Harley. "Let's hear them," she said.

"'Ye are Blood of my Blood, and Bone of my Bone,'" recited Harley. "'I give ye my Body, that we Two might be One / I give ye my Spirit, 'til our Life shall be Done.'"

Kelly smiled. "Well, I guess you and I are now married."

"No, don't worry about that," said Harley, as they continued to walk. "But notice the coming together of body and spirit in the vows. This is the heart of Celtic Christianity."

"That's an improvement over Jesus letting sinners of the hook, so that they can keep on sinning."

"I agree," said Harley. "The Bible is serious about forgiveness, but also about justice." *The truth requires both,* he remembered from his dream.

"Funny how that was never stressed at Ransom Methodist."

"It should have been."

"How about your clergy sex abuse scandals? They prove to me that the church still doesn't have this right. And I tell you, we Wiccans will keep growing unless you figure this out."

Reaching Harley's room, Kelly helped him to get back in bed. He thanked her again for saving his life, and then told her how much he appreciated her visit.

"You're welcome, Harley," she said at the door. "Feel better. I'll go home and do a candle service for you." He looked perplexed, so she added, "For your healing."

Harley appreciated her good intentions, but recoiled at the thought that witchcraft would be done on his behalf. He was torn by wanting her help and not wanting her help, and this tension caused a pain to shoot through his chest. *This can't be another heart attack, can it?* He took a deep breath and the pain began to subside. "Kelly," he said, "before you leave, I need to say something." He was discovering that life was incredibly fragile, and he shouldn't leave anything unsaid. "I want to apologize to you for being part of the group that excluded you. You know, the clergy group."

Kelly gave a slight nod, thought for a moment, and then looked Harley straight in the eyes. "You acted in ignorance," she said softly. Harley noticed that she didn't excuse him or forgive him.

"I hope I'll see you back in Occoquan soon," he said. "We can talk more."

"I'd like that," she replied, and then stood still for a moment, pondering something. "Harley, I'll tell you about Cornbluff," she said. "But not today." And then she vanished.

16

Darkness was coming fast, as Tie-dye Tim drove Harley home from the hospital in the town's pickup truck on Wednesday afternoon. Harley's heart was being treated by medication, along with a plan for outpatient cardiac rehabilitation, and he was happy to have avoided surgery. But he couldn't help but feel discouraged by the gloom that was settling on the heavily forested hill that fell from Lorton to the Town of Occoquan, and by the lack of sparkle on the Occoquan River. Daylight Saving Time had ended, which meant that the sun was setting at around five o'clock, leading to a long stretch of dark evenings. *Very Celtic,* he said to himself. *Darkness and light, suffering and celebration, illness and health—all are part of God's creation, complex and confounding as it is.*

"Thanks so much for the ride, Tim," Harley said, as they pulled into town.

"No problem. Good to get you back."

"And thanks for fetching my car as well."

"Actually, Kelly took care of that. She was going to the gym, so I gave her your spare key. John dropped her off on Monday, and she drove your car home that night."

"That was nice of her," said Harley. *Witches helping pastors. Only in Occoquan!*

"So, how are you feeling?" Tie-dye asked.

"Physically, not bad. No chest pain. But I have to admit that I'm a bit down. A heart attack is a wake-up call."

"Yeah," nodded Tim. "I've heard that people can get depressed."

"*Memento mori,*" said Harley as the truck arrived at his house.

"Huh?" said Tie-dye.

"Medieval Christian spirituality," said the pastor. "It means, 'remember that you have to die.'"

Tim laughed and then punched his friend on the arm. "I want to party with *you*!"

"Reminds me that I'm not in control," said Harley, remaining serious. "I thought I was doing well with my exercise, but then boom—heart attack!"

"Yeah, that running can get you. That's why I avoid it."

"Oh well," said Harley. "Could have been worse."

"For sure."

"Hey, Tim, before I head inside, let me ask you: Did you hear anything about the kid who got shot?"

"Yeah, Jason Weiss. He got out of the hospital over the weekend. Has his arm in a sling, but he is healing quickly. Why do you ask?"

"Just curious," said Harley. "I know his mother."

"Well, guess what? The mayor wants me to hire him as a part-time maintenance guy. Thinks it would be a goodwill gesture to the coven, and would improve the image of Occoquan as well."

"How do you feel about that?"

"Okay by me," said Tie-dye. "I can always use the help, especially as we continue to clean up from the flood. I talked with the kid on Monday, and he seems all right. Kind of sullen, but that's par for the course."

"And how about his shooter? Who was it?"

"Our own Beau Harper, claiming self-defense. His gun was registered, and he had a concealed carry permit."

"So, nothing will happen to him?"

"Hard to say," said Tie-dye. "I'm no lawyer, but I know that people can use force to protect themselves from attack. Virginia is what you call a 'stand your ground' state. If you don't provoke the attack, you don't have to run from it. But I'm not sure that fits the bill here. There's probably going to be a lot more investigation."

"Do you think that Jason wanted to hurt him?" Harley asked.

"No doubt. The Christians were being pretty nasty. I bet he wanted to strangle him."

∼

"Welcome home, Harley," said Leah Silverman, giving him a kiss on the cheek. "Good to see you with your clothes on!" She had visited him several times in the hospital, and now she was cooking dinner for him on his first night back in Occoquan.

"Yeah, I thought you were getting tired of my hospital gown," he replied, stepping through the front door of her condominium on the ridge above town.

"You wore it well, but I prefer you in your Duke sweatshirt," she said, poking him gently in the chest.

"Blue Devils . . . *forever!*" he said, handing her a bottle of Chianti.

"Perfect," she said, inspecting the label. "I've made us a lasagna to celebrate your return."

"Smells good. Shall I open the wine now?"

"Please do. Let's have some cheese and crackers while the lasagna finishes cooking."

They sat in a living room filled with sleek mid-century modern furniture. Harley had always admired her taste, and envied the disposable income she had as a single, professional woman. "Is this new?" he asked, as he sat down on a blue-spruce sofa.

"Yes, thanks for noticing. Just got it delivered last week."

"I'll try not to spill my wine on it."

"I trust you."

Harley picked up a piece of cheese, put it on a cracker, and popped it into his mouth. While chewing, he noticed the music that Leah had playing in the background: Chicago. After swallowing, he said, "That music is a trip down memory lane."

"*Chicago's Greatest Hits*," she said. "Takes me back to junior high school."

"Right about that. '25 or 6 to 4.' I never knew what that song was about."

"Me neither. But the tune is impossible to forget."

"I played this album for my daughter Jessica once," Harley reminisced, feeling a pang of sadness. "She was unimpressed."

"I'm not surprised," said Leah. "It would have been like your parents playing you a dusty old record from the 1930s."

"Don't be mean," said Harley. "You know this is good stuff."

"So, how are you doing with your cardiac rehab?"

"Not bad. I'm on a program of exercise, watching my nutrition, managing my stress. It's stuff that we should all be doing, heart attack or not."

Leah handed him a bowl of grapes and said, "Eat some of these, along with the cheese."

"Yeah, got to eat heart-healthy."

"And I guess you'll have to slow down for a while."

"Definitely," Harley nodded. "I'll need to pace myself for the next few weeks. Won't be volunteering to do any flood cleanup."

"That work has taken far longer than anyone would have expected. One night of flooding has led to weeks of work, and we've still got a long way to go."

"I'm surprised at how many shops are still shut down."

"I really feel for the business owners," said Leah. "I know they are working hard to get back in time for Christmas shopping."

Harley thought back to the flood and to the chaotic weeks that followed. In particular, he thought of his pizza dinner with Leah, at which he had been so dismissive of her concerns for the environment. He said, "Leah, I owe you an apology."

"For what?" she asked.

"For the way I acted at our dinner, at the pizza place. I wasn't myself."

Leah nodded. "You were struggling with something, for sure. But you seem better now."

"I do feel better," Harley agreed. "My thoughts and feelings are not so jumbled. But I am sorry about the way I reacted to you over dinner."

"What do you mean?"

"I was so dismissive of what you said about . . . what was it . . . the Creation Care . . ."

"Creation Care Council."

"Yes, that's it. You seemed to want to get me and my church involved, and I shot you down."

"Well, you didn't seem to care," she admitted. "But I wouldn't say you shot me down. I've continued to work with the group. We've been doing some good stuff."

"Like what?"

"Well, for one thing, we've been investigating whether runoff from developed areas might have contributed to our flood."

Harley pondered this for a moment and then asked, "But don't they have rules for stormwater?"

"Yes, they do," said Leah. "But that's why we are investigating. We need to know what rules were in place when the development was done, and whether the rules were followed. If stormwater is not absorbed or controlled, it can lead to catastrophe."

"Like September."

"Exactly," Leah agreed. "The problem is, the whole situation is very complicated. In a natural state, the land can absorb most of the rain that falls. Parking lots and other hard surfaces cause the water to run off and cause flooding. But when development is done over time, with different rules at different times, it can be hard to point to a particular culprit. Sometimes the area just reaches a tipping point, and disaster strikes."

"Have you found anything in particular?"

"Not yet," said Leah. "But we are poking around."

Harley sat back on the couch and thought for a moment. He recalled conversations about the coven and its leaders, and then said, "Leah, have you talked with John Jonas?"

"No," she said.

"Well, you might want to. He and his group have an interest in the environment, although our clergy group pushed them away."

"You did?"

"Yeah, we did, although I kind of regret it now. Anyway, the coven wants to be involved in environmental stuff, and John works for IT in the county government. Maybe he can help get you some information."

"Good idea, Harley," said Leah. "I'll reach out to him."

At that point, the bell rang on the kitchen timer, letting them know that it was time for dinner. The two of them stood up, and as they did, the song "Colour My World" began to play on Chicago's Greatest Hits. "Remember this one?" asked Harley.

"Greatest slow dance song of all time," said Leah.

"Shall we dance?" he asked.

"Why not?" she said. They took each other's hands and pressed their bodies gently together.

"Junior high dances," Harley recalled, moving Leah slowly around the living room. "When this song would come on, I would desperately look for a partner. Those were my first chances to get close to a girl, actually have physical contact."

Leah smiled. "I was a target for guys like you—I would have been in seventh grade, and you would be in . . . what? Ninth? But for me, the contact never thrilled me. I would have my eyes on the other girls on the dance floor."

"When did you know?"

"Know what?"

"That you were a lesbian?"

"Well, I didn't even know that word," Leah admitted, as they swayed together. "But I knew where my attention was going. And it wasn't toward guys."

"Junior high was a confusing time, straight or gay."

"You are right about that," Leah said.

Harley looked her in the eyes and smiled. Even though she would never have romantic feelings toward him, he sensed that she was enjoying the dance as much as he was. As two people without partners, alone in the world, the physical contact felt good.

Thursday morning, Harley was back in the office for the first time in a week. His ten o'clock appointment was with Juan Erazo, who had covered for the pastor on Sunday.

"*Muchas gracias, amigo*," said Harley, as Juan poked his head in the church office.

"*De nada*," said the affable Honduran, stepping inside. "Happy to help."

"Coffee?" asked Harley.

"Of course!"

"So, how did the Sunday service go?" the pastor asked, as he poured his guest a cup.

"Very well," said Juan, taking a seat. "You had already written the order for worship, so the only thing I had to do was follow your script."

"And preach, of course!"

"Well, yes," said Juan. "But my sermon was a very personal message. I talked about our mission trip." Then, seeing anxiety in Harley's eyes, he said, "Don't worry, I didn't talk about you. It was all about my experience, all very positive."

Harley thanked him, and then said, "I bet the congregation enjoyed it. And I really appreciate you filling in for me."

"My pleasure. I used to lead worship as a young man in Honduras, so it comes very naturally."

"So, what's been happening here in Occoquan?"

"You can see that the carpenter has the new steeple framed on the church. And progress is being made with the flood cleanup around town, although it's very slow."

"Yeah," said Harley. "Tie-dye has his work cut out for him."

"Unfortunately, the cleanup is not the only challenge I'm seeing."

"What do you mean?"

"I'm concerned about an increase in gang recruitment at the high school," said Juan. "Kids in the Latino Students Association are more scared than ever. Remember how I told you that there might be drugs being sold out of *el Castillo*?" Harley nodded. "Well, I think I've seen several gang members here on the streets of Occoquan."

"That's too close," said Harley. "How do you know they are in a gang?"

"Their tattoos—*la garra*, Satan's claw."

Harley felt a chill. "Too close," he said again.

Juan sipped his coffee and then said, "I'm trying to keep very cool about this, *muy tranquilo*. I don't want to overreact. But I am worried about my kids, and worried about our town. This is an evil force, all around us. Very demonic."

Harley could see the fear in Juan's eyes, and a hint of anger as well. Occoquan had been hit by a powerful and destructive flood, but this was an even darker and more threatening force. "What can we do?" he asked.

"Hard to say. I lost a nephew to a gang in Honduras, so this is very emotional for me. Very personal. I would go after anyone who threatened one of my kids. Yes, I'm an old man, but I would not hold back."

"You would use violence?" asked Harley. He noticed Juan's arms, rock solid from years of swinging hammers and turning wrenches.

"I would want to," said Juan. "But I don't know. I try to be a Christian, but I really hate these gangs for what they do to our kids."

"What other options do we have?"

"The police have an anti-gang task force," Juan said. "I could go to them if I had any good information. But the gangs are very secretive, and they do their evil in the dark."

"You are right," Harley said. "Works of darkness. Maybe your challenge is to answer the call of the Bible, from Ephesians."

"What's that?"

"'Take no part in the unfruitful works of darkness,' says the apostle Paul, 'but instead expose them.'"

"Good words," said Juan. "But easier said than done."

"*Es verdad*," said the pastor.

∼

That night, Harley took his first walk through the town since returning from Saint Brigid's. The evening was cloudy and cool, and he strolled slowly westward on Mill Street, trying to comply with his cardiac rehabilitation guidelines. *I won't be jogging for a while,* he thought to himself, feeling nervous about getting back on a treadmill. The agony of his last run was still too fresh.

The shops were all closed, and the restaurants were in the process of shutting down. Only a few cars remained on the street, belonging to the relatively few bar patrons who would be out on a Thursday night in November. As Harley passed the lot where the candle shop had stood, he saw that the debris of the building had been completely hauled away, and it looked as though the site was ready for redevelopment. *I wonder where Beau Harper has moved?* Harley figured that he must have found a place nearby, since he was present for the Halloween protest. *Maybe he should have moved away, and spared Jason Weiss a bullet in the shoulder.*

At that moment, a figure appeared in the light of the gas streetlight in front of him: Beau Harper. *Speak of the devil!*

"Harley, is that you?" he asked.

"Beau! What are you doing?"

"Taking a walk. Same as you."

"I'm just surprised to see you, right in front of your old place."

"Well, I'm living with my sister up in Lake Ridge, for the time being. But I still have my Occoquan PO box."

"I figured you were still in the area."

"Heard you were in the hospital," said Beau. "We prayed for you at New Life Church."

"Well, that was nice of you."

"Tony said you had a heart attack."

"Yes, that's right," said Harley. "Fortunately, a mild one."

"Thank God for that."

Harley wanted to bring up the Halloween protest, but he didn't know how to do it. Beau was being so kind to him that it would feel rude to ask about the shooting and its aftermath. But Beau didn't give him an opportunity.

"You need to be careful out here," Beau warned him.

"What do you mean?"

"I've seen gang members here in Occoquan."

Harley nodded and said, "I've heard about that."

"I'm always armed," said Beau, pulling back his jacket and patting his handgun. "You can't be too careful."

"Has anyone had trouble?" asked Harley.

"Not yet," said Beau. "But something is brewing. I've seen Jonas the witch talking to Latino kids on the street. Evil is all around. I think the witches and the gangs are in some kind of alliance."

"Really?"

"Satan's claw. It was on the dead guy. And I've seen it on the street."

"I don't know about an alliance," said Harley, "but you're right: We need to be careful."

"I'm just saying, as a fellow Christian, take care of yourself," said Beau. Patting his gun again, he said, "I wouldn't hesitate." And then, resuming his walk, he looked over his shoulder and said, "I've got your back."

Harley continued his stroll toward River Mill Park, which was lit by a row of streetlights on the wooded side. On the side by the river, the path was shrouded in darkness. He decided to walk on the lighted side to the end of the park, and then turn around. But he never got the chance.

Halfway into the park, he heard voices coming from a spot ahead of him, in the darkness of the river side. Two people were talking in heated tones, a man and a woman. Harley stopped, wondering if they had seen him in the light, but they remained oblivious to him, consumed by their argument. The man was trying to keep his voice down, but the woman was getting more animated and upset. Harley felt frozen in place, not wanting to move and attract attention, but not wanting to eavesdrop either.

Then, when the woman shouted and the man responded, Harley realized who they were: John Jonas and Kelly Westbrook. A second later, Kelly pushed John away and began to walk toward the entrance of the park. Harley knew that he would have to get moving, to avoid detection. He walked as quickly as he could toward Mill Street, probably too fast for his weakened heart.

When he got back to his townhouse development, he stood on the dock by the river to catch his breath. He had avoided being seen by Kelly and John, but he still felt very unsettled. Across the river, he saw the glow of a light from *el Castillo*.

17

The cappuccino marble bench outside Sterling Methodist Church was like a block of ice, sucking the heat out of Harley's body as he sat there in silence. The past month had been chilly, but the first serious cold of the season arrived on Thanksgiving Day, when the temperature dropped to twenty-nine degrees. Harley was visiting the burial site of his wife Karen and his daughter Jessica in the memorial garden outside the Sterling church, a plot that was full of color in the summer, but brown and gray in the late fall. Their ashes had been interred after they died in a European terrorist attack in 2016, a loss which caused Harley to spiral downward in grief and anger until his bishop was forced to move him from Sterling to Occoquan. There, he had a chance to heal and to recover, but not without serious personal challenges. *Memento mori*, he thought to himself, *remember that you have to die.*

"The landscaping team ought to clean this place up," he said out loud as he looked around the memorial garden, under a cloudy sky that was the color of lead. Fallen leaves covered the ground, along with debris from the flowers that had died at the end of the season. The brick walkway that snaked into the garden area was also obscured by leaves, although Harley used his foot to clear the two bricks that mattered to him: Memorial pavers with the names Karen Anne Camden and Jessica Louise Camden. Seeing his daughter's paver, he recalled that she had always hated her middle name—"so old-fashioned!" she said—and never used it. But it had been the name of Harley's mother, a softhearted and caring woman, so it mattered to him. Jessica had inherited his mother's compassion, so he was glad that she carried the name forward.

"Karen and Jessica, I don't think I've been here since spring," he said to the pavers. "Since the anniversary of your deaths." They had died during

Holy Week, so he always returned for a visit between Palm Sunday and Easter, feeling that it was a particularly good time to focus on death and resurrection. "A lot has happened. A flood, a death, damage to the church, a mission trip—a trip which I can hardly remember. Strange experiences with witches, rumors of gang activity, a Halloween shooting, and then a heart attack!" *Too much darkness,* he thought to himself, *not enough light.*

He looked around to make sure he was alone in the garden, which he was. No one but he was spending time in the church yard on a freezing Thanksgiving morning. He wondered if he should be speaking aloud, and then thought to himself, *why not?* He blew on his hands to warm them, smiled, and asked, "So how have things been with you?"

No one answered, of course, although the wind began to whistle as it whipped around the edge of the church building. He imagined their faces, alive and well and unmarked by nails from the bombs that had disfigured and killed them. Harley started to shiver as he sat on the marble bench, but he wasn't quite ready to get up. "I am so thankful for you two," he said. "I miss you so much. Thirty years with you, Karen; twenty with Jessica—the best years of my life. The very best. A day doesn't go by that I don't think of you. There is such a big hole . . ." Harley's voice caught, and his eyes teared up. *It's the little things,* he thought. *Karen's smile across the breakfast table. Jessica's stories at dinner. The sound of one of them singing in an upstairs room. The balloons that would appear on their birthdays.* He thought he would miss the big things, but it's the little things.

"When I had my heart attack," he whispered out loud, "I saw a white light. And in that light, I thought I would see your faces. I stared into it, and was disappointed that I didn't see you. Part of me wishes that I had stayed dead, so that I could finally see you. Does that sound strange? Kind of morbid?" He paused, and then said, "I don't care. I mean it. I really do." *Being dead is better than being stuck in a town with witches and gangs and a murder that could have been committed by anyone . . . even Juan or Beau.* Getting up from the bench, he moved to his family's pavers and knelt down to touch them. "God take care of you," he said to them, "until I see you."

∽

Harley pushed his car over the speed limit as he drove down Route 123 to Occoquan, hoping to make it to Riverview Bakery by noon. The Bayatis kept it open on Thanksgiving morning, and they had a line out the door as people bought pies, rolls, breads, and pastries for their dinners. Harley had been invited to celebrate Thanksgiving with Mary and Paul Ranger, and he had offered to bring a pumpkin pie. If he didn't get to Riverview on time, he'd have to show up empty-handed.

Fortunately, the roads were clear and Harley pulled into a spot in front of the bakery with ten minutes to spare. Opening the front door, he saw Fatima Bayati at the cash register and her daughter Sarah behind the display case.

"Pastor Harley," said Fatima with a big smile. "Happy Thanksgiving!"

"You, too, Fatima. I'm glad I made it."

Both women wore colorful headscarves and white baker's smocks, and the two seemed happy to see Harley. The pastor had become very close to the family the year before, when they had struggled with the murder of their oldest child Norah. "If you had come earlier, you would have had to wait," said Sarah. "I'm glad you are here now, with the crowd gone."

"Me too," said Harley. "Hope you are not sold out."

"What are you looking for?" asked the father of the family, Muhammad, as he pushed through the swinging doors from the back of the shop. He wiped his hands on his smock and then extended a hand across the counter for a handshake. "So good to see you, my friend." Muhammad had a brown face with deep lines, bushy eyebrows, and a fringe of gray hair around the back of his head. He had been on a hunger strike when Harley first met him in the Prince William County Adult Detention Center, and had been very thin at the time. But since his release, Muhammad had returned to a normal weight, although he was naturally quite slender. Norah's mysterious death and Muhammad's incarceration had been a major part of the drama of Harley's first few months in Occoquan, an experience that had created a strong bond between the pastor and the family.

"I was hoping for pumpkin," said Harley, fearing the worst as he looked at the nearly empty display case.

"Well, you're in luck," said Muhammad. "We sold out of apple pie, but made extra pumpkins, just in case. Sarah, run in the back and get Pastor Harley a pumpkin pie."

"Thank you," said Harley. "That's a relief."

"So, where will you be celebrating Thanksgiving?" asked Fatima, as Sarah fetched the pie.

"Mary and Paul Ranger's," he said.

"That's good," said Fatima. "Mary always takes care of her pastor, doesn't she?"

"She is very kind," Harley said. "She doesn't want me to be alone on a day like this."

"Occoquan is lucky to have her," added Muhammad. "She runs the post office well."

"Indeed, she does," said Harley. "So, what are your plans for this afternoon?"

"We will close up shop in just a few minutes," answered Fatima. "Then we'll go upstairs and continue to prepare our Thanksgiving meal. The turkey is already in the oven."

"We did not have Thanksgiving in Iraq," said Muhammad. "But it is a holiday that we have come to enjoy very much. We always have a turkey, but everything else is Iraqi cuisine."

"That's good," said Harley. "When I was growing up, an Italian family on my street always had pasta with their turkey!"

"Thanksgiving is for everyone," Fatima said. "It's the one true American holiday, good for people of any faith, any culture. We'll be joined by the Ayads again this year, and they'll bring something Egyptian to add to the meal."

Youssef and Sofia Ayad ran a jewelry store in Occoquan, one that served many of Harley's parishioners. They were Coptic Christians from Egypt, and had become close to the Bayatis as they shared the experience of running small businesses as immigrants. Although Muslims and Coptic Christians had become increasingly antagonistic towards one another in Egypt, the Bayatis and the Ayads were very friendly in Occoquan, largely because they had shared so many meals together.

"Please give them my best," said Harley, as Sarah returned from the back of the shop, carrying a pie in a white cardboard box. Then he asked, "Sarah, where is your brother today?"

"You know that Omar is studying law enforcement, right? Well, this morning he is doing what they call a 'ride along.' Do you know what that is?"

"Riding in what? A police car?"

"Exactly," said Sarah. "He rides along on a normal shift to learn about an officer's duties and responsibilities."

"Is it dangerous?" asked Harley.

"Shouldn't be," said the sister. "Not on Thanksgiving morning, anyway."

"He'll be back by dinner," said Fatima, as Harley handed her the money for the pie. "I don't want him to miss Thanksgiving."

"Hope not," Harley said, taking the change and putting it in their tip jar. "Please say hello to him." Then he thanked all three and said that he would get out of their way so they could close up.

"We are thankful for you," said Muhammad, locking the door behind him.

∽

Mary Ranger opened the front door and welcomed Harley at exactly two o'clock. Her small brick house was filled with the savory smell of a roasted turkey, which made Harley's empty stomach rumble. "Right on time," she said. "Come on in."

"I appreciate the invitation," said the pastor. "Happy Thanksgiving."

"Same to you," said Paul from the archway between the dining room and the kitchen. He had a slight smile on his thin face, and was wiping his hands on a kitchen towel.

"Your place looks beautiful," said Harley, looking around the combination dining room and living room. "I really like your family pictures—I remember your granddaughters from our boat ride last summer. You've decorated it so nicely, and everything is spotless. How do you keep your furniture looking so nice?"

"Well, the cleanliness is not my doing," admitted Mary. "We have a cleaning lady, a young woman from El Salvador. Does a great job."

"I could probably use some help in that department," said Harley. "Everything in my place looks pretty dingy."

"Can I get you a glass of wine?" offered Paul.

"Now, Paul, go easy," said Mary. "You know that Harley has been in the hospital."

"No, it's okay," said Harley. "I have to watch what I eat and drink, but a glass of wine won't hurt."

"All right," said Mary. "Good nutrition is part of rehab."

"I should be fine today," Harley said. "Turkey is low-fat, and vegetables are good. Everything in moderation."

"Have a seat," said Mary, guiding him into the living room while Paul delivered his wine. "You two talk while I put the finishing touches on dinner."

Paul sat down in an overstuffed chair, on the other side of a coffee table containing several picture books of the Holy Land. He had also poured himself a wine. "I won't make you carry any heavy boxes today," he said, "given your heart attack."

"I appreciate that," said Harley, holding up his glass in a toast. He recalled that Paul had mentioned getting together, after Harley had discovered his collection of vintage erotica. But Paul had never followed up, and he had dropped off in church attendance in recent weeks. *Perhaps the porn has returned to the darkness of the basement,* thought Harley, *and Paul has followed.* "Take no part in the unfruitful works of darkness," said his fellow Paul, the apostle.

"I see that work is progressing on the steeple," said Paul.

"Yes, it should be done soon. We hope to rededicate before Christmas."

"Sounds good," said Paul, sipping his wine. "As a town, we need that steeple restored. It is such a landmark. Every time I drive by it, I think of the flood."

"I do, too. When it is restored, we'll feel like we are getting back to normal."

"Funny how buildings have become important to me," said Paul.

"What do you mean?"

"Well, when I was working full-time, I never paid much attention to them. But now that I am retired, I spend a lot of time here in town, and I find myself watching what is going on with the buildings, for better or for worse."

"You've seen a lot this fall."

"You're right," nodded Paul. "The flood did so much destruction, especially downhill. And while a lot of the buildings are coming back, some may never be repaired. It's a shame, I think."

"Well, I guess the owners make business decisions," said Harley. "Is a building worth repairing . . . or not?"

"There is just so much history in the structures. When they are demolished, it's all lost."

"You really seem to care about this."

"As I said, it's a recent interest," said Paul, taking another drink. "I took early retirement last year from the Library of Congress, and I retired to doing nothing. That was a mistake." Harley smiled. He had heard the same thing from many parishioners who retired without a plan in place. "So, I started to look for something to do. I *needed* something to do."

"That's for sure," said Mary, poking her head in from the kitchen. "Three minutes till dinner."

"I found a part-time job with Jefferson Jones," Paul said. "Doing maintenance on his properties. I enjoy the work, and it's gotten me interested in buildings."

"Jefferson told me that you were taking care of the castle."

"Yes, that's one of them. Strange place."

"What's it like?" asked Harley.

"You've seen the outside, with its turrets and arrow slits. The inside is really nothing special, although the plate-glass windows in the living room give a spectacular view of the river."

"What about the basement?" asked Harley.

"Well, that part *is* unusual. Carved out of solid rock, which I understand created a perfect space for wine storage."

"That's what I heard, as well."

"The walls are rock, but a plank floor was put down at one point. I guess no one wanted to walk on a cold stone floor. Jefferson tells me that there is a trap-door in the floor, which enables you to go down to a smaller sub-cellar. There is some abandoned furniture in the basement, and a lot of old wine storage racks. I've never moved any of it around, so I'm not sure where the trap-door is."

"Have you ever heard anything?" asked the pastor.

"Heard anything?"

"In the basement," said Harley. "Voices? Wailing sounds?"

"No," said Paul, surprised by Harley's question. "Never. When I go down there, it is silent as a tomb."

"As a tomb." Interesting description. Harley was about to question him further, but he caught himself. Not wanting Paul to think that he was unbalanced, he said, "It's just that I've heard some spooky stories."

"Yes, we do have some ghost stories around here," Paul agreed. "But I've never seen or heard anything unusual at the castle."

At that point, Mary called the two men to the dinner table and asked Harley to say grace over the slices of turkey that had been put on the plates. After they sat down, Mary passed around mashed potatoes, green beans, and a boat of steaming gravy. Harley took a generous helping of each. "Fresh rolls," added Mary, passing a basket, "from the Bayatis."

Harley realized that this was his first home-cooked meal since his lasagna at Leah's house. Most of his meals were frozen dinners that he microwaved at home, or were fast food—ordered and eaten at a local restaurant. *No wonder I had a heart attack.* Rarely did he get to enjoy a meal that had been carefully prepared at home, by someone as hospitable as Mary Ranger. "This is all very delicious," said Harley, after eating for a few moments in silence.

"Thank you," said Mary. "I'm glad you are enjoying it." Then she added, "And let me thank you for visiting Doris in the hospital."

"You're welcome," said Harley, wiping his mouth with a cloth napkin. "Although my memory of the visit is fuzzy. It was before my heart attack, and seems like ages ago."

"Well, it meant a lot to her."

"How could you tell?" joked Paul, knowing Doris's reputation as a pit bull.

"Be nice," said Mary to her husband. "She has a good heart."

The three continued to eat and talk about life in the town, which Mary knew well from her perch at the post office. One news item she shared, which was of interest to both Paul and Harley, was that the flood damage seemed to be accelerating the redevelopment of the riverfront. *That's good news for Jefferson Jones,* thought Harley, *especially with his days being numbered.* The postmistress said that a member of the town council had shown her some architectural renderings of the riverfront, and it looked very attractive—brand-new buildings designed to fit with the older structures around them. Mary and Paul both had second helpings of the dinner, but Harley declined, not wanting to violate his cardiac rehab guidelines. "I want to save some room for dessert," he said.

Then the doorbell rang. "Speaking of dessert," said Mary, "I have a surprise for you." She got up, went to the door, and opened it. In walked Doris King and Leah Silverman.

"Happy Thanksgiving!" said Doris, looking more vital than she had in the hospital.

"I ran into Doris and Leah in the post office," explained Mary, "and invited them to join us for dessert. They can help us with Harley's pumpkin pie."

Mary. Doris. Leah. They hadn't been together since Harley's dream, in which their faces glowed in the cauldron's fire. "When shall we three meet again," Mary had asked in the dream. "In thunder, lightning, or in rain?" *How about Thanksgiving?*

Harley got up to welcome them, and ended up giving both visitors a hug. He realized that he had nothing to fear from them—the three were mature and powerful women, pillars of the community. But he knew that through history, many older women were unfairly accused of being witches, especially those who were childless, stubborn, or contentious. Of the three women in front of him, only Mary had a child, and every one of them could be contentious. *Witches*, thought Harley. *In another era, these three might be turned into scapegoats and burned at the stake.*

"The hags are happy to be here," said Leah with a smile.

"Oh, come on," said Paul. "You look great."

"No, she's right," said Harley, making a connection he had never made before. "Don't think of a hag as being an ugly old woman, a witch. Think of a hag as *hagios*."

"Meaning what?" asked Mary.

"*Hagios* is Greek for 'holy' or 'saint,'" Harley explained. "As in the name of the great old cathedral in Istanbul, *Hagia Sophia*, 'Holy Wisdom.'"

"Leave it to the divinity school nerd," teased Leah.

Mary looked skeptical. "Is that *really* where the word 'hag' comes from?"

"Probably not," Harley admitted. "But you three have holiness in you. You've been saints to me, at some important times. Thanks for being my hags."

18

On the Monday after Thanksgiving, the Occoquan River was a muddy brown, smooth as glass. Harley stood by the wooden railing of the town dock and looked out over the water, taking a brief detour as he walked to church to start his day. *Lifeless,* he thought to himself. In warmer months, fish would be jumping and birds would be swooping. Spiders would be building webs on the dock railing, flies would be buzzing around, and long-legged insects would be daintily walking on the water. But not that day. Any signs of life were well hidden on that cold November morning.

He felt a twinge in his chest, and wondered if his heart was acting up. *Could this be another attack?* Although his doctor was pleased with his cardiac rehab, Harley felt vulnerable. He knew that life was a fragile thing, and he had seen parishioners die at every age and stage. But his knowledge had always been conceptual, right up until the moment he tumbled off the treadmill, clutching his chest. Now he knew, without any doubt at all, that he would eventually be *lifeless*—as inert as the Occoquan River that day.

"Harley!" said a voice from the small park behind him. Harley turned and saw Tie-dye Tim and Jason Weiss sitting in the Town of Occoquan golf cart. They were both wearing navy-blue coveralls under the official town work coat, but aside from the uniform they were opposites: Round-faced and smiling Tim had rosy cheeks and a gray beard, while skinny and sullen Jason had acne and long, straight, greasy, brown hair.

"Good morning, guys," said Harley, as he left the boardwalk and headed toward them. He needed a distraction from his reflections on mortality.

"First day for the new guy," said Tie-dye as he hooked a thumb toward his partner. "Jason Weiss, meet Harley Camden."

"Nice to meet you," said Harley, extending his hand.

"I know about you," said the young man, shaking hands but remaining expressionless. "My mother has told me about you."

Harley wasn't sure how to interpret his words. "She's an excellent waitress," he said. "Always takes good care of me."

"Jason is here on what the high school calls 'cooperative education,'" explained Tim. "I'm supervising him and giving him on-the-job training. He gets academic credit and money."

"Sounds good," said Harley.

Jason shrugged and said, "Gets me out of school."

"He'll be here all day on Mondays," said Tim, "and on some Saturdays, when we need weekend help."

"How are you feeling?" asked Harley, pointing to Jason's shoulder. "I hate that you got shot."

Jason didn't respond immediately. He looked at Harley, trying to assess his sincerity. Then he said, "I'm okay."

"He got out of the sling last week," said Tim. "But don't worry: I'll go easy on him for a while."

"So, what's up at town hall?" asked Harley, trying to change the subject.

"I talked with the sheriff this morning," said Tim. "He told me that the official report on the flood death was released on Friday. Medical examiner says that the man, Enrique Garcia, died of blunt force trauma to the head, before the flood. They suspect a gang killing. Maybe drug related."

"That stuff is getting too close," said Harley.

"But get this," said Tim. "The folks at New Life Church aren't accepting it. They heard the news and jumped into action after their service yesterday. They want to blame the witches because of the man's satanic markings."

"That's BS," said Jason.

"They are calling the death a satanic sacrifice," said Tim.

"No way," Jason said, shaking his head.

"I'm just reporting what I've heard," Tim explained.

Harley waited for Jason to respond, but the teenager just sat in the golf cart with his arms crossed. Finally, Harley asked him, "What makes you so sure?"

Jason shot him a dirty look. "They are not that kind of people."

"What kind?" probed Harley.

"Killers," said Jason. Then, touching his shoulder, he said, "Not like the Christian who shot me."

Harley nodded and said again, "I really do hate that you got shot."

Jason uncrossed his arms and put his hands on his knees. "The people in the coven are trying to live good lives," he said. "I don't know a lot about them, but everything I've learned is good."

"Like what?" asked Harley, as gently as he could. "I'm not trying to argue. I really want to know."

"Well, for starters, they don't see God as some dude with a white beard in the sky," he said. "God is not outside us. If there is a God, he is inside us."

"I've heard that," said Harley. "It's a pagan understanding."

"What do you mean?" asked Tim.

"For pagans, divinity is inside the world, not outside it," explained Harley. "The gods are part of creation, not external creators. Religion is immanent rather than transcendent."

"Now you are losing me," said Tim, holding up a hand.

"Me too," said Jason.

"Sorry," said Harley. "I'm just commenting on what Jason said. In Christianity, God is a creator, separate from creation. He is transcendent. In paganism, on the other hand, the gods are part of creation. Immanent."

"That confuses me," said Jason, "like a lot of the religious crap I've heard over the years. But I like what the members of the coven say. I understand the idea of having power inside me."

"So, how does it work?" asked Harley. "When you do rituals, does this power help you? Does it make you stronger?"

"I don't know," said Jason. "I told you that I don't know a lot, yet."

"Sorry," said Harley, backing off.

"But I like the people," said Jason, "and they seem to be helped by their religion. That's more than I can say for the church."

Harley pondered this for a moment, and then said, "I understand the attraction. I really do. But it's the opposite of what I believe—I am convinced that God is outside me."

"'Spirit of the living God,'" Tim began to sing, softly. "'Fall afresh on me. Melt me, mold me, fill me, use me.'"

"You know that song?" asked Harley.

"Sure thing," said Tim. "We sang it at your church, just a few weeks ago. A real earworm. Doesn't that hymn mean that God is inside us?"

"Well, not exactly," Harley said. "The Spirit comes from the outside. Then it moves inside us, fills us, uses us."

"Still, you can see why people want God on the inside."

"Sure," said Harley, nodding. "I understand completely."

"'Spirit of the living God,'" Tim sang, completing the verse, "'fall afresh on me.'" Then, looking at his watch, he said to Jason and Harley, "We better get moving. There is a lot of weekend trash at River Mill Park."

"I don't agree with the church people," said Jason, going back to the beginning of the conversation. "I think the dead guy was killed by a gang. He was probably *in* a gang. Probably had something to do with drugs."

Hoping that Tim and Jason would stay put, Harley asked, "Is there a lot of that around here?"

"Sure," said Jason. "And I hate it. I hate drugs, and I hate the people who sell drugs."

Harley was surprised. Seeing Jason on the street, he might think he was a drug user. "Why's that?"

"Don't you know?" Jason said. "Didn't my mother tell you? My father is in jail for dealing. He ruined my mother's life."

Recalling the situation, Harley said, "I'm sorry. That must be awful, for all of you."

"Whatever," said Jason. "He's a loser."

"I'm going to get us moving," said Tie-dye Tim, turning the key in the ignition.

But Jason held up his hand, asking Tim to stop. "I want to say something," he said to Harley. "You've been a good friend to my mother."

"You're welcome," said Harley.

"I've got no use for Christians," said Jason. "But my mom says you are nice to her at the restaurant. I appreciate that."

∽

After walking up the creaky wooden steps to his office on the side of the church, Harley opened the door and saw the message light flashing on his answering machine. "One new message," said the automated voice after he pressed the button. "Harley, it's Leah. Thanksgiving was fun. Glad we could get together. I just got some information that I'd like to share with you. Can you meet me at Lake Ridge Coffee at eleven?"

Harley smiled when he heard her suggestion of Lake Ridge Coffee. That was the place that Leah had casually outed herself to Harley the previous year. Back at Duke, Harley had always wondered why their relationship had not become romantic. He guessed that it was because she was Jewish and he was Christian, a divide only widened by the fact that he was studying to be a pastor. They went their separate ways after graduation, reconnecting at a Duke reunion and then in the Town of Occoquan. Soon after becoming neighbors, he heard about Pat—a love of Leah's who had died too young. He assumed that Pat was Patrick. Then Leah and Harley got together at Lake Ridge Coffee.

"Pat and I spent a lot of time here," Leah said. "She loved it."

"She?" said Harley, bewildered. He didn't think he had heard her right. "Wait a second. Pat was a woman?"

"Of course," said Leah.

Harley stared at her, feeling his thirty-year-old assumptions beginning to shift, like ancient rocks beneath his feet. Then the movement stopped, and the puzzle of their perplexing personal history suddenly made sense.

"Pat was Patricia," said Leah. "You know that I am a lesbian, right?"

"Uh, no, I didn't," he said, sheepishly.

Leah laughed. "Harley, how could you not know?"

"I just didn't," he said. "Never occurred to me."

The experience had taught Harley that he didn't always see things clearly, even when they were right in front of him.

Harley picked up the phone and called Leah back, agreeing to meet her at eleven. He was always happy to see her, and the appointment gave him something to look forward to on a Monday morning. *Wonder what she'll be disclosing*, he asked himself. *Couldn't be more earth-shaking than last year's revelation.*

Harley organized his sermon notes and worship bulletin from the day before, stapled them together, and stuck them in a file marked "Christ the King Sunday 2018." The church year was a cycle, rolling endlessly through the seasons in a predictable pattern, and he knew that he'd want to go back to his notes in future years. He had left a hymnbook on his desk, so he leafed through it as he began to think about the service that lay ahead. *First Sunday in Advent. The beginning of the church year.*

Harley knew that the word Advent meant "coming," and it was the season in which the church prepared for the coming of Jesus Christ. But it was more than a time to get ready to celebrate his birth at Christmas. Advent was also a season to reflect on the earth-shaking second coming of Jesus at the end of the world, and to ponder the fiery message of John the Baptist, who prepared the way for the ministry of Jesus. So, the Advent season was not only about sweet baby Jesus—the arrival of Christ was always preceded by shock and awe.

Harley picked up a Bible and found the lesson suggested for the First Sunday in Advent. "There will be signs in the sun, the moon, and the stars," said Jesus in the Gospel of Luke, "and on the earth distress among nations confused by the roaring of the sea and the waves. People will faint from fear and foreboding of what is coming upon the world, for the powers of the heavens will be shaken."

My God, thought Harley as he read the lesson. *Signs in nature. Distress. The roaring of the sea and the waves. Fear and foreboding. That's been our life in Occoquan.* He put down the Bible and tipped back in his chair, beginning to think about the shape of the upcoming service. While he didn't typically focus on the end of the world in his Sunday sermons, the combination of recent events and the words of Jesus seemed to demand that he go in that direction.

The phone rang and he picked it up. On the line was a woman from the community who needed a gas card to fill her tank and get to work. Harley had talked with her several times before, so he knew her story and assessed that the need was legitimate. He said that he thought he had one, and that she'd be welcome to have it if she could come to the church and pick it up. He moved around some papers on his desk until he uncovered it. She agreed to stop by before eleven.

Where was I? Hymnbook. Bible. Advent service for Sunday. He was about to get back into service planning when he saw the corner of the journal from his archaeological dig in Honduras, unearthed by his search for the gas card. He realized that he hadn't looked at it since he read a passage to Bill Stanford before their departure on the mission trip, so he picked it up and began to read. He had shared the very first entry with Bill, but had put it down and forgotten all about it. This time, he decided to go a little farther, so he read the next entry, and then the next. It transported him back to the summer of 1986, when he was a twenty-six-year-old graduate of Duke Divinity School, and he found the book to be impossible to put down. The journal was like a time machine, taking him back to a critical turning point in his life, a six-week period in which he was done with his education and about to embark on a lifetime of parish ministry. Harley kept flipping the pages, amazed at the journal's strange blend of wisdom and naivete, right up until the church doorbell rang. *Who's that?* he wondered. And then he remembered: *Gas card.*

Glancing at the clock, he saw that it was time to leave for his coffee with Leah, so he pulled on his coat, grabbed the gas card and dig journal, and headed for the front door of the church. Walking through the dark Sanctuary, he wondered, *How could I have blown an entire hour with this old journal? Meant to get the Sunday service planned.* But he knew how irresistible a book could be, as long as it was not the book he was supposed to be reading. Over the course of his life, he had attacked numerous books and read them cover to cover, usually when he was supposed to be writing a sermon or preparing for a church meeting. *Oh well, nothing is wasted. Leah is going to be interested.*

Harley met the needy neighbor at the Sanctuary door, gave her the gas card, and wished her well. Then he zipped up his coat, walked to the parking lot, climbed into his car, and headed up the hill to Lake Ridge, where Leah was sitting at a table by the front window.

"Harley," she said with a smile. "Hope you don't mind that I ordered for you."

"You know how I like it." The small shop was a warm refuge from the chilly morning, and the aroma of freshly-ground coffee filled the air.

"Smells good in here, doesn't it?" she asked, as Harley sat down across from her at a café table.

"The smell is what first attracted me to coffee," he said, as he took off his coat. "I worked at a golf course in high school. Had to get up at five in the morning on Saturdays to make coffee for the golfers."

"Early for a high schooler."

"You're right," he said. "I had tasted coffee once or twice, but didn't like it. Too bitter. But I always found the aroma to be intoxicating. Eventually, I started drinking it just to wake up. And then I developed a taste for it."

"And now you're hooked," said Leah.

"Total addict."

The waitress delivered two coffees: Black for Harley and a latte for Leah. "Cheers," she said, lifting her cup.

"Same to you," he said before they took their first sips. "Leah, I know that you have some information for me. But first, let me show you something." He reached into his coat pocket and pulled out his dig journal.

"What's that?" she asked. "Looks old."

"From my dig in Honduras, the year after we were in Israel."

"I remember keeping a dig journal."

"Yes, you'd be familiar with a lot of it. But as I was reading it this morning, I came across something that surprised me. The entry didn't mean a lot to me in 1986, but now it seems important:

> *Grad student Nancy is not focused on either the religious life or the political history of Copán. Instead, she wants to know how the community grew and declined, and what strain the inhabitants put on the environment. She told me that the population growth during the last decades of the classical period caused tremendous deforestation and degradation of the land.*

"Interesting," said Leah. "I didn't know that you were working on environmental issues."

"Neither did I. My focus was elsewhere, and it didn't stick with me. But it seems from this entry that the Mayans disappeared because of what they did to the land."

"Makes sense," said Leah. "I don't know much about Mayans, but I'm guessing that deforestation would do more long-term damage than warfare."

"That seems to be what this grad student was working on."

"It actually connects with the reason for my call," said Leah. "And a lot of what I'm working on with the Creation Care group."

"Really?" said Harley. "So, this is not another big personal revelation, like last year?"

Leah laughed. "No, nothing like that. I'm the same as I've always been." And then she teased, "Most of my friends didn't have to be told."

"Most of your friends are pretty smart," said Harley, sipping his coffee.

"Here, I've got something to show you." She pulled a folder out of a large bookbag and put it on the table. "You asked me to connect with John Jonas, and I did. Since he works for the county, he was able to access the zoning documents and building permits for developments up the hill from Occoquan." As she opened the folder, Harley saw a document related to Justice Plaza.

"What did he find?" asked Harley, feeling a sour taste in his mouth.

"This one was built in the 1970s," said Leah. "I think you've seen it. Maybe you've even been there. I think it was a factor in the flood. You know that it's a large enclosed mall with an enormous parking lot—I'm talking acres of blacktop."

"That creates a lot of run-off, I know. But could a parking lot cause a flood?"

"Not by itself," said Leah. "The storm was extraordinary, dumping huge amounts of rain. But Occoquan was hit hard because the lots at Justice Plaza acted like a funnel, directing an enormous volume of water toward the town."

"Makes sense," said Harley. "The thing is, there is a lot of commercial development up there. Why is this one being singled out?"

"Here are the rules for this type of development," said Leah, pulling a page from beneath the Justice Plaza specifications and putting the two documents side by side. "If you look at the regulations for parking lots, you can see that the lot at Justice Plaza is way bigger than should have been allowed. There were not many regulations for storm water management at the time, but even the most basic requirements were ignored. And even the mall itself should not have been built there—the area was not zoned for commercial development."

"What do you think happened?" asked Harley.

"Something irregular," said Leah. "Kind of hard to put a finger on it now. But my guess is that money traded hands—the builder may have bribed someone in county government to get the place built. Or maybe it was political. Contributions could have been given to a candidate in exchange for approval. In any case, Justice Plaza seems dirty."

"And you know who built it, don't you?" asked Harley, feeling sick to his stomach.

"Afraid so," said Leah, pointing to the name on the document: "Occoquan's own Jefferson Jones."

19

"We are in trouble," said the Secretary General of the United Nations. "We are in deep trouble with climate change." Harley read these words in *The Washington Post* as he ate a burrito, one that had been unevenly heated by the microwave in his townhouse kitchen. As he sat at his kitchen table and chewed on a still-frozen chunk of his dinner, he read a story on the UN Climate Conference in Poland. Global emissions of carbon dioxide were reaching record levels, scientists reported, with increases in China, India, and the United States.

Emissions were a problem, yes, but they were not as disturbing as what he saw that afternoon in a clearing in the woods not far from Occoquan. Taking a walk before sunset, he hiked into an area across the river, going deeper into the woods than he had ever gone before. Cresting a ridge, he came across a small field that had been cleared to be a cemetery, one that was dotted by several dozen weathered headstones. Someone had been maintaining the site, but not very well. Tall grass had grown up around most of the markers, the stones were black with algae, and the area looked especially lifeless under the gray autumn sky.

Then Harley noticed some movement at the far end of the clearing. At first, he thought that he was seeing a herd of deer coming out of the woods, but he quickly realized that it was a small group of people, dressed in robes and carrying a long wooden box. Harley stepped behind a tree to avoid being seen, and watched as four of them put the box down on the ground. *Was this a funeral procession?* He thought that it was strange that there was no tent in the field, as there would typically be for an interment, and no sign of a grave. He squinted to get a better look, and then recognized the robes as being similar to the ones worn in the Halloween ceremony. *Wiccans!* And then he saw one of them lower his hood. *John Jonas!*

A cold breeze rustled the branches around him, causing the few remaining dried-out leaves to flutter. Harley watched as four of the people opened the lid of the box and removed a body. The corpse was naked, but Harley was too far away to determine if it was a man or a woman. The body was laid down on the grass, and the lid was restored to the box. Then the four robed figures put the body on top of the box, lying naked and exposed to the sky, like a sacrifice placed on an altar. *What are they doing?* Harley saw no evidence that the body was going to be buried. Then the group of Wiccans, about eight in number, began to walk away from the corpse toward the tree line. *Was this a pagan sacrifice?* John was moving in Harley's direction, so he slipped deeper into the woods to escape detection. Hiding behind a large rock, Harley watched as the witches took positions at the tree line, forming a large circle around the corpse. They stood, in silence and stillness, waiting.

After about ten minutes, Harley noticed six large black vultures beginning to circle above the clearing. Two more joined them, then another pair and another. Like a tornado they spiraled downward and landed on the body, beginning to attack it and tear flesh from bone. The dozen vultures were feasting on the fresh meat, flapping their wings and fighting with each other over the most valuable cuts, playing their grisly role in the decomposition of carrion. The Wiccans remained motionless, not wanting to disturb the violent liturgy that was playing out before them. Harley couldn't stand to watch it, however. Caring for the dead had always been important to him as a person, as well as being a core responsibility as a minister, and this ceremony felt like the desecration of a corpse. With his stomach turning, he backtracked slowly into the woods, and then picked up the trail that took him back to Occoquan.

After an unsatisfying dinner, Harley sat in the darkness of his kitchen, sipped a beer, and reflected on the day. Everything in and around him seemed to be in a state of chaos, from his wounded heart to his troubled town. His cardiac rehab gave him no guarantee of good health, Occoquan remained vulnerable to catastrophic flooding, gangs were dealing drugs and killing people at will, the witches were feeding human flesh to vultures, and carbon emissions were growing around the world at an alarming rate. Harley wanted so badly to get something under control, even just one aspect of his personal or professional life. But stability remained elusive. He still hadn't figured out why he had acted so strangely on the mission trip, and every time he stepped on a treadmill, he felt worried about having another heart attack. In so many areas, he was fragile and vulnerable—even his confidence in the pulpit was fading fast. The previous Sunday, when he preached on "distress among nations" and people fainting "from fear and foreboding of what is coming upon the world," the congregation had been unimpressed. "Nice Christmas message," said Andy Stackhouse at the door. The retired military man said that he came to church for inspiration, not for doom and gloom.

"We are in trouble," said the Secretary General of the United Nations. *Yes,* thought Harley as he drained the last of his beer, *I am in trouble.*

After putting his dinner plate in the dishwasher, he picked up his stack of mail and quickly rifled through it. Among the bills and junk mail was a Christmas card from Tawnya Jones, his first card of the season. The front had a black baby Jesus—the infant version of the mighty Jesus in the stained glass of Riverside Methodist Church—and inside was a personal message. Tawnya thanked him for accommodating her family reunion in October, and for being a good friend to her and her family. "You've been a great support to my father," she concluded, "especially during his illness."

Harley sighed. Although he was grateful for the affirming words, the mention of Jefferson caused his heart to sink. *What am I going to do about Jefferson?*

Looking out his kitchen window into the gloom, Harley thought that another walk would do him good. Putting on a lined jacket, he opened the kitchen door and headed down the cast iron steps on the side of the house. The cold air stung his skin, but also invigorated him. When he hit the sidewalk, he thought *yes, this feels great—get the body moving again.* Gas streetlights flickered as he strode westward toward River Mill Park, and a few strings of Christmas lights added color to the street.

He walked past the vacant lot that had become a muddy delta on the day of the flood, and noticed that a fresh layer of gravel had been put down on the ground. *That's progress,* he thought, *but the brew pub is still dark.* Being on the river side of the street, the pub had suffered significant damage, and contractors had been hard at work for more than two months. Harley was sure that the owners, unable to make money unless the doors were open, were feeling deeply discouraged. *No pale ale, no profit.*

Harley passed the lot where the candle shop had been, and then looked up at the apartment building where John and Kelly lived. No lights on the top floors, so he assumed they were out. Then he passed the town museum, a small stone building that had once been part of the Occoquan mill, and walked downhill to the pedestrian bridge. The walk was feeling so good that he figured he would cross the bridge, walk the road that cut through the woods on the other side of the river, and then return home by the large concrete bridge on the eastern edge of town. That would be a one-mile loop—good after-dinner exercise.

But when Harley got halfway across the bridge, he stopped. He could hear the river rushing beneath him, a sound that was both soothing and threatening. Yes, running water was a beautiful thing, part of the music of the natural world. It sang of refreshment and cleansing and new life—that's why Christians used water in the sacrament of baptism. But the river also sent a message of danger and destruction and death, a theme that was equally present in Scripture. The authors of the Bible had a healthy respect for water, expressed in the Book of Psalms when the writer cries out, "Save me, O God, for the waters have come up to my neck." *Nothing refreshing and soothing about that.*

Harley looked over the railing at the rushing black water below, and thought of how destructive the recent flood had been. A residence had been destroyed, businesses had been crippled, and untold items had been ruined in flooded basements throughout the town. And now, with global temperatures rising and glaciers melting, the rising seas were going to encroach on coastal areas around the world—including the Town of Occoquan. *Was the September flood just the first of many? Would the destruction continue? Are the mighty waters going to wipe us out?* Harley knew that miners used to carry canaries with them when they went underground, realizing that if methane gas or carbon monoxide reached a dangerous level, the canary would die before any human would get sick. Occoquan was the canary in the coal mine for the larger region, an early indicator of climate change danger. *Perhaps this town will be the first to go, when the fountains burst forth and the windows of the heavens open.*

Through his first minutes of walking, Harley had felt invigorated. But now, with his thoughts spiraling downward into ruminations on flooding, he was back to feeling fragile and vulnerable. *Save me, O God,* he thought as he peered down into the swirling blackness, *before the waters come up to my neck.*

"Beautiful stars," said a voice behind him. Surprised, he jerked his head upward, spun his body around, and tipped awkwardly against the bridge railing. Kelly Westbrook had appeared, as if by magic.

"Kelly!" he stammered, his heart pounding. It took a second for him to catch his breath, and then he said, "You trying to give me another heart attack?"

"Sorry," she said, smiling. "You were lost in thought, so I *had* to sneak up on you."

Harley shook his head and said, "You witches are mean."

"Yeah, that's our reputation. But don't keep looking down, Harley."

"Huh?" he said, confused.

"Look up!" she insisted, turning him around and pointing up at the eastern sky. "Orion," she said.

The stars were brilliant on that cold, clear night. The constellation Orion covered the eastern sky, and its stars were the brightest of the lights scattered across the sky like diamonds on black velvet.

"Spectacular," said Harley. He realized that even in a time of deep darkness, some lights were permanent, unchanging, eternal—completely unaffected by earthly affairs. His spirits began to rise again.

"I love nature," said Kelly, standing next to him and gazing up. "I feel like I can count on it, even when people let me down."

"The stars never change," said Harley. "We need that."

"So, what are you doing out here tonight?" she asked.

"Taking a walk. I wanted some air. Thought I'd make the loop over the bridge, through the woods, and then back across the Route 123 bridge."

"May I join you?"

"Sure," said Harley. "Some company would be great."

Kelly had her auburn hair pulled back in a ponytail, and her pale skin seemed to glow in the dim light. She was wearing form-fitting exercise pants and a quilted winter jacket, an outfit for a vigorous walk, and Harley hoped he wouldn't slow her down. "Shall we?" she said, pointing toward the dark woods on the other side of the bridge.

"I do love walking this time of year," Harley said, as they turned onto the road that took them through the trees.

"I once saw a couple having sex in this clearing," said Kelly, pointing to the roadside.

"Really?" said Harley.

"Yes, it was about this time of year, so there wasn't anyone else on the road."

"Must have been cold."

"They had coats over them, but they were definitely doing it."

"The wonders of nature," said Harley, grinning.

"Look at Occoquan," she said as they continued up the hill. "You can see it so clearly when the leaves are off the trees." Windows glowed in restaurants, houses, and apartments, and reflections of their light danced in the water below.

"I ran into John right here," said Harley, pointing to the large rock that had become their bench.

"He likes to hike these woods," she said.

"He put a curse on some moths," Harley told her. "They were flying around, and then they fell to the ground."

"That's not a curse," she said, shaking her head. "That's science."

"What do you mean?"

"Did he shake his car keys?"

"Yes."

"Those moths are hunted by bats," she explained. "The moths have evolved the ability to hear the sounds that bats make when they are flying through the air. You know that bats navigate by sound, right? Their sounds are ultrasonic, so we humans can't hear them."

"But the moths can?"

"Right. The moths hear the sounds, and they drop to the ground, like they are dead. That way, the bats can't catch them in flight."

"Interesting," said Harley. "But what does that have to do with car keys?"

"John knows that the shaking of car keys can mimic the ultrasonic sounds that bats make. He shook them to trick the moths into thinking that bats were coming after them. That's why they dropped to the ground."

"But what about the words that John said, the curse?"

"That was just BS," said Kelly. "He was messing with you. The moths heard the car keys, nothing else."

"Interesting," said Harley. "I wish he had just told me about the bats and the moths."

"Well, he's a BSer," Kelly said, a hint of frustration in her voice. She motioned him forward and they continued their walk up the hill.

"How long have you two been together?" asked Harley.

"We're not together anymore," she said. "I moved out."

"You did?"

"Yeah, I've got an apartment in the Hammill Hotel." Harley knew the old red brick building, on the corner of Union and Commerce Streets.

"Very historic," he said.

She nodded. "Built in 1804. Good bones, but the owner needs to update it."

"Well, I'm sorry that you split up."

"I'm not," she said.

The two walked in silence until they came alongside *el Castillo*, which was down the hill to their right, surrounded by trees. "I wonder what goes on in there," said Harley.

"What do you mean?" asked Kelly.

"It's supposed to be empty, but I've seen lights at night. I just wonder: Are there people hiding in there? Dealing drugs? Doing . . . who knows what?"

"I don't know," said Kelly. "I've never seen any activity." Harley wondered if he could trust her. After all, she *was* a witch. Maybe the coven was involved.

"It just seems suspicious," said Harley.

"Well, John is concerned about drug dealing in the area, and he's never said anything to me. He hates drugs. His younger brother died of an overdose."

"Oh, no. I'm sorry."

"Yeah, it was bad," said Kelly. "Happened right before we met, over in Woodbridge. John doesn't drink or do drugs, and he's even more organic than I am. Because of his brother, I think."

"So does John talk with those people?" asked Harley. "With drug people? Does he . . . confront them?" He remembered what Beau Harper had told him about the Latinos and John, and he imagined a standoff between those kids and a Grizzly. *Not a fair fight.*

"I don't think so," said Kelly. "I know he has talked to the police a few times. Once or twice, he saw some things in Occoquan that concerned him, so he reported it."

"See something, say something," said Harley, repeating an old cliché.

The two of them made it to the concrete Route 123 bridge and began to walk back to the Town of Occoquan, their steps illuminated by streetlights. As they strolled on the pedestrian pathway, they came across a large fish, dead on the concrete, with one glassy eye staring up at them.

"That's weird," said Harley, wondering what a fish was doing forty feet above the water. "It couldn't have jumped up here." His mind raced to the supernatural, causing him to wonder if some strange force was at work, distorting the normal rhythms of nature.

"No," said Kelly, "It didn't jump. Some bird plucked it out of the water, and then dropped it."

"Oh," said Harley. "Of course." Once again, what seemed strange turned out to be entirely normal.

"The fish was probably too heavy to carry," Kelly said.

"Speaking of birds," said Harley. "I saw something strange today."

"Really? What's that?"

"It was in a clearing in the woods. John was there, along with some Wiccans. I don't think I saw you."

"No, I was at the gym."

"A body was placed on top of a casket and fed to the vultures."

Kelly didn't seem surprised. "A sky burial," she said.

"A what?"

"A sky burial. It's not pagan, but comes from Tibetan Buddhism. Since the dead body is an empty vessel, there is no reason to preserve it. Some members of our group prefer it, because it seems natural."

"Seemed disrespectful to me. And maybe even illegal."

"Not that I know of," said Kelly. "Sky burials are always done in a remote place, and then the bones are put in a coffin and buried in a cemetery."

Harley realized that he may have left the scene too early. "It did happen in an old cemetery," he admitted.

"Yeah," said Kelly, "we have learned that we have to follow the law about burials. But some cemeteries, like the one in the woods, are what you would call a 'green' cemetery. Remains can be put in pine boxes and buried in a natural way. No embalming, no preservation of the body."

"Ashes to ashes," said Harley. "Dust to dust."

"I can imagine it freaked you out."

"A bit," he admitted. "Do you know who was being buried?"

"A member of the group had a relative who died," she said. "Someone John knows better than I do."

"Makes sense that he was there."

"Speaking of John," said Kelly, "I really don't think he is involved with drug people. But I cannot say for sure."

"Why do you say that?"

"Well, I've learned I can't trust him," she said, suddenly looking vulnerable. To Harley, the change made her even more beautiful, and he wanted to hear more. But she looked down at the path and fell into silence.

"If you ever want to talk, my door is open," he said as they walked down into town. Harley had never counseled a witch before, but there is a first time for everything.

"Good night, Harley," she said, splitting off from him to return to the Hammill Hotel. "Thanks for the walk."

That night, Harley dreamed of a huge black vulture, spiraling downward out of the sky. As it descended, it burst into flames and turned into a radiant eagle that unfurled its bright and powerful wings as it settled down onto the earth. *Earth Eagle?* Then it molted, shedding its fiery feathers and becoming an angel—one that was holding a heavy chain and a brass key. The angel plunged the key into the ground, turned it, and through the dirt of the ground lifted up a heavy trap door that marked the entrance to a dark and bottomless pit. From behind the angel, a serpent appeared with blazing eyes and needle-sharp fangs. *Kelly Westbrook? No . . . Satan.* His muscular body coiled and tried to strike, but the angel seized the serpent and bound him with the chain. Then he threw the devil into the pit, to be sealed inside for one thousand years.

When the period of captivity was over—*one second is like a thousand years, and a thousand years are like one second*—Satan was released. He continued his deceptions as the age-old father of lies, tricking whole armies into marching with him into battle. But as soon as they took up arms, fire came down out of heaven and consumed them. *Sky burial.* The devil who deceived them was thrown into a lake of fire and sulphur to be tormented forever, along with the cowardly, the faithless, the polluted, the murderers, the fornicators, the sorcerers, the idolaters, and the liars. And then there appeared a new heaven and a new earth, containing a lush and verdant garden in a city.

When Harley woke up at dawn, his dream was still quite vivid. He couldn't tell what was real and what was fantasy, or who was an ally and who was an opponent—Occoquan had plenty of vultures, eagles, cowards, liars, and even some sorcerers. But he knew that he wanted to be on the side of the angels, rather than in the army of the father of lies. As he climbed out of bed, he realized that his first action had to be a confrontation with Jefferson Jones.

20

Heavy rain fell all weekend, causing the river to swell to the highest level since the September flood. The congregation of Riverside Methodist Church filled the entrance to the sanctuary with wet umbrellas, and the mood of the Third Sunday of Advent was gloomy, as sheets of rain rattled the windows throughout the service. The mournful tune of "O Come, O Come Emmanuel" fit the bleakness of the day very well, and people sang it like a dirge. In the middle of his sermon, Harley noticed that entire words in his manuscript had exploded like starbursts on the page, and he wondered—in a moment of panic—if his mental instability was returning. But then another word erupted in front of his eyes, and he saw that it was caused by a drop of water, coming down from the high cathedral ceiling. The roof was leaking, right over the pulpit!

"Excuse me," he said to the congregation, interrupting his own sermon. The people looked puzzled until he pointed to the ceiling and said, "We've got a leak." Gathering up his manuscript, he began to move from the pulpit to the lectern, and when he made it halfway across the front of the church, he had an inspiration. Grabbing the baptismal bowl from the stand in front of the lectern, he carried it back to the pulpit and placed it on top, to catch the falling water.

"I'll be available for baptisms at the end of the service," he quipped, and then continued his message from the lectern.

At the end of the service, Andy Stackhouse was kinder than he had been two Sundays before. "Nice visual aid for your John the Baptist sermon," he said with a grin. "Water from heaven, falling right into the baptismal bowl."

"Took a lot of preparation," Harley said, shaking hands at the door.

"Really brought your words to life," said the old Navy man.

The rain continued all Sunday, and when Harley woke up on Monday morning he wondered if the river had overflowed its banks. Climbing the stairs to the top level of his townhouse, he looked out the window and saw that the Occoquan River was the color of a latte, topped by swirling foam that spun in enormous whirlpools as it moved quickly downstream. But fortunately, the river had stayed where it belonged, not flooding the town. *Small blessings,* thought Harley. Heading down to the kitchen, he turned on the radio and heard that the region's annual rainfall record had been broken over the weekend, making 2018 the wettest in 129 years. *No surprise there.* Having heard that climate change was causing weather events to become more and more severe, he wondered if this record would be broken repeatedly in the years that lay ahead.

Harley stepped onto the porch outside his kitchen to pick up his newspaper, and pulled his winter robe tightly around him. Looking to Mill Street, he saw the Town of Occoquan golf cart heading toward him. It contained only one passenger: Jason Weiss. His greasy hair draped over the collar of his official town work coat, and he looked bored.

"Jason, good morning!" said Harley, waving.

Jason pulled his cart to the curb and hit the brake. "What's up?" he asked.

"Not much. How's the town after the rain?"

"Tim has got me checking the storm sewers. Making sure they are clear."

"That's good," said Harley. "I bet they get clogged."

"I guess," said Jason, shrugging.

"How's your mom doing?" asked Harley. He was staying away from lustful thoughts, but still felt an attraction to her.

"Okay. Working hard. Getting ready for Christmas."

"Yeah, that's just a little over a week away."

"Not that it matters to me," said the young pagan.

"Well, you've got your winter solstice coming up."

"My what?"

"Winter solstice," said Harley. "Yule."

Jason looked mystified.

"Want to come up for coffee?" asked Harley.

"I should be working," said Jason.

"I'll talk to Tim," said the pastor. "It's cold out. Come in for five minutes."

Jason climbed out of his golf cart and trudged up the wrought-iron stairs. He looked conflicted, not wanting to trust this Christian minister and yet feeling a certain confidence in his mother's assessment of the man. Plus, he could use a cup of coffee.

Harley ushered him into the kitchen and closed the door behind him. Then he offered Jason a chair by the small kitchen table and poured him a steaming cup of coffee. "Cream and sugar?" he asked.

"No, black," said Jason.

"Same as me," said Harley, sitting down across the table from him. "So, you are still learning about winter solstice?"

"I guess," said the young man, not wanting to reveal his ignorance.

"Winter solstice is an ancient pagan celebration," said Harley, sipping his coffee. "It's held on December 21, the longest night of the year."

"So that's coming up," said Jason.

"Yes, this Friday."

"What's it all about?"

"It's a ritual to welcome back the sun," said the pastor. "After December 21, the sun returns and the days get longer and longer."

"That makes sense. So, what do people do?"

"I'm no expert," said Harley, "but I think some pagans burn a Yule log. Set up a holiday tree. Get out the mistletoe."

"Sounds a lot like Christmas."

"Yeah, sure," said Harley. "Christians adopted a lot of pagan practices into their Christmas celebrations."

"They stole them?"

"Sort of," said Harley. "Christians have always seen the glory of God in the beauty of the world. The return of the sun is part of God's creation, and should be noticed and honored. The beauty of an evergreen tree and a piece of mistletoe—same thing. We Christians have simply added our worship of Jesus to our worship of God the creator."

"Still, it sounds like stealing."

"At times," said Harley, "Christians used pagan celebrations as a time to hide. When Christianity was illegal in Rome, Christians used the Roman Saturnalia as a time to celebrate the birth of Jesus. While the Romans were partying, Christians were worshiping the baby Jesus."

"That's pretty clever," admitted Jason.

"So, you see," said Harley. "Christians are not always the strong guys, the bullies, the oppressors. Sometimes we have been quite vulnerable, and have gone along to get along."

"Tell that to Beau Harper," said Jason.

"Right about that," admitted Harley.

"Tim tells me that Beau got in trouble with the sheriff," said Jason.

"Really?"

"Yeah, he was giving some Latino kids a hard time. They got scared and went to the sheriff."

"Why do you think he bothered them?"

"Probably thought they were gang members."

"Yes, I know he is worried about gangs."

"Anyway, they were not causing trouble, but he didn't like them hanging around the park. Sheriff told him to leave them alone, and to leave the law enforcement to him."

"Sounds about right," said Harley.

Then Jason looked at his watch, pushed back from the table, and said, "I better get back to work. Thanks for the coffee."

⌒

When Harley arrived at church, the phone was ringing in his office. "Harley, it's Andy," said the voice on the line.

"How are you doing, Captain?" said the pastor.

"Good until yesterday," said the man. "I thought we were done with water problems, but I guess not." Andy had directed the cleanup of the church basement after the flood, and was now jumping on this latest problem.

"What should we do?" asked Harley.

"Well, we need someone to get on the roof," said Andy. "But not me. And not a volunteer. Too dangerous. I know a roof guy, and I'll try to get him to take a look early this week. The skies are finally clearing."

"Thanks, Andy. I really appreciate it."

"No problem, Harley. We've got to get a patch on it, at least. You can't have water on the pulpit."

"Right about that, especially at Christmas. Keep me posted, will you?"

"Sure thing," said Andy.

At that moment, a knock came at the door, so Harley said goodbye and hung up the phone. *Kinda busy for a Monday morning.*

Opening the door, he saw the tall redhead Bill Stanford, the dentist who had organized the Honduras trip. "Harley, got a minute?" he asked.

"Sure, Bill. Come on in."

"I was just driving to the office, talking with a friend on the phone."

"Want to sit down?" asked Harley.

"No, this will just a take a minute. This friend is a doctor who also does mission work in Honduras, so we talk from time to time, compare notes and whatnot. Anyway, she asked me if anyone on our team had used Melial."

"Melial?" said Harley. "That's what I was taking, right? Anti-malaria?"

"I thought so," said Bill, nodding. "It's a fairly new drug, and I had never heard of it. But I thought I remembered that you had used it. So here is what she told me: Melial has been found to cause hallucinations."

"Really?"

"And not only that," said the dentist, "but psychological effects such as anxiety and depression."

"Could it have caused my . . ."

"Absolutely," said Bill. "I think your troubles on the mission trip were all caused by Melial."

"Huh," said Harley, thinking back on the past few months.

"The good news is that the symptoms go away when you stop taking the medication."

"Well, that was true for me," said the pastor. He hadn't been cursed, and he hadn't been crazy. He had simply suffered from a bad drug interaction.

"Harley, I am really sorry that you went through that," said Bill. "And I apologize for anything I said or did that was insensitive to you."

"You had a right to be upset."

"Still, I feel badly," said the dentist.

"I forgive you," said Harley, putting his hand on Bill's shoulder. "I know I made the trip very difficult for you. You didn't deserve to have to manage *un gringo loco*."

"*Gracias, mi pastor*," said Bill, smiling.

That afternoon, Harley sat down with Jefferson Jones in his office on the fifth floor of a modern steel-and-glass building in Woodbridge. Harley had called him after his walk with Kelly Westbrook and requested an appointment to talk about Justice Plaza and the flood. Jefferson responded by saying that his first open slot would be eleven days later, and Harley immediately jumped to the conclusion that the developer was trying to avoid him. But then Jefferson explained that he was undergoing chemotherapy and had a part-time schedule, spending time in the office just a few days a week. When Harley walked into his wood-paneled office and saw how gaunt Jefferson had become, he knew that the man had been telling the truth.

"I want you to know that I have no regrets about building Justice Plaza," said Jefferson, sitting in a high-backed executive chair behind an expansive glass-topped desk.

Harley sat in a comfortable chair with leather upholstery and padded arms, in front of the desk. Jefferson's secretary had brought Harley a cup of Kona coffee, and then left the room so that they could talk in private.

"But I have heard reports about the causes of the flood," said Jefferson, sipping a sparkling water. "Now I feel guilt—tremendous guilt—about constructing something that did damage to the town." He sighed, sat silently for a moment, and then added, "A town I love."

"Your mall was certainly a factor in the flood," said Harley, feeling compassion for the dying man, "but it was not the only cause."

"It was a major factor," confessed Jefferson. "I admit it. But I need to tell you why I did what I did."

Harley had always known that Jefferson was a complicated man, and his motivations were bound to be complex. "I want to hear it."

"I had such hatred for the landowner that I wanted to destroy his property," said the developer. "Wipe it out. He had a big farmhouse, where the KKK would meet. I knew about it as a boy, and it terrified me. The house was surrounded by acres of fields where he grew corn, and a large wooded area where he would hunt. The rumor was that he and his fellow Klansmen had lynched a man there."

Harley shuddered. "I can understand your fear," he said. "And your hatred."

"When the man got in trouble with his property taxes," Jefferson continued, "I began to assemble my money. I watched and I waited, preparing to do anything I could to buy his house and his land. When the property went on the market in a tax sale, I was the highest bidder. I put everything I had into the offer, and I was successful."

"You got justice," said Harley. "And you built Justice."

"Yes, that's what I called it," Jefferson nodded. "But I should have called it Revenge. I wanted to destroy his land and make him suffer. I built the biggest shopping center in the area, and surrounded it by an enormous parking lot. I cut down all of his trees and paved over all of his fields. I cut corners on stormwater management—I admit it—and I bribed some officials to get permission to build the biggest possible parking lot." He paused to sip his water, and then continued. "When the landowner drove by the mall, I wanted him to see black—endless black parking lot, built by a black man. And I wanted him to be green—green with envy that a man he looked down on was getting rich off his land."

Harley sat in silence, feeling Jefferson's passion. He knew that the old man had done wrong, but he found that it was hard to blame him.

"I wanted everyone to love Justice Plaza, full of beautiful stores with abundant parking. No one—black or white—would struggle to find a space, even at the peak of the Christmas season." Jefferson smiled slightly, thinking back.

"I'm sure it was a great place," said Harley, "but those parking lots? Not good . . . not good for the environment."

"That's true," admitted the old man. "'Impervious surfaces,' as they say. The water runs right off them. Justice Plaza turned into a funnel, channeling the flood waters down the hill."

"Much of it. Although some of the water came from elsewhere."

"Yes," said Jefferson, "but if Justice Plaza had remained fields and woods, Occoquan would have been spared."

"You're probably right," said Harley, remembering again what Juan had told him about the brake light mechanism. Jefferson's actions didn't have the effect he thought they would have—he thought he was pushing a racist neighbor, but he was actually releasing a flood.

"My anger got the best of me. It was righteous anger, but it clouded my judgment. I wanted to destroy a man, and I ruined a town."

Harley sat in silence, absorbing his words. But then he felt he needed to offer some grace. "We're not ruined," he said. "We'll rebuild."

"I may not live to see it," Jefferson said, with a catch in his voice. "I want to do something. I want to try to make things right."

Harley thought for a moment and then said, "You still own Justice Plaza, right?"

"Yes."

"Could you improve the parking at Justice before you sell it? Put in some of those things—what do they call them?" asked Harley. "Retention ponds? Could you change the pavement so it is not impervious?"

"I suppose," said Jefferson. "It would be expensive."

"Yes, true."

"But it would be the right thing to do."

"You're a rich man," Harley stated. "You know you can't take it with you."

"So true. Making some improvements would ease my mind, before I go."

"You pursued justice before," said Harley. "Now choose righteousness."

Jefferson's eyebrows went up. "What do you mean by that?"

"Righteousness is right relationship. Right relationship with God, and right relationship with the people around you."

Jefferson pondered these words for a moment, and then said, "I'll do something. I want to be right: Right with God, and right with Occoquan."

21

The shortest day of the year was ushered in by a night of heavy rain, followed by thick fog on the river. Harley looked at the calendar in his kitchen and saw that it was Friday, December 21, the day of the winter solstice, when sunset occurred just a few minutes before five in the evening, creating the longest of nights. The night was huge for pagans, and it was meaningful for many Christians as well, especially those who gathered for "Longest Night" services that focused their prayers on dark times—the death of a loved one, the loss of a job, living with cancer, or adjusting to a separation or divorce. Churches had discovered that the Christmas season was not a bright and happy time for every member of the congregation, and such services gave people opportunities to acknowledge their pain and pray for healing and help. Since the days became longer and longer after the winter solstice, there was reason to believe that light can return and darkness can be overcome.

But Riverside Methodist Church was not offering a Longest Night service that evening, so Harley was simply getting ready for another day at the office, one that would be filled with preparations for the Fourth Sunday of Advent and Christmas Eve, which were on back-to-back days. As a pastor, he hated when Christmas occurred too close to a Sunday, creating confusion between the message of Advent and the story of Christmas. Much better was when Christmas fell on a Wednesday or Thursday, creating enough space so that the two seasons could maintain their integrity. *Easter is always on a Sunday,* he mused, *so why can't Christmas always be on a Wednesday?* Yes, he knew that December 25 was tied to the Roman Saturnalia, which had been a convenient time for early Christians to celebrate the birth of Jesus. *But since the date itself has no religious significance, why not just move it to a convenient day of the week?* Sipping his morning coffee, he wondered about the possibility of such a change, and the daunting logistics of getting every major Christian body to agree to make the shift. *Where would I even begin? With my congregation, my clergy group, my bishop? Or should I go big and send a suggestion directly to the pope?*

Harley imagined the change to the calendar: Easter Sunday, Christmas Wednesday. *It started right here in Occoquan.*

Realizing that the idea would go nowhere, Harley rinsed his cup in the sink, straightened his tie, and pulled on his winter coat. Stepping onto the porch, he looked north toward the river and watched the fog move slowly eastward with the current. Everything around him looked damp and dreary, wet from the night of rain and unable to dry out because of the blanket of fog. Looking at the side of his house, he noticed that even the whimsical colors of his Victorian townhouse were muted, their brilliance no match for the gloom. Walking down his wrought-iron stairs, he saw that mud covered his sidewalk, and puddles dotted the parking lot, making the dark day even more depressing. Harley knew that abnormal rain was becoming the new normal in the Washington area—yet another unwanted consequence of climate change.

Dodging the puddles, he stepped into Mill Street and set a course for the church. After turning the corner onto Washington Street, he ran into Paul Ranger, the man whose dark and damp basement matched the feel of the day. "Take no part in the unfruitful works of darkness," said Paul to the Ephesians, "but instead expose them." Harley realized that he had done nothing to expose Paul Ranger's works of darkness, nor had he even discussed them. Maybe he had failed as a pastor in this regard, and maybe not—after the relocation of the erotica, Paul had certainly failed to follow up with him. But in any case, vintage porn was not Harley's biggest concern on that particular day.

"Good morning, Paul," he greeted him.

"Same to you," said the thin man.

"What are you up to today?"

"Christmas shopping," said Paul, pointing to the jewelry store owned by Youssef and Sofia Ayad. "I want to get something for Mary."

Harley nodded, feeling a rush of sadness. He had no one to shop for since the deaths of his wife and daughter. As much as he disdained the commercialization of Christmas, he missed being able to surprise his wife with a special piece of jewelry, something unexpectedly luxurious, under the tree. "Nice," he said to Paul. And then he followed with the question, "Got a minute?"

"Sure," said Paul. "I don't think they open until nine."

"At Thanksgiving, you said you had never seen or heard anything unusual at the castle."

"That's right. It's creepy . . . but quiet."

"I've seen some lights there at night," Harley said.

"Really? I've never seen that."

"Never?" pressed Harley.

"No. Why would I? I just do maintenance. I never go there at night."

"Well, I'm convinced that something is going on in the place."

Paul paused for a moment, wondering what Harley was thinking. Then he said, "If I saw anything, I would certainly tell Jefferson. Maybe even call the police."

"So, here's what I'm wondering: Can I go to the castle with you? Go inside?"

"That's kind of odd, Harley," said Paul. Now it was Harley's turn to pause. Paul continued by asking, "Are you doing some kind of investigation?"

"No," said Harley, shading the truth. "I'm just curious."

"Well, I guess," Paul said. "No harm in it. I'll be stopping by tomorrow morning, just to make sure everything is in good shape. Check for leaks and whatnot."

"Could I join you?"

"Okay. Meet me at my house at ten."

∽

After a long day of service preparation and sermon writing, Harley's back was hurting, his vision was blurry, and he was feeling weary. His coffee pot was empty, but he knew that caffeine was not going to help him. What he needed was some exercise. So, at about half past three, he returned home, changed his clothes, and then powered his car up the hill to his gym in Lorton. The place was buzzing with activity, the polar opposite of his lifeless church office, and Harley felt invigorated by the change of scenery. Looking around the cavernous big box, he saw people on treadmills and stationary bicycles trying to shed a few pounds before the holiday, and at first he wondered if he would be able to find a bike for his workout. But then he wandered into the cinema studio and found one in the first row, so he was able to pedal hard for an hour while watching the Christmas classic *Home Alone*, one his favorites. While most people enjoyed the pratfalls of the thieves being tortured by the resourceful little boy, pastor Harley always got teary-eyed at another scene: The Christmas Eve conversation between the old man and the boy in a nearly-empty church.

"You've been a good boy this year?" asks the old man.

"I think so," says the boy.

"You swear to it?"

"No."

"I had a feeling," says the old man. "Well, this is the place to be if you're feeling bad about yourself."

Emerging from the darkness, Harley blinked as his eyes adjusted to the bright light of the main floor. He wiped his face with a towel and decided that he needed to rehydrate, so he walked toward the juice bar that was located near the entrance. He ordered a mango smoothie and then turned around to see if there was an empty seat in the café area. Sitting in the corner, by herself at a table for two, was Kelly Westbrook. She was looking down at her hands, and seemed upset.

With drink in hand, Harley walked slowly to the table, not wanting to startle her. "Kelly?" he said.

She looked up with puffy eyes. "Hey, Harley," she said without smiling.

"May I join you?" he asked.

She paused a moment but then said "Okay," and pointed to the chair in front of her.

"Happy Yule," he said as he sat down.

"Same to you."

"Got any plans?" he asked.

"Not really," she said. "There's a gathering, but I'm not going."

Harley sipped his smoothie in silence. He didn't want to pry.

"Not up for it," she said, completing her thought.

"Well, I've been gearing up for Christmas," said Harley. "Busy time."

"Yeah, I bet."

"Everybody loves Christmas. Larger crowds than Easter."

"Does that surprise you?" asked Kelly.

"Well, Easter is much more important as a religious holiday—you know, there wouldn't be Christianity without the resurrection. But Christmas is a bigger holiday all around, with the parties and concerts and presents. No one goes shopping for Easter presents!"

"Right about that," said Kelly, smiling slightly.

"So, I always find Christmas to be more stressful. All of the other activity makes the season much busier."

Kelly nodded, but sat quietly. Her mind was clearly on other things. Then, to make conversation, she asked, "How was your workout?"

"Good," he said. "An hour on the stationary bike. In the cinema."

"That helps the time to pass quickly," she said, "but at lot of people slack off in there."

"I bet," said Harley. "There's no instructor like you, cracking the whip."

"Well, you want a good workout, don't you?"

"Sure thing," said Harley. "I try to crank up the resistance, even when I'm watching a movie."

"How many calories did you burn?"

"About four hundred," he said.

"Not bad," she said. "I'll give you a passing grade."

Harley finished his smoothie and then asked, "Do you have another class today?"

"No," she said. "I'm done. I'm just killing some time before a staff meeting at six."

Sensing that she was struggling, he wanted to do something to help. After all, he owed her: She had saved his life. Taking a chance, he said, "Want to go for a walk?"

"A walk?" she said.

"Yeah. Just around the area. There's a park next door. I've got nothing until dinner, and you are killing time till six."

Kelly wasn't sure what he was up to, but she felt a walk might do her good. After thinking for a second, she said, "Why not?"

The two of them pulled on their winter coats and headed for the door. When they stepped through the glass doors, Harley pointed to the sky and said, "There it is. Sunset. The longest night begins."

"Solstice," said Kelly. "Tomorrow, the light returns."

The afternoon was unseasonably warm, so they didn't have to zip up their coats. "It's been a strange day," said Harley. "Did you hear the thunder and see the rainbows?"

"No, I didn't," said Kelly. "I was teaching classes all day."

"It was weird," Harley said as they walked toward the park. "The storms got me up from my desk and looking out my window."

"'When shall we three meet again,'" said Kelly, "'in thunder, lightning, or in rain?'"

"You like Shakespeare?" Harley asked, surprised.

"That line, at least."

"Well, we certainly had some thunder."

"Glad it is over now," she said, looking at the scattered clouds that were drifting across the sky as the sun dropped below the horizon.

"Absolutely," said Harley as they took the path into the woods. "I am so done with rain."

The two of them walked for a minute in silence, side by side, and then Harley glanced at her. In profile, with her auburn hair pulled back in a ponytail and her gaze focused forward, she looked like a Roman statue, except for a hint of color in her porcelain cheeks. Suddenly, she turned to him and said, "I left John because of his lying."

Harley nodded, not knowing what to say.

"I cannot tolerate lying," she said forcefully.

Harley said, "I understand."

"You know the dead man, Enrique?" she asked him. "I found his phone number on John's phone. I had asked to see his phone, to get the number of a friend. He gave it to me, and while I was scrolling, I saw two names I had never seen before, Jesus and Enrique."

"Okay," said Harley.

"I said, 'Who's Jesus?' John looked surprised, but smiled and made some crack about Jesus Christ. Then he said, 'Just kidding: A guy I know, a guy at work.' Then I asked, 'Enrique?' John paused a second, just a second too long, and then said, 'He's at the auto shop.' I sensed he was lying, so I checked it out. I stopped by the auto shop the next day, and there was no Enrique."

"John just made that up?"

"Right. So, I confronted him again, and he said that Enrique used to work there, but now he was gone. I called BS on that, and told him to give me the phone. I wanted to call the number and see who it was. He gave me the phone but he had deleted the number."

"That must have made you mad."

"You have no idea," Kelly said, her green eyes flashing. "I was furious. I told him that we had to be truthful with each other—that's something I had *always* said to him. I said that I thought that the Enrique on his phone was the dead man, and I wanted to know why it was there. He said again it was the auto guy. I said no—it's got to be the dead Enrique."

"What did he say to that?" asked Harley.

"He just said no, it's not. Said he didn't know that Enrique. I asked if he knew anything about the death. He told me, 'Just what the police said—gang versus gang.'"

"You know," said Harley, "I've heard that John has been seen in the street, talking to Latinos."

"Yeah, I asked him about that, and he said that he was talking to them about their tattoos."

"Did you believe that?" asked Harley.

"Not really. He's a liar, and the Enrique thing—the last straw. After he wouldn't tell me the truth about the phone number, I left."

The two continued to walk, and the woods around them became darker and darker. Then Harley said, "I get that being truthful is really important to you. Why is that?"

She thought for a moment, and then said, "It goes back to Durham."

"Back to your childhood?"

"Yes," she nodded. "Back to Ransom." Although the evening was not cold, Harley felt a chill go down his spine.

"You want to talk about it?"

"I guess so," she said. "The truth is important, so I'll give it to you straight. Remember Pastor Cornbluff?"

Harley nodded and said, "Yes."

"Well, he molested me. When I was a child, he took me alone into his office, saying he wanted to show me something special. Then he hugged me and put his hands up my skirt and inside my underwear."

Harley stopped walking and muttered, "Oh, God." His stomach was turning.

"I knew it was wrong, so I broke free and ran out of the office," said Kelly, face to face with Harley. "I found my mother and told her all about it. Guess what? She didn't believe me. I told my father, and he didn't believe me. I told the truth, and no one believed me."

"That's terrible," said Harley.

"Sure is," said Kelly, putting her hands on her hips. "I felt completely powerless, isolated and alone. Worst years of my life."

"I believe it."

"Then," Kelly continued, "years later, I met my first witch. I was in college, and a woman who was a couple years ahead of me told me that she was Wiccan. She said that women are often powerless in this world, but witches have power. She said she practiced magic—she could cause changes to occur, based on her will. And she believed in both a God and a Goddess, which sounded good to me. There I was, a victim of abuse in the church, feeling powerless and alone, looking for something to believe in, hungry for people I could trust. Wicca became my path."

Harley stood in silence, absorbing the force of her words. He felt deep shame about what the church had done to her, and how abuse by a pastor had driven her into witchcraft. "I am so deeply sorry," he said to her. "What was done to you was a violation of my faith."

"Well, as you know, I'm not alone," she said. "Many kids have been abused by pastors."

Harley nodded, knowing she was speaking the truth. But he didn't want to be passive. "So, tell me," he said. "How has Wicca helped you?"

"It has been my spirituality," she said. "Wicca, you've got to understand, is not so much a religion as it is a way of life. It puts me in touch with nature and its cycles, and gives me a sense of control. I'm drawn to its magic, which gives me access to the forces of nature. I try to practice good magic, focused on healing and protection. I'll only curse someone if they curse me."

"And how has it turned out for you?" asked Harley.

Kelly seemed a bit surprised by the question. "What do you mean?"

"Has it worked?"

"Well, I like to be in touch with nature," she said.

"So do I."

"But, to be honest," she said, looking down, "it hasn't really worked."

"Want to sit down?" asked Harley, pointing to a park bench.

They sat side-by-side, and Kelly looked down at her hands. "I have tried to practice all the rituals, but they don't seem to have an effect. My spells don't work, on myself or anyone else. I want light, but my world just gets darker and darker."

"Sounds awful," said Harley.

"Maybe my will isn't strong enough," said Kelly, turning toward him.

"Maybe you've been praying to the wrong God."

"I've got no *use* for your God," she snapped, her words echoing through the woods.

"I understand," said Harley, pausing for a second. But then, after taking a deep breath, he said, "Let's talk about Jesus. He would condemn what was done to you. Absolutely. Do know what Jesus said about a person who causes one of his little ones to stumble? He should have a millstone hung around his neck, and he should be thrown into the sea."

"Sounds about right," said Kelly.

"Here's the thing about Jesus," said Harley: "Not only does he speak the truth, but he *is* the truth. Jesus takes what is true about life and puts it in human form: Reverence, humility, strength, compassion."

"Those are part of Wicca as well," Kelly said.

"If Wicca has access to the truth, I don't doubt it," said Harley. "But Jesus embodies these qualities. By that, I mean that he makes them incarnate—in human flesh. I believe that Jesus is both fully human and fully divine, the perfection of the natural world. Jesus lived on earth, but gave us a window to heaven."

Kelly sat quietly, staring into the darkness of the woods in front of her.

"It also matters to me that Jesus was abused," Harley said. *Laid on him was the iniquity of us all.* That got Kelly's attention; she turned and gave him a quizzical look. "Jesus was beaten and hung on a cross after being abandoned by his friends. Jesus experienced the same kind of pain and isolation and darkness that we feel. He understands what we go through and empathizes with us. He didn't come to have power over us, but to suffer with us. To be a suffering servant."

Kelly absorbed this for a moment and then said, "Okay." She paused again, and then said, "Sounds good, in theory. But if Jesus is a suffering—what did you say, 'suffering servant'?—why do some of his followers cause so much suffering?"

"I don't know," admitted Harley. "We are sinners, each and every one of us. That's why Jesus is not just a suffering servant, he's a savior."

"So, people keep sinning," she said, "and he keeps saving?"

"Some people do keep sinning," admitted Harley. "But most of us want to follow his way, understand his truth, live his life. We need to be forgiven, yes, but we also try to walk in his way."

Harley realized that he needed to speak in a way that was less theological and more personal. "Kelly, I want to know the truth as much as you do, because Jesus says that the truth will make you free. I want to know the truth about what is going on in *el Castillo*, because it might be connected to all of the violence around us. The truth might actually save us."

Kelly sat quietly for a moment, thinking about what Harley was saying. Then she looked at her watch and said that she had better get back to the gym. "I do sometimes think," she said quietly, "that I need help from something outside of myself."

Harley nodded and said, "That's the core of what I believe: I need power from outside. I cannot make life right, all by myself."

"I'll think about this," said Kelly, touching Harley's left hand.

"This is a good night for that," said Harley.

"Why is that?"

"Tomorrow, the light begins to return. That's why we are about to celebrate Christmas. Jesus is the light, coming into the world."

The two of them got up and walked back to the gym, under a moon that was brilliant and almost full.

22

When Harley opened the door to leave his house on Saturday morning, a young woman in a headscarf was standing on his porch. "Merry Christmas," she said, smiling broadly. "I was just about to ring your bell."

"Sarah, come in," he said. As always, he was struck by how much she resembled her mother Fatima, not just in appearance but in mannerisms.

"No, I really shouldn't intrude," she said. "I just wanted to bring you a present."

"Well, at least get out of the cold," he insisted. She stepped inside the kitchen and Harley closed the door behind her.

"We want you to have this coffee cake," she said, handing him a bakery box with a green and red ribbon, "as a thank you."

"You shouldn't have."

"No, we want to," she said. "You are a good customer and a good friend."

"My pleasure," said Harley. He put the box on the kitchen table, untied the ribbon, and opened the box. The cake was still warm, and it filled the air with the aroma of sugar and cinnamon. "Smells delicious."

"We hope you have a very nice Christmas," Sarah said.

"This gift will help," said Harley, smiling. "It is nice of you to think of me at this time of year."

"Jesus is important to us," said the young woman. "The story of his birth is in the Quran, you know, and he is mentioned more than anyone else in the book."

"I wasn't aware of that."

"Yes, he plays a very special role," said Sarah. "He is the last prophet before Muhammad, and we believe he will return in a second coming."

"Interesting," said Harley. "I was preaching on that just a few weeks ago."

"But for me," Sarah added, her brown eyes sparkling, "he is much more... personal. When I hear the name of Jesus, my heart fills with love and light." Harley was surprised to hear her say that, and it struck him that many of his own church members didn't have such feelings for Jesus. "Yes, he is the most loving of the prophets for me," she continued, "the most tender, the most beautiful, the most inspiring."

"I'm glad to hear that," said Harley. "I hope that his birthday will be a very special day for you."

"We will think of you, and your congregation, on Christmas Day," said Sarah. "And now, if you will excuse me, I need to get back to the shop."

"Of course," said Harley, opening the door for her. "I'll follow you out." They walked down the steps together, and the two of them separated on Mill Street. As she headed back to the Riverview Bakery, headscarf cascading like water over the rocks in the river, Harley felt thankful for his friendship with Sarah and her family, a completely unexpected gift of his time in Occoquan. *And her passion for Jesus—what a surprise! A Muslim was loving Jesus, right after a witch was talking theology. What is the world coming to?* Looking up, he saw that the longest night of the year had been replaced by brilliant blue skies, with a brightness that hurt his eyes after so many dark and rainy days. Yes, the light was beginning to return, slowly but surely. In fact, the length of daylight on Saturday was going to be one whole second longer than the daylight on Friday.

∽

Turning the corner onto Commerce Street, Harley arrived at Paul's house just a few minutes after ten o'clock. Paul was standing outside in his coat, talking to Jason Weiss, who was sitting in the Town of Occoquan golf cart, wearing a heavy coat and wool cap.

"I was beginning to wonder about you," said Paul to Harley.

"Had an unexpected visitor."

"It's your busy time, I know," said Paul.

"How are you doing, Jason?" asked Harley.

"Okay," said Jason, shrugging. "A little cold to be working outside today."

"What does Tim have you doing?"

"Mostly trash pickup," said the young man. "The cans fill up during the shopping season."

"I bet," said Harley. "I hope business is getting back to normal."

"Mary says it is still a bit off," Paul interjected. "At least that's what the merchants tell her."

"She would know," said Harley.

"So, you want to head over to the Castle?" asked Paul.

"Sure thing," said Harley. And then, feeling an impulse to include Jason, he asked the teenager, "Want to drive us?"

"Uh," said Jason. "Guess so. Beats picking up trash."

"We won't be long," promised the pastor.

The Town of Occoquan golf cart was a stretch version, with two seats in the front, a section for tools and trash cans in the middle, and a bench seat at the back, allowing riders to hop on and ride backwards. Harley let Paul have the seat next to Jason, and then he climbed on the rear and said, "Let's roll."

The three of them buzzed down the hill to Mill Street and then headed west toward the pedestrian bridge. Merchants were opening their shops, no doubt hoping for good sales on the last Saturday before Christmas, a shopping day blessed by clear skies and snow-free streets. Harley waved to a few of them from his perch on the back of the cart, and then grabbed the side rails for stability when Jason made a sharp right turn toward the bridge. Although the span was not wide enough for a car or a truck, it handled the golf cart quite easily, and Harley got a thrill out of speeding across the bridge and listening to the wooden planks clattering underneath him. For a second, he was transported back in time, to when the pedestrian bridge was the only bridge in Occoquan, capable of handling all of the traffic coming down from the City of Fairfax. It was a narrow, two-lane steel bridge that spanned the river and allowed motorists to drive south on Ox Road, cross into the Town of Occoquan by the old mill, and then make their way toward Richmond. But then Hurricane Agnes hit the bridge with a wall of water and knocked it off its piers. *A disaster*, thought Harley, *and maybe not the last.*

After crossing the river, they drove up the hill on the northern shore, passing the ancient rocks that had been looking down on Occoquan for hundreds of millions of years. Then they zipped down the driveway to *el Castillo*, and fishtailed slightly when Jason slammed on the brakes at the bottom of the hill. "Sure beats walking," said Harley.

"What's this place all about?" asked Jason, seeing the strange building up close for the first time.

"Long story," said Harley. "Built by a wine merchant about forty years ago. But it has a unique basement, carved out of solid rock. And people say it's spooky."

"That's just talk," said Paul, walking toward the heavy wooden door.

"Well, I'm curious," Harley said. "I want to see it for myself."

"Me too," said Jason, hopping out of the cart.

Paul removed the padlock from the door and opened it. They entered and walked around the deserted living room, inhaling the smell of newly installed wall-to-wall carpet. "Jefferson just had the carpet put down," Paul said as he poked his head into the kitchen, checking to make sure everything was in good order. "He really wants to sell this place."

"Check out the view," said Harley to Jason. The two of them looked through the plate glass windows at the sparkling Occoquan River. With no leaves on the trees, the panorama was spectacular. But when Harley dropped his gaze to the lifeless winter grass that extended to the shoreline, he felt a wave of dread, rising out of nowhere. *Is that where the little girl drowned?* His eyes darted back and forth along the rocky shore. *But wait, no. That was not real. Or was it?*

"Best view in town," said Paul, walking up behind them. "Although, technically, this is not in town."

"Still, pretty nice," said Jason.

Harley wanted a change of focus, so he asked, "Can we see the basement?"

"Why not?" said Paul. He led them to a door near the entryway, and opened it. Flipping on the lights, he began to walk down a set of wooden stairs into the rock basement, followed by Harley and Jason. Rough-hewn walls surrounded them on all four sides, with no windows for natural light. The only illumination came from two bare bulbs in ceiling fixtures, which left the corners of the room shrouded in darkness. Reaching the plank floor, Harley sensed that the basement was much cooler than the first floor of the house, and it seemed to be drafty. Putting the palm of his hand on the stone wall, he sensed that air was coming through cracks in the rocks.

"It's like a cave," said Jason. Harley flipped the light switch at the bottom of the stairs off and on, just to get a sense of how dark it was.

"Used as a prison during the Revolutionary War," said Harley.

"Again, just talk," said Paul.

"No, that's a fact," said Harley. Then, with a smile, he added, "But not something you put in the real estate listing."

The three men wandered around the room, listening to the planks of the floor creaking under their steps. "Creepy," said Jason as he looked around the space. "So cold. So quiet."

"Wait a second," said Paul. "That's different."

"What?" asked Harley.

"That old table. It used to be against the wall. Now it is over there."

"Who moved it?" asked Jason.

"I have no idea," said Paul. "It's where a storage rack used to be." The three men walked to the table, and began to inspect the floor beneath it. Harley spotted something.

"You said there was a trap-door, right?" he asked.

"Yeah," said Paul.

"Well, I think we found it," said Harley. "Under this table." *The angel plunged the key into the ground, turned it, and through the dirt of the ground lifted up a heavy trap door that marked the entrance to a dark and bottomless pit.*

"Cool," said Jason. "Let's open it."

Paul didn't want to get in trouble with Jefferson, but his curiosity got the best of him. "Guess it wouldn't hurt," he said, pushing the table to one side. Harley found a finger-hole at the edge of the trap door, and used it to pull the door open. Steps had been cut into the rock below, leading down into a sub-cellar that was six feet long, four feet wide, and about three feet deep.

"Looks like a grave," said Jason.

As Harley finished opening the trap-door, Paul descended the steps into the darkness beneath them. "What the hell?" he said, reaching down and picking up a package of powder that was the size of a brick. "Drugs?"

"I hate drugs," said Jason. "I don't want to be here. I'm leaving."

At that point, the three heard voices coming from upstairs. Someone was entering the house. A man called out, "Who's in here?"

Jason recognized the voice and whispered to Harley, "It's John." Another man spoke with a strong Spanish accent.

"It's me, the caretaker," Paul replied. "I'm down here." Harley could tell that he was frightened but trying to sound calm.

The two men stomped down the wooden stairs, clearly annoyed to find people in the house. The first man down was a Latino, carrying a bat. Right behind him was John, who was surprised to see Harley and Jason.

"*Mi bola!*" shouted the Latino, pointing at the drugs. He looked to John, who shrugged his shoulders. Turning back to Paul, he demanded, "*Dámela!*"

Not understanding Spanish, Paul just stood there holding the package. The Latino lifted the bat and moved towards him, saying again, "*Dámela!*"

Harley intervened by translating, "Give it to . . ." But Paul panicked and dropped the package into the sub-cellar. *The serpent's muscular body coiled and began to strike.* Charging Paul, the Latino began to swing the bat in a long and powerful arc, causing Paul to cover his face in a ridiculous defensive gesture. Harley rushed towards Paul to shield him, and in that split second he remembered a completely unexpected line from Scripture, the one about the Lord laying on one man the iniquity of all. *That's me,* thought Harley, surprised by his clarity of thought. *Receiving the iniquity of this Latino and Paul and . . .*

The bat cut through the air, but it seemed to be moving in slow motion. *One second is a thousand years and a thousand years are one second.* Time seemed to be standing still as Harley threw his body into the spot between Paul and the bat. *The suffering servant. The lamb being led to slaughter . . .*

Harley prepared for impact.

Then the lights went out, plunging the entire room into total darkness. Harley's forward momentum knocked Paul down, and as the two of them tipped over they heard the bat swoosh above their heads. But they didn't simply fall to the floor. They kept tumbling into the pitch-black sub-cellar, where their impact was cushioned by a huge pile of drug packages. As they hit the ground, a cloud of powder enveloped them. *Painful . . . but not heart-attack painful.*

Up above, the lights came back on and John Jonas grabbed the drug dealer, pulling him away from the sub-cellar. The man took a short swing at John with the bat, hitting his upper arm and driving him back. This created a face-off between the Latino and John, but then Jason joined the fight, fueled by his intense hatred for drugs and drug dealers and anyone who reminded him of his father. He cursed the Latino and drew his attention away from John, and the Latino responded by swinging his bat back and forth, between John and Jason, unsure of how he should defend himself or how he should attack. The three were at a stand-off, but none of them was going to back down, fueled as they were by rage and adrenaline.

Then, the sound of police sirens filled the air. The Latino looked for a way out, saw the stairs and raced up in a panic, only to be met by six Prince William County Police officers, guns drawn.

Violence had erupted, quickly and unexpectedly, and now it was over.

Harley and Paul climbed out of the sub-cellar, bodies aching from their fall but grateful to be alive. "You look like a ghost," said Harley to Paul, pointing at the dusting of drugs all over his body.

"You too, pastor," said the caretaker, massaging his elbow. "My right arm is killing me. I am way too old to be taking falls like that."

John had gone up the stairs behind the Latino, leaving Jason to help the two men. "You guys are lucky," he said as he brushed them off. "That bat could have messed you up."

"Right about that," said Harley. "Who turned off the light?"

"John did," said Jason. "Turned it off and then turned it back on."

"Wonder why," asked Paul.

"I guess to protect you," said Jason. "I don't think he wanted that guy to hurt you."

"I'm confused," said Harley, rubbing his aching head. "It seemed like they were together, but maybe not."

At that point, two police officers came down the stairs, yelling at them to lie down with arms extended and hands visible. Their guns were out and they were all business, determined to establish control over the situation. After patting them down and ascertaining that they had no weapons, they allowed them to sit up for questioning.

"What were you doing down here?" asked the first officer, a burly guy whom Harley recognized as the officer from the day of the flood. *Great, him again*. Paul introduced himself as the caretaker, and said that he, Harley, and Jason were on a routine maintenance visit.

"Routine?" said the second officer. "So why are you covered with powder?" The cop had a right to be suspicious.

"It seems to be drugs," said Paul, brushing his arm. "We discovered them in the sub-cellar, right before that guy attacked us."

"Show us," said the second officer, pulling out a huge flashlight.

Harley and Paul stood up slowly, aching from their fall, with an assist from Jason. They moved slowly toward to trap door, not wanting to make any moves that would agitate the officers.

"That's quite a stash," said the burly officer, peering down into the sub-cellar.

"You say you found them today?" asked the second.

"Just a little while ago," said Paul. "I've been down here many times, but I had never opened the door to the sub-cellar. Had no reason to."

"We'll have to take you to the station for a statement," said the first officer. "A team will come to secure this area."

"Who owns the house?" asked the second officer.

"Jefferson Jones," said Paul. "He's not involved in any of this. He's just trying to sell the house."

"We'll need a statement from him as well," said the burly officer.

As the five of them walked up the wooden stairs to the first level, Harley asked the second officer, "Who is the guy who attacked us?"

The officer didn't seem to want to answer at first. Instead, he asked, "Who are you?"

"Harley Camden. Pastor of Riverside Methodist Church."

"Really?" The information came as a surprise and seemed to soften the officer's attitude. "His license says Jesus Alvarado. Do you know him?"

Harley shook his head and said, "Never seen him before." As they walked out of *el Castillo* into the bright sunshine, Harley was amazed by the number of law enforcement officers that had assembled. There were three squad cars with lights flashing, and the back seat of one car contained Jesus Alvarado. Two officers were talking with John Jonas, another was placing the baseball bat into an evidence bag, and another was sealing off the area with police tape. As Harley looked around the scene, a large police panel truck rolled down the driveway. *Probably a group of specialists to deal with the drugs.*

"Is that your golf cart?" asked the burly officer.

Jason raised his hand and said, "Yes."

"Take out the key and leave it here. You can get it after your statement."

"Yes, sir," said Jason, clearly intimidated.

"Don't go anywhere," said the officer. "We'll transport you to the station in just a minute."

"Are these drugs going to hurt us?" asked Paul, pointing to himself and Harley.

"Probably not," said the officer. "As long as you did not ingest them."

"Not intentionally," said Paul.

"But just to be safe, our specialists will check you out," he said.

Harley, Paul and Jason stood outside *el Castillo*, feeling shocked and overwhelmed by the drama that had unfolded since their arrival at the house.

"Looks like your trash pickup will have to wait," said Harley to Jason, trying to lighten the mood.

"Tim will be mad," said the young man.

"Yeah, at first," said Harley. "But he'll understand. This is a big deal, what just happened here."

"You're right," nodded Paul. "A major drug bust. Biggest ever for Occoquan, I'd say."

"And you had a role in it," said Harley to Jason. "You helped the police to get their guy."

For a moment, Jason quietly absorbed what they were saying, and then whispered, "Guess so."

"Guys!" said John Jonas as he walked over to the three men. "Looks like we are all going downtown. We'll have to make statements."

"Who is that guy . . . Jesus?" asked Harley.

"A bad *hombre*," said John. "A leader of MS-13. I think he is going away for a long time."

"Did you know him?" Jason asked.

"Not really," said John. "Knew who he was. Knew him enough to get him over here." Harley was grateful to John for his actions, but was perplexed by his relationship with Jesus.

"So those are his drugs?" Paul asked.

"Looks like it," said John. "And that's not all. That bat of his? I saw blood on it."

"Blood?" asked Harley.

"Yeah, but not yours. He never hit you. Must belong to someone else. The police are going to check it out."

23

"He died in his sleep," said Tawnya Jones on the phone, her voice cracking. She called Harley while he was eating breakfast on Sunday morning, thinking he would want to get the news before he went to church. "He had been getting weaker every day, and then the police came to his home to get a statement about the drugs in the house across the river. That really upset him; you know how he likes to be in control of everything."

"Yes, I do," said Harley. He pictured the man sitting in his executive chair behind his expansive glass-topped desk, saying, "I wanted him to see black—endless black parking lot, built by a black man." Jefferson Jones was one of the most strong-willed people he had ever known, whether fiercely negotiating the price on a distressed piece of property or generously funding a legal defense fund for an Iraqi immigrant. Jefferson always knew what he wanted, and pursued it relentlessly. Harley would miss the intense, complicated, rat-faced old man.

"He went to bed after giving them his statement. When I stopped by in the afternoon, he pulled me close and said, 'Everything is falling apart.' I said, 'No, Dad. It will be okay. You had nothing to do with it.' He just closed his eyes and sighed."

"Tawnya, I am so very sorry," said Harley. "I know how close you were."

"At least I told him I loved him."

"I'm glad you did. Those moments are precious, and you never know which one will be the last."

"You're right," said Tawnya. "Look, I'll let you get to church. Just wanted you to know." Harley thanked her for calling, but wondered if Jefferson's intentions for Justice Plaza had died with him.

Worship at Riverside Methodist Church began outside the front door of the Sanctuary, under the recently repaired and repainted steeple. About a hundred worshipers spilled off the steps, across the sidewalk, and into the street, which didn't really matter on a quiet Sunday morning. "This is the Fourth Sunday of Advent," said Harley to the church members standing around in coats, hats and gloves. "We begin our worship with the rededication of our steeple, which points us to God and draws people to this church. Our psalm today is number eighty: 'Restore us, O God; let your face shine, that we may be saved.' We give thanks today that our steeple has been restored, thanks to the generosity of our congregation and the hard work of many skilled craftsmen. We dedicate it to the glory of God, with the hope that it will stand tall and strong for many years to come."

"No more steeple rot," shouted Sid Bennett, who had inherited the role of jokester from Arvin Natwick. A handful of people laughed, a few gave him dirty looks, and Harley invited everyone to move inside.

After an opening hymn and prayer, Harley cleared his throat and read the Scripture lesson for the day. "A reading from the twenty-second chapter of Revelation," he said.

> *Then the angel showed me the river of the water of life, bright as crystal, flowing from the throne of God and of the Lamb through the middle of the street of the city. On either side of the river is the tree of life with its twelve kinds of fruit, producing its fruit each month; and the leaves of the tree are for the healing of the nations.*

Harley closed his Bible and looked out over a sea of perplexed faces. Paul and Mary Ranger were in her usual pew, but Paul had his right arm in a sling after his fall into the sub-cellar. Bill Stanford had resumed his weekly attendance after discovering the cause of his pastor's bizarre behavior, and he shared a pew with Tie-dye Tim Underwood. Juan Erazo and Gretchen Bennett were sitting side-by-side, having bonded over their mission trip experience, and next to Gretchen was her husband, Sid. And much to Harley's surprise, both Leah Silverman and Kelly Westbrook were sitting in the back row. Everyone was curious about what Harley would say about such an unusual passage of Scripture.

"An ancient philosopher named Seneca gave this advice," said Harley, beginning his sermon: "Let all your efforts be directed to something, let it keep that end in view." Harley sensed that his church members had no idea who Seneca was, so he added, "Seneca was a Roman philosopher who lived just a few years after the ministry of Jesus." Then he returned to his text, saying, "Seneca was right, and his insights were picked up many years later by Steven Covey in his best-selling book, *Seven Habits of Highly*

Effective People." Harley saw some nods when he made this reference, so he continued by saying, "Covey suggests that one of the keys to successful and effective efforts is to 'begin with the end in mind.'"

Harley knew that this opening was not setting the house on fire, but it contained a point that he needed to make. "The Scripture I have chosen for this morning helps us to begin with the end in mind. It is designed to direct our efforts to something important, and to keep that end in view." Looking around, he saw that the people were staying with him, but he sensed that he needed to focus their attention as quickly as possible. "Tomorrow is Christmas Eve, as you know. Deck the halls! Don your holiday apparel! Finish your shopping . . . *please!* We will gather here tomorrow night to celebrate the birth of Jesus, and to hear the story of Joseph, Mary, Bethlehem, the shepherds, and the angels." With these words, Harley was offering the assurance that he had not forgotten about that beloved story—he was simply saving it for Christmas Eve. "That is the *beginning* of the story of Jesus, and we will celebrate it with lessons and carols. But since we need to begin with the end in mind, this morning I am giving you . . . *the end.*" Now he sensed that he had their attention. *Begin with the end in mind.*

"Yes," he continued, "today's Scripture is the end of the story. It is the goal to which God is moving, from the first day of creation to the end of time. In the Book of Revelation, an angel shows John the river of the water of life, bright as crystal, flowing from the throne of God and of the Lamb through the middle of the street of the city. At the end of time, there will be a river, clean and refreshing, as bright as crystal. It will flow from a throne shared by God and by the Lamb of God, Jesus Christ. And this river will flow through the middle of the street of the holy city. Notice what we see here: A river in the middle of a city. A river that flows through an inhabited area, much as the Occoquan River flows through our town. But is *our* river as bright as crystal? I'm afraid not."

Departing from his sermon text, Harley looked straight at his church members and said, "We've got a problem, here in Occoquan and around the world. I read this morning that ice is melting at a rate of fourteen thousand tons of water per second, contributing to rising sea levels. I cannot even begin to picture what that looks like, fourteen thousand tons of water per second, but I can imagine that it is going to have an impact. NASA is reporting that seas have been rising by about three millimeters each year. That seems small, on a yearly basis, but it will add up." Pointing north towards the Occoquan, Harley asked, "How long will our river stay within its banks? Some scientists are saying that sea levels could rise three feet by the year 2100. Three feet! Friends, we have a problem, a serious problem." In the sea of faces in front of him, Harley saw only one smile, and it was on the face of Leah Silverman, who was clearly agreeing with his message. "Climate change is real," he continued. "Temperatures could rise between two and ten degrees Fahrenheit over the next century, causing destructive heat waves and extreme weather events. We've seen that this fall, haven't we? Our town has been slammed by an extreme weather event. We are still recovering from it."

Feeling that his congregation was with him, he returned to his text. "If the relationship between the river and the city was nothing more than a scientific thing, I would not be preaching on it. But because it matters to God—because it appears in the Bible—I have to proclaim it to you. God wants there to be harmony between water and cities, and between plant life and human developments. That is why the next line from Revelation says, 'On either side of the river is the tree of life with its twelve kinds of fruit, producing its fruit each month; and the leaves of the tree are for the healing of the nations.' Consider that very carefully: In the middle of the city, on either side of the river, is the tree of life. The city and the river and the tree of life all live in harmony. And the leaves of the tree are for the healing of the nations."

Harley paused to let that message sink in. "Begin with the end in mind. Begin your celebration of Christmas with an awareness of where Jesus is leading you. Jesus is moving toward a throne in a city that has a remarkable balance with a river and a tree of life. He wants you to work for such a life of balance as well." With that line, he saw a smile on the face of the witch, Kelly Westbrook. *She likes balance, for sure. City, river. Heaven, earth. Physical, spiritual.* And then shifting his attention back to Leah, he remembered that she was not interested in saving souls, but in saving the earth. *Well, maybe I can do both.*

"Many of you know that I had some psychological problems in Honduras this year," he continued. "They were caused by a drug interaction, but that's a story I can tell some other time. What I want to share with you today is a discovery I have made about the Mayans, a people that had an advanced civilization in the Copán region many years ago. I just came across a journal entry I wrote when I was on a dig there in the 1980s, an entry that I think speaks to us today.

> *What caused Copán to collapse? The expanding population of the city caused people to move to the hills and mountains around the Copán Valley, and there they stripped the trees off the slopes to make room for agriculture. This caused massive erosion of the soil, and the lack of trees allowed disastrous floods to sweep through Copán during the rainy season. Skeletal remains from this period*

show evidence of malnutrition and infectious diseases. The end of the kingdom probably occurred around 822. After this time, people continued to live in poverty in Copán, but over time they moved away from the ruined valley. The end came not from unhappy gods or defeated kings, but from a population that failed to live in harmony with nature.

Again, Harley paused. "That was my journal entry from over thirty years ago," he said. "But I think it has a message for us today, just like the ancient Book of Revelation has a message for us today. The Mayan kingdom in Copán was destroyed by failure to care for the environment. The people failed to live in sustainable ways. Our town was almost destroyed this fall by a flood caused by excessive development and a failure to manage water runoff." Harley had included a line in the sermon about Jefferson Jones and the problems with Justice Plaza, but he skipped over it out of respect for the grieving family.

"We have got to change our ways," he continued. "We have got to begin with the end in mind." He went on to make suggestions about how the people of Riverside could do a better job of caring for the environment by replacing inefficient light bulbs at home, turning off computers at night, and eliminating unnecessary car trips. He also invited them to form a "green team" at the church—one that would promote recycling, replace energy-inefficient equipment, and create a community garden.

After taking a sip of water, Harley returned to the Scripture lesson. "Notice that Revelation says that the leaves of the tree are for the healing of the nations. The tree of life desires our healing. God desires our healing. Jesus desires our healing. And not just personal healing, but the healing of the nations. The mission of Jesus that began on Christmas morning has an end in mind: The healing of the nations. Jesus wants to do this healing work, and he invites us to join him in that healing work. It means forgiving those who hurt us. Working for reconciliation in our personal lives and in our community and world as well. Feeding the hungry, sheltering the homeless, welcoming strangers, and visiting those who are in prison. Healing is what the mission of Jesus is all about. Begin with the end in mind."

Harley wasn't sure how Kelly would feel about the events that had occurred in *el Castillo,* since John Jonas had played such a central role. But on Saturday night he had added the story to his sermon, feeling that it fit his message well. He plowed ahead, even though Kelly was sitting in the congregation and she might not like it: "Perhaps you have heard about the events that occurred yesterday in the house across the river, 'the castle.' Paul Ranger is the caretaker there, and he took me with him on a maintenance visit. While we were there, a drug dealer entered the house and threatened us with a baseball bat. Our neighbor John Jonas acted boldly to help us, and spared us from serious harm." Harley omitted the part about inserting himself between the bat and Paul, not wanting to make the story about himself. "In the end," he said, "the police arrested the drug dealer and confiscated a huge stockpile of illegal drugs. They are also holding the dealer because he may have used his bat on someone else in our community—time will tell. The brave actions of the police have made our community a safer place. They have done the work of healing." *And the leaves of the tree are for the healing of the nations.*

Knowing that it was time to conclude the sermon, Harley said, "I look forward to being with you all tomorrow, as we celebrate the birth of Jesus. But as we do, let's remember that Christmas is simply the beginning of the story. The story continues through Christ's ministry, his death, his resurrection, his ascension, and the work he is doing to lead us all toward his heavenly kingdom. Let's begin with the end in mind, and put his heavenly values to work in our earthy lives. We can do the work of healing—as individuals, as a congregation, as a nation, and as a world. We can work for harmony between people, as well as harmony between our cities, our rivers, and the natural world around us." Then, looking for a biblical way to wrap up his message, Harley quoted the very last words of the Book of Revelation: "The grace of the Lord Jesus be with all the saints. Amen."

∽

Kelly shook Harley's hand at the door, and then she said, "My first church service in many years. Not bad."

"You like the sermon?" he asked. "Message of balance?"

"I didn't agree with everything," she said, "but that won't surprise you."

"Not surprised at all."

"Well, I'll see you around," she said, moving gracefully through the door.

"Can you talk?" he asked, hoping she would stick around.

"Sure," she said. "Now?"

"Give me a minute," said Harley. Kelly stepped aside and let him finish greeting the church members as they passed through the door. Harley got a few "nice sermons" from the polite people in the congregation, but he could tell that he missed the mark with most of them. Only Leah Silverman gave him a fist bump for his environmental message, and then suggested he use the Hebrew concept of *Tikkun Olam* in the future—a Jewish idea about repairing the world. "See you next year," she joked, fully aware that she visited Harley's church on rare occasions, usually around the holidays.

When the Sanctuary was empty, Harley asked Kelly to wait while he took off his robe and put on his winter coat. Then the two of them walked to the pizza place near River Mill Park. The restaurant had been heated up by the pizza oven, providing a cocoon of warmth on the cold December day.

"Want a glass of wine?" asked Harley as they sat down.

"Not a drinker," said Kelly, "but help yourself."

"I think I need one," said the pastor. "Didn't hit a home run this morning."

"Well, baseball is a game of failure," she said. "Maybe preaching is the same."

"Hit four out of ten and you get into the Hall of Fame."

"Exactly," she said.

They studied the menus, put in their order, and then Kelly pulled out a devotional book. "I got this in the lobby of your church," she said.

"Really?" said Harley. "I mean, 'good.' The books are there for people to pick up."

"I opened it to this story from the Book of Acts," she said.

> We met a slave girl who had a spirit of divination and brought her owners a great deal of money by fortune-telling. While she followed Paul and us, she would cry out, 'These men are slaves of the Most High God, who proclaim to you a way of salvation.' She kept doing this for many days. But Paul, very much annoyed, turned and said to the spirit, 'I order you in the name of Jesus Christ to come out of her.'

"Interesting story," said Harley, wondering how Kelly would react to it.

"I wouldn't say I have a spirit of divination," she said. "Like I told you before, my rituals don't seem to have an effect. My spells don't work."

"But still, you feel . . . what?"

"I feel a bit like that girl," said Kelly, softly. "I want to get out, go in a new direction."

"There is always a way," Harley assured her.

Kelly stared down at the devotional book, looking vulnerable. "So, to get free of a power, you just speak in the name of Jesus Christ?"

"That's it," said Harley. "We cannot fix our problems by ourselves. We need a power from outside ourselves. The best of these powers is Jesus."

"Why is he the best?" she asked.

"Because Jesus is nothing less than God," said Harley. "Really big. Really powerful. All things in heaven and on earth were created in him. One of the lines from the Bible that I like best is 'in him all things hold together.' Jesus is the glue. He holds everything together."

"I sometimes feel I need that."

"One of the names for God is 'I am who I am,'" explained Harley. "That's the name that God uses when Moses meets God at the burning bush. That says to me that God is the most real thing in the universe—God is who God is, and God will be who God will be. This God is whole, undivided, honest."

"Honesty is key," said Kelly, staring at Harley with her deep green eyes.

"You could say that God has integrity," said Harley. "I am who I am."

"That's what I'm looking for. And that's why I couldn't be with John."

"If God is 'I am who I am,'" Harley continued, "then those who oppose God are the opposite. A name for the devil might be, 'I am *not* who I am.' No integrity. Fragmented. Divided. Dishonest."

"I wouldn't go so far," said Kelly, "to say that John is evil."

"Nor would I," said Harley, holding up his hands. "Everyone has the image of God inside him. But there are people who follow a fragmented, divided, dishonest path."

"That's what John has done," said Kelly. "He has chosen a dishonest path, a path of lies."

Harley knew she was angry at John, and might be coming down a bit too hard on him. "But don't you think he showed some good actions yesterday, at *el Castillo*?"

"I don't know," she said. "I wasn't there."

"He acted to save me," said Harley. "I'm grateful to him for that. He could have let that guy Jesus break my head."

"Okay. But what happened before he saved you?"

Harley thought for a second, and then said, "Paul, Jason, and I were in the house, and then Jesus and John came down the stairs."

"So why were they together?" asked Kelly.

"I don't know," Harley said. "They just were." He still knew nothing about John's relationship with Jesus.

Their drinks were delivered: A glass of red wine for Harley and a cup of hot tea for Kelly. "I just think," said Kelly, "that you should get an answer to that question. Things may not be what they seem to be."

24

Harley could feel that rain was on its way to Occoquan as he left his townhouse and walked to church, under clouds that looked like they were made of dirty, unprocessed cotton. *What else but rain,* he thought, *after the wettest year in a century?* Although it would have been nice to start the New Year with a blanket of snow, one that would put a thin veneer of purity on the town, he knew that the temperatures in the forties wouldn't allow it. The day would be rain, nothing but cold rain, starting at about noon and soaking the muddy streets and sidewalks.

Harley always worked a half day on New Year's Eve, because people would stop at the church to drop off donations before the end of the calendar year. Church members that hadn't attended a single service all year would appear at his office and give him checks dated December 31, to be able to claim charitable contributions. Once, at his previous church, a member whom he hardly recognized had come to his door and handed him a check for ten thousand dollars. So, it was certainly worth his while to put in a few hours at the office, before the year ran out.

Christmas Eve had gone very well, with a large crowd of people gathering to sing carols, hear the story of the birth of Jesus, and join their voices for Silent Night, while holding candles in a darkened Sanctuary. The tradition at Riverside was to sing this carol without accompaniment, so at the end of the service the organ was shut off and the lights were dimmed. Harley walked to the Christ candle on the Communion Table and used it to light his own taper. Then he held up his light and spoke words based on the Gospel of John, "Jesus is the light of all people. The light shines in the darkness, and the darkness cannot overcome it." Then the choir filed past him, using their tapers to take the light from his, and as they walked down the center aisle, they began to sing Silent Night. Members of the congregation lit their tapers from the choir, and then passed the light down each pew as they joined their voices in the carol. By the third verse, the faces of all of the church members were illuminated by candlelight, and their voices blended in the sweet and haunting melody. Harley felt privileged to stand at the front and look out at the glowing congregation, a group of people who were determined—despite their many flaws and failures—to carry the light of Christ into the world.

But the first Sunday after Christmas was an entirely different story. When Harley entered the Sanctuary to start the morning service, he wondered where all of his committed Christians had gone. The congregation was just a handful of people, and the singing was anemic. Harley cut a few paragraphs out of his sermon, and no one seemed bothered when he pronounced the benediction before the end of the hour. "It's just the poor people here today," said Sid Bennett, shaking hands at the door. When Harley looked mystified, Sid said, "All the people with money are on vacation!"

After entering the church on Monday morning, Harley walked through the Sanctuary and picked up the stray bulletins that had been left in the pews. There wasn't much of a mess to clean up, given the poor attendance the day before, so he wouldn't have much to do in order to prepare the place for the first Sunday of the new year. Taking stock of the dimly lit room, he saw that the poinsettias in the front of the Sanctuary were beginning to wilt, and a garland of greenery had fallen off the front of the organ. The Christmas wreaths in the windows were still fresh, but they didn't seem nearly as festive as they had just a few days before. Even the black Jesus in the stained-glass window appeared lifeless that morning, with no bright sunshine to light his face. Realizing that he wasn't going to find much inspiration in the Sanctuary that morning, Harley moved quickly to his office and turned on his desk light and his computer. Then he started up the coffee pot, hoping that a shot of caffeine would pull him out of his funk.

As the coffee was gurgling, a knock came at his door. "Just a second," called Harley, realizing that he hadn't unlocked the outside door of his office, the one that provided entry at the top of the wooden stairs. Turning the lock and opening the door, he expected to see a church member with a check. But instead, he saw Abdul, looking grim.

"Good morning, pastor," said the powerfully-built man with the shaved head. He appeared larger than ever in his wool coat, and he towered over Harley. "Do you have a minute?"

"Of course, Abdul. Please, come in." Harley motioned for him to enter, and said, "I haven't seen you for months."

"No," he said, gravely. "Not since the cleanup."

"Let me take your coat," said the pastor. "I certainly appreciated your help after the flood." When Abdul slipped out of his coat, Harvey was struck again by how muscular he was, with a huge neck and upper body. A wave of fear flowed through him, and he hoped that Abdul had come in peace. "Please, have a seat."

The big man settled into a wooden chair in front of the pastor's desk. "I apologize for not making an appointment," said Abdul.

"No problem," said Harley. "Care for some coffee?"

"No, thank you."

Harley poured himself a cup and then sat down in the companion chair that was facing Abdul. "I want you to know," said Harley, "that you have my sympathy. Jefferson was a good man."

"Yes, he was," said Abdul. "To me, he was a *great* man."

Harley sipped his coffee and then nodded. "Yes, I know he meant a lot to you."

"Next to my conversion to Islam," said Abdul, "Meeting Jefferson was the most important event in my life."

"He helped you, and you helped him."

Abdul looked out the window for a moment, thinking. Then he said, "My debt to him will never be repaid."

Harley thought back over his own life, recalling the mentors that had assisted him in school and in ministry. Many had been helpful, but none had served as a Jefferson Jones to him. That realization made him feel sad. "Such a person is precious," said Harley, softly.

"Priceless," said Abdul.

Harley took another sip of coffee, and then said, "I talked with Tawnya after he died, but then I got busy with Christmas. How is the family doing?"

"They are grieving," said Abdul, "and the holiday season has made things difficult and complicated. They are still planning the funeral." This surprised Harley, since Jefferson had died more than a week earlier. But he also knew that it was hard to make arrangements over Christmas.

"Yes," said Harley. "I understand."

"This brings me to one reason for my visit," said the man. "Tawnya wanted me to ask you if the funeral could be here at Riverside."

"I don't see why not," said Harley. "I would be honored."

"Is Saturday available?"

Harley got up, checked the church calendar, and then said, "Yes. The Christmas decorations will still be up, but the service can be here."

"That should be fine," said Abdul. "The family will be pleased, since this was the church building that Jefferson grew up in."

"Please have the funeral director get in touch with me," said Harley, sitting down. "And Jefferson's pastor as well. We'll do it right."

"You have my thanks as well," said Abdul. "Now, on to item number two. I understand that you and Jefferson had a conversation about Justice Plaza."

Harley's fear returned, and he felt himself beginning to perspire as he wondered if Abdul was going to berate him for putting pressure on a dying old man. "Yes, we did," admitted Harley.

"I am solely responsible for our business," he said, "now that Jefferson has passed." *Here it comes,* thought Harley, *Abdul is going to assert himself.*

"His will leaves a portion of his fortune to his family," said the big man, "which is appropriate. But a sizable amount remains with the business, under my control." Harley braced himself for the news that Abdul would not tolerate any interference in matters related to the business, and that the property would be sold in its present state.

But Abdul said, "I want you to know that I will execute all of Jefferson's wishes with regard to Justice Plaza. I will make sure that all of the storm water issues are rectified prior to the sale of the property."

A wave of relief flowed through Harley. Not only had Abdul come in peace, he had come in righteousness. Jefferson was going to be restored to right relationship with Occoquan.

∽

Another knock came on Harley's door at about eleven, pulling him away from his work on the bulletin for Epiphany, the church's celebration of the day when the wise man brought their gifts to Jesus. *Must be a church member,* he thought as he got up, *a person bearing gifts.*

Once again, he was wrong. "Hi, Harley," said Kelly, standing in front of him in a ski jacket and winter hat. "I was just walking by and saw your car."

Harley smiled. "Want to come in?"

"No, just saying hi."

Harley hadn't seen her since before Christmas, and he was surprised by how happy her appearance made him. *Maybe she has some powers she isn't aware of.* "Let me get my coat," he said. "I could use some fresh air."

The two of them walked down the wooden stairs and across the church parking lot. The clouds were even heavier than they were at the start of the day, and rain was clearly coming. "We better not walk too far," said Kelly, "or we'll get wet."

"How about a quick walk to the park and back?"

"Sounds good," she said.

"I enjoyed our lunch," said Harley, as they turned left on Mill Street and walked west.

"Me too," she nodded. "And your church service. It felt . . . okay."

"I'm glad," said Harley. "You are welcome any time."

"It wasn't easy for me to be there," she admitted, looking straight ahead, "but some good things happened. I want to learn more."

Harley knew he had to choose his words carefully. "Jesus is the key, as far as I am concerned," he said. "He brings power. And peace."

"I think I need that," Kelly said, turning to Harley. "I don't have it inside myself."

"You can ask for it," he said. "Put your trust in him, and he will help you. Jesus promises that he will do whatever you ask in his name."

"Anything?" asked Kelly.

"Well, anything in line with God," said Harley. "Anything that can help your faith, your life, your salvation."

"Salvation?" asked Kelly. "That's a word I never liked. Too judgmental."

"I know," said Harley. "Some people use it that way. But salvation is basically being saved—saved from anything that can hurt or destroy you."

"I always thought it meant going to heaven instead of hell," Kelly said.

"Well, yes," said Harley. "But we need to be saved in this life as well."

Kelly pondered this as they walked along Mill Street, approaching town hall. Then she said, "How do I ask for help?"

"Check this out," said Harley, motioning her to a park bench in front of the hall. They took a seat and Harley pulled out his smartphone. After doing a quick search, he said, "You can pray these words. They come from a hymn."

Kelly looked at the screen and read out loud:

Come, my way, my truth, my life:
Such a way, as gives us breath;
Such a truth, as ends all strife;
Such a life, as conquers death.

For a few moments, she looked at the screen in silence. Then Harley said, "It's a prayer to Jesus. The Bible says that Jesus is the way, the truth, and the life."

"'Come, my way, my truth, my life,'" said Kelly, quoting the hymn.

"Jesus is the way," said Harley, "the way that gives us breath."

"Find your breath," said Kelly, repeating her own fitness instructions. "Jesus is the truth."

"The truth," nodded Kelly.

"And the life," said Harley. "The life that conquers death."

"Salvation," said Kelly.

"Not original to me," said Harley. "Like I said, it's a hymn. But I do believe it."

"I'll give it a try," said Kelly. "Will you send me the link?"

"Sure," said Harley, tapping the screen of his smartphone. Her email popped up automatically, saved from her first message—the one that carried the threat of attacks and curses. *What a difference a few months make.*

"You know," said Kelly, "I'm still not sure about your religion, but I like what you are saying about Jesus. Way, truth, life."

"He's a window," said Harley. "A window to heaven. Also, a window to the world. I see him as the balance—God in human form, Creator in creation."

Kelly sat in silence for a moment, looking straight ahead, then turned to Harley and said, "I'm open." After that, she looked at the sky, got up, and motioned for Harley to join her.

"Well, we've got a whole new year in front of us," said Harley.

The two of them passed in front of the stone building housing the Occoquan museum at the edge of the park, and Harley looked up at the dark clouds that were moving in from the west. Then, as they approached the corner of the museum, John Jonas appeared in front of them.

"John!" said Kelly, startled.

"Hello, Kelly," said John, seeming pleased to have scared her. And then, after a pause, "Hello, Harley."

"What are you doing here?" asked Harley.

"Just coming back from a hike," he said, holding up his walking stick.

"Well, you surprised us," said Kelly.

"Life is full of surprises," said John.

"I don't think I've seen you since the police station," Harley said. "Thank you for the help you gave us in the castle."

"Glad to help," said John, sounding proud.

"But I do want to ask you," Harley continued. "What were you doing there?"

"What do you mean?"

"What were you doing there in the first place?" said Harley.

"That's easy," said John: "Getting Jesus arrested."

"Explain that," said Kelly.

"I suspected he was the killer, so I peeled him away from his gang and alerted the police."

Harley scratched his head and said, "How did you do that?" He knew that John had been talking with Latinos around town, but didn't know what he had been saying.

"I started talking with him and his *amigos* about a year ago," said John.

"You speak Spanish?" asked Harley.

"*Hablo un poco.* Got through four years of Spanish in high school."

"What did you talk about?" asked Kelly.

"*La Bestia,*" he answered. "They seemed impressed that we honor the same god."

Harley shivered, and not from the temperature. "Go on," said the pastor.

"We also like baseball bats," said John with a crooked grin. "I hit softballs, and they beat new gang members. Which I think is insane, by the way. But when I saw them walking through town, swinging their bats, I figured I'd copy them. I got a bat like theirs and used it as another connection point. We would come at each other, bang them together, wrestle them from each other's hands. *Machismo,* you know."

"*La Bestia* and bats," Kelly said. "What a bond."

"Speaking of bats," said John, "I got to know some cops while playing softball. Guys on the anti-gang task force. Told them I'd call them if I saw anything suspicious in Occoquan. See something, say something."

"That's good," said Harley, seeing the puzzle beginning to come together.

"On my walks along the river, I had seen Jesus going in and out of the castle, sometimes at night," John continued. "So, when I ran into him on Saturday morning, I told him that a lot of other people were going in and out of the place. He said, 'No, I'm the only one with a key.' He told me that his sister cleaned for the caretaker and his wife, and she made a copy of the key for him. I said to him, 'I swear to you, I've seen other people.'"

"Wait a second," said Harley. "Are you saying that Jesus got a key to the castle from his sister, who cleans for Paul, and that's how he stored his drugs there?"

"Right," said John with a grin. Harley was amazed at how the pieces fit together.

"But you were lying to him," said Kelly.

Her accusation wiped the smile off John's face, but just for a moment. "So what?"

Kelly didn't say a word. Then Harley broke the silence by saying, "Go on."

"Anyway, I told him that since we both serve *La Bestia,* we should go check it out, just the two of us. No one else, so we don't attract attention. I had my bat, and I told him to go get his. While he was doing that, I called the cops and said that MS-13 was breaking and entering."

"The task force was on alert?" Harley asked.

"Not exactly," said John. "They had spread the word. The officers who responded knew that I was a good guy."

"Did you know Harley was there?" asked Kelly.

"Hell, no," said John. "I planned on sending Jesus down the stairs with the bat and then slipping out to meet the police. Running into Harley, Paul, and Jason—that was icing on the cake."

"That makes it sound a bit too sweet," said Harley, still aching from his tumble into the sub-cellar.

"Oh, I had your back," insisted John. "I was the one who turned off the light."

"You're lucky no one got hurt," Kelly said.

"Anyway, I just heard from a contact in the police department that some blood and hair from Enrique were found on the bat, and Jesus has been charged with murder. That's sweet, isn't it? Jesus is going away for a very long time."

"Do you think he is guilty?" Harley asked.

"Sure, but does it matter, really? One drug dealer is dead, and the other is going to prison. That's all that really matters."

"I disagree," said Harley, shaking his head. "I think the truth is what matters." As he said these words, a cold rain began to fall.

"What about the bat?" said Kelly, glaring at John. "The baseball bat. The one that Jesus was swinging, the one that had Enrique's blood on it. I think it belonged to you, John. Is it yours?"

Is it his? Harley wondered. *Is it, or isn't it?* He wanted John to respond, but he didn't trust him to tell the truth. *I am not what I am, says the father of lies.* Another window was opening, one that revealed only deep darkness. *Sure, he could have switched the bats. Would have been easy to do.*

"Is it yours, John?" said Kelly. "Tell me the truth."

John could have beaten Enrique to death, dumped his body by the river, and then put the murder weapon in the hands of Jesus.

John didn't answer. He just gave Kelly a wicked smile and walked away.

Acknowledgments

Monsignor Bill Parent is a life-long friend and Roman Catholic priest who challenged me, on my fortieth birthday, to attempt the Marine Corps Marathon. He had run several marathons before, so he gave me some pointers and turned me loose, helping me to complete the event after eight months of training. I ran a marathon a year through my forties, and then switched to sprint triathlons and Century (100-mile) bike rides. Bill awakened in me an appreciation for fitness and faith, along with the challenge of keeping body and soul together. I am grateful for the theological conversations we have had over the years.

Another marathon man is Jay Tharp, a friend since college and a former federal prosecutor. Jay and I have completed several marathons together, as well as a number of sprint triathlons. Like Harley Camden, we are keenly aware of the challenges of staying in shape in our early sixties, and we keep pushing each other to swim, cycle, and run. I am grateful to Jay for the review he did of this book's legal issues, a service he also provided for *City of Peace* (Köehler Books, 2018), my first book in the "Mill Street Mysteries" series.

Since an important element of this book is Harley's mission trip to Honduras, I knew that I would have to include some Spanish. My daughter Sadie Brinton, who attended a partial Spanish-immersion school as a child and then majored in Spanish literature at Duke University, was a big help in correcting my rudimentary knowledge of the language. Sadie has also been an insightful critic and enthusiastic cheerleader since I first dreamed up Harley Camden and put him in the Town of Occoquan, Virginia.

Peter Panagore is a friend and classmate from Yale Divinity School, and we have encouraged each other as writers throughout our ministerial careers. His near-death experience as a young man is recounted in his book

Acknowledgments

Heaven is Beautiful: How Dying Taught Me That Death Is Just the Beginning, and it provided powerful inspiration for a pivotal scene in *Windows of the Heavens.*

Another friend and writer is Vik Khanna, an exercise coach and health educator who was co-author of my book *Ten Commandments of Faith and Fitness.* Vik devised the "Fitness Trinity" of endurance exercise, strength training and good nutrition that plays a role in this book, as Harley Camden and other characters try to keep body and soul together.

My knowledge of the archaeology of Copán, Honduras, comes from numerous visits to the site while participating in church mission trips with the "Men y Mujeres on a Mission" of Fairfax Presbyterian Church. I was fortunate to have a sabbatical in Copán Ruinas in the summer of 2017, and I benefited from the insights provided by William F. Fash and Ricardo Agurcia Fasquelle in their book *History Carved in Stone: A Guide to the Archaeological Park of the Ruins of Copán.* I love the people of Honduras, and am grateful for the warm hospitality they provide whenever I visit. *Gracias, mis amigos.*

I first heard the hymn *Come, My Way, My Truth, My Life* while a student at Yale Divinity School, and it has been an inspiration to me for over thirty years. First a poem by Welsh poet George Herbert (1593–1633), it was set to music by British composer and hymn tune writer Ralph Vaughn Williams (1872–1958) as part of his *Five Mystical Songs* (1911). The hymn works not only as a song but as a prayer, which is how Harley employs it in this book.

Some readers might wonder if a town such as Occoquan could suffer an unexpected and devastating flood after one night of heavy rain. While I hope that Occoquan never experiences such a tragedy, nearby Ellicott City in Maryland was damaged badly by floods in 2016 and 2018. In 2016, an evening of heavy rain caused streets to flood, buildings to collapse, and cars to be swept away. A National Guardsman was killed in the flooding. Then, in 2018, eight inches of rain fell in the course of two hours, and Ellicott City flooded again. Speculation about the cause of the flooding included overdevelopment of the area around the historic city. Coincidentally, the Ellicott family has connections to both locations: Nathaniel Ellicott (1763–1841) owned the mill in Occoquan, while three of his brothers were millers in what is now called Ellicott City. The floodwaters that destroy the candle shop in *Windows of the Heavens* rush down Ellicott Street on their way to the Occoquan River.

Thanks to Matthew Wimer, the Managing Editor of Wipf and Stock Publishers, for agreeing to publish the book under their Resource Publications imprint. Abby Carlson has done a very fine job for me as a proofreader.

ACKNOWLEDGMENTS

Linda Carlton has created my author's website www.henrygbrinton.com, and Shari Stauch has been an excellent advisor in the marketing arena. Thanks to my wife Nancy Freeborne Brinton, who is a constant support as I peck away at my computer, and to our children Sadie and Sam, who love to visit us in the Town of Occoquan. I am grateful to Mayor Earnie Porta and our neighbors in the Victorian townhouses of Gaslight Landing, as well as to all of the residents of Occoquan who have responded so positively to the stories I have set in our community. May the *Windows of the Heavens* open for all readers of this book—not in catastrophic flooding, but in new insights about life, death, and our need to care for God's creation.

Made in the USA
Middletown, DE
08 July 2023

34623300R00116